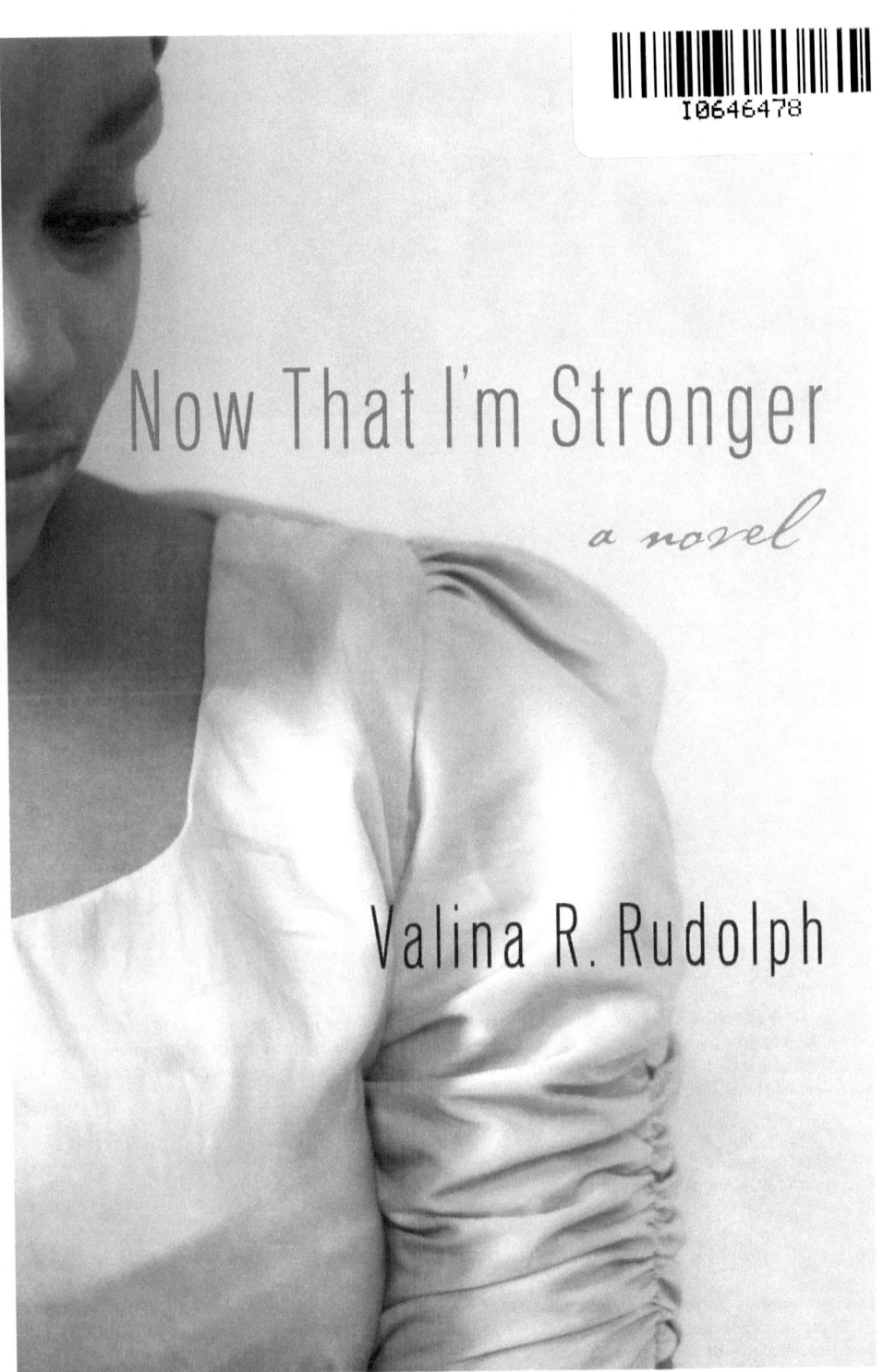

Now That I'm Stronger

a novel

Valina R. Rudolph

MoVal Press

Now That I'm Stronger
All Rights Reserved.
Copyright © 2014 Valina R. Rudolph
v2.0

Cover Photo © 2014 Christine Van Bree. All rights reserved - used with permission.

ISBN: 978-0-578-13290-7

PRINTED IN THE UNITED STATES OF AMERICA

This book is dedicated to my husband,
my best friend,
and my number one supporter.
I'm fortunate that all of those titles belong to one person.
Mohammed Addo

Chapter 1

The bus ride was unbearable, more so because we weren't allowed to carry electronic devices—no phones, iPods, or handheld games—to pass the time. As usual, the fifty-five seater was filled to capacity. The majority of the passengers were women, I noticed, all going to see their loved ones—brothers, fathers, baby daddies. We were taking a direct route to one of the maximum-security prisons that littered upstate New York, Upstate Correctional Facility.

Part of the punishment was for the families. On sentencing day, when the judge announced where the inmate would be housed, the family found out how many hours a month they would be prisoner on this bus. And sometimes the trip was simply too far and made regular visitation impractical.

I was starting to recognize some of the faces; some were regulars like me. They made idle chit chat with one another. "How long is yours in for?" "Are you allowed private visits?" I tuned it all out. Looked out the window and watched the cars speed by. I didn't belong here anymore than my father belonged there.

The name of the prison was more than fitting because it was definitely upstate. There was no traffic and the trip would still take no less than six hours. Six hours of breathing in the smell of nicotine mixed with the dirty bathroom odor seeping out from under the closed door in the back of the bus. I swallowed hard trying to push back a wave of nausea. I could taste the bitterness in the back of my throat. Even a Dramamine wouldn't have helped. And yet, for the past eight months I had been making the trip religiously, two Saturdays a month. Ever since those twelve people that I had never seen before in my life, but were supposedly my father's peers, had found him guilty.

The trial had only lasted four days. Four days of arguments, objections, and evidence. I sat next to my aunt, my father's younger sister, and watched her cry. I didn't cry; I knew it would be fine. I knew that it was all some type of horrible mistake and that my father would be coming home soon. The jury didn't even take a full day to make up their minds, no doubt in a rush to complete their civic duty so they could get back to their lives. My father's life would never be the same.

My father had been in jail almost a year awaiting trial, and in my mind I was planning a homecoming party for him. Balloons. Cake. But there he stood in his prison uniform listening as the verdict was read. Guilty.

I felt numb. Everything that I knew to be true and right in the world fell away. My father turned to me and mouthed, "I'm sorry."

More kids left my neighborhood for prison or the morgue than for college. Not many people reached my age, eighteen, without having some interaction with the criminal justice system. The word justice was obviously being used in the loosest sense of the word. Growing up in my 'hood I had seen my fair share of bad people. I had seen my share of criminals. My father was the one that had taught me how to spot them and how to avoid them. It was more than simply, "Don't talk to strangers." It was, "You see that guy over there? He's a dealer. Stay away from him. And that guy, don't ever buy anything he tries to sell you." And his golden rule, "Never go into anyone's apartment without telling me first."

Because of his guidance all of these years, I considered myself a good judge of character. And now those twelve people wanted me to believe that my father was one of them, one of the bad guys.

My father was a construction worker. It was seasonal work; sometimes he worked seven days a week and other times he was home for months at a time. He didn't seem to mind; he said it gave him more time to spend with me. My father and I have always been very close. My mother died of complications while giving birth to me. But between my father and my aunt I never wanted for anything. Well, actually, I did go through a phase where I wanted a sister. I begged my father for a sister, someone to play with and share my secrets with. But no such luck, it was always just him and I. He was the one that I would share my secrets with; he was my best friend. And these people sat in a room for a few days and learned about my father through lawyers and thought that they could judge him. They thought they knew him better than me?

My aunt had sent me with 150 dollars to put into my father's commissary. She had not seen him since the day of his sentencing. It was a long trip and she had her kids to take care of. She sent money, though, and she always took his collect calls. I lived with her. She only lived two buildings over from the building I grew up in with my father.

My father had lived in the projects his whole life, and his mother, too, and probably her mother before that. You would think project apartments were passed down by will. The thing was, once you were in there, it was hard to get out, especially if it was all you had ever known. But I was the one who was going to break the cycle for my family. I was going to get out and do something positive with my life.

Daddy had told me that he wanted us to live close to my aunt. As I got a little older, I realized why. Whenever I had some question on what he considered a women's issue, he would send me to her. It was kind of funny; sometimes I would ask him things just to see him get nervous and watch him start to stutter.

My father is a big guy. If you didn't know him he could be quite intimidating. He was always physically fit because of his construction job, but he was tall, too, 6'4" or so. He had a reputation in the neighborhood; not a bad one, but people just kind of knew not to mess with him, I guess. And that trickled down to me.

I will never forget the time that he pulled some guy out of his car because the guy had driven up beside me as I walked down the block. Some pimp from the neighborhood. I knew better than to speak to him, but my father thought he would make a point. He was sitting out in front of the building waiting for me to get home from school when he saw the guy drive up and try to get my attention. My father came running. Before the guy had a chance to press down on the gas pedal, he was being pulled out of his car and hitting the pavement. He was on the ground so quickly he probably didn't know what happened. I never had a problem with him again.

My father was always my protector. Now he was in there surrounded by criminals 24/7 with no one to watch his back. Who was going to protect him?

"Oh crap," I said under my breath, realizing that I had made the same mistake yet again. In addition to the no electronics rule, there was a long list of rules that visitors to Upstate Correctional had to follow. I always forgot the same one: no underwire. I would have to go into a little room and remove my bra, getting more than a little acquainted with one of the guards. I told myself not to complain because at the end of the day I could leave. My father had 137 more months to serve before he would walk out of there. I wondered why they counted in months instead of years; that just makes it seem longer to me.

Chapter 2

As if all the hours on the bus weren't enough, it took at least another hour to make it through security. When I was finally ushered into the visitor's room, I sat at a table, which was kind of like the long tables that used to be in my high school cafeteria. Come to think of it, the metal detectors were kind of like the ones in my high school too. After a few more minutes, men started entering the room. People shouted so their loved one could find them in the crowd. The massive swarm of prison orange made finding my father like a game of *Where's Waldo.*

After my father was sentenced I began watching prison documentaries. As the men flocked into the visitation area, I would see how many prison gang tattoos I could identify. I had counted sixteen by the time I finally spotted my father. I stood and waived him over to me. The guard quickly shouted at me to remain seated. He rested his hand on the butt of his baton. His breathing fogged up the Plexiglas face shield that he was wearing.

My father sat down in front of me and blew me a kiss. This was a maximum security prison so there was absolutely no physical contact allowed, unless you were married to an inmate, passed an extensive background check, and the particular prisoner was not on any type of restriction. Oh, and of course there was a waiting list. Like so many others, my father and I didn't fall into that category, so physical contact was not an option. I would have loved a hug, just to have his arms around me. Instead, I grabbed his air kiss and put it in my pocket. He smiled.

I hated this because there was so much pressure to find something interesting to talk about. Talking about the weather or making other small talk just wouldn't do.

"Hey Brie, how are you?"

"I'm okay daddy. How are you?" I said, at the same time I noticed a small purplish bruise at the top of his forehead, almost hidden by his hairline. He'd lost weight. I tried not to stare.

"I'm fine," he said. "How's Aunt Jackie?"

"She's good. The boys are keeping her busy. They are so bad!"

He smiled. "Yeah, they are a handful. When you were younger we use to swap for the weekend. I would take them out to do something manly and she would take you out shopping or something."

I smiled. "Yeah, I remember"

"But they are kids. What are they, nine and eleven now?"

"Yeah"

"They are supposed to drive her crazy at that age. I wish their deadbeat loser father was around to help. Being a single parent is not easy."

I never really liked their father. Sometimes Aunt Jackie and Daddy would go out and he would babysit us. He was mean and always screaming at us. I had wished he would disappear. I'd close my eyes and wish for it every time I saw him. The only thing I wished for these days was for my father to come home. But no amount of wishing or hoping could accomplish that. That didn't stop me from trying.

I tried to think of other things to talk about with Daddy. I told him about the money that I had put in his commissary. He looked embarrassed. It was awkward.

"So have you talked to your lawyer lately?" I asked.

"Nope."

"You have to stay on top of him, Daddy. Otherwise he is not going to do anything."

"There is nothing he can do, Brie." He looked so defeated; I hated seeing him like this. I decided to change the subject to make it easier on the both of us.

"I registered for nursing school," I said. "I start classes at the end of August."

"Oh, that's good. You will be good at that."

"So are you dating anyone?" my father asked casually. This must've been one of the hardest things for him, being in there and not being able to keep an eye on me. I didn't answer right away. I gave him a sly look, toying with him a little. There was a No Dating While In High School policy in my house, but I had graduated high school a semester early and he'd amended the rule to no dating before you're eighteen. I had turned eighteen six months ago and he was trying to amend the rule again. He was very strict with that sort of thing.

"Well..." I said, pausing again.

"Brianna!" He shouted with a look on his face that was an equal mixture of surprise and fear.

"I'm just kidding, Daddy." He didn't look convinced. "For real, I'm not dating. I'm not. I won't make any promises about how long that is going to last, but for now I have no intention of dating anyone. There is too much going on. And with school starting soon I won't have time for that."

And who would I date anyway? I wondered. I'd had one or two crushes while in school but none of them amounted to anything. I wanted to be with someone who was ambitious. Someone who could understand that I wanted to make something out of my life. But like I told my father, "I'm not looking for a relationship." I figured if someone worth my time and energy came along, I would realize it.

I talked with Daddy about things that were going on back home.

We discussed whether it was a good idea for me to work while in school.

A guard announced over the loud speaker that visitation would be ending in fifteen minutes. I always felt every last minute of the six hours it took to get there, but as soon as I got there time began to fly by. I'm sure it was only like that if you were on this side of the gate. On the other side, my father's side, it must have been like time was standing still.

"Listen, Brie," my father said, putting on a serious face that made me nervous. "I don't want you to make the trip up here anymore. I don't like you riding on that bus and this is no place for a young girl like you to be. I will call and write you, but I don't want you to come up here anymore." He looked down at his hands as he spoke. If I didn't know better I might have thought he was praying. We were not a religious family. The only time we went to church was for funerals, but in my neighborhood that was quite often, so maybe that counted for something.

"I don't want you to see me in here like this. This is not how I want you to remember me."

"We will have plenty more memories when you get out, Daddy. I'd rather see you like this than not at all."

He just shook his head. So I continued, "Anyway, I am sure your lawyer will figure out a way to get you out of here soon."

He looked at me then. Tears streamed down his face. I don't think I had ever seen him cry before, not even when he got sentenced.

So the other thing about these visitations was that I was in a huge room with dozens of conversations going on at the same time. Sometimes the background noise made it hard to hear. Half the time I was reading Daddy's lips instead of actually hearing his voice. So when I heard him say, "I did it," I knew I must have heard him wrong.

"What?" I said cupping my hand behind my ear.

"I did it," he repeated. "I did what they said. I'm not getting out,

Brianna. Not anytime soon. You have to live your life. Focus on school and making a life for yourself. I love you so much, Brianna."

The loud buzzer sounded indicating that visitation was over. He stood as a guard came to escort him out.

I stood, my heart thumping in my chest. I ignored the guard's order to sit back down.

I pointed an accusatory finger at him. "You say that I shouldn't visit," I shouted. "That this is no place for me. This is no place for you either, Daddy! You don't belong here either!"

He looked at me one last time. The sadness in his eyes broke my heart. I collapsed back in my seat as he turned and walked away. My body shook with the force of my cries.

I needed a brown paper bag. I couldn't catch my breath. My cries were not the silent type. They were loud and painful. I didn't care who was watching. I don't know how I made it home that night. I don't remember anything; it's like I was in a trance. I kept playing my father's words over and over in my head. "I did it... you don't belong here... this is no place for you."

Chapter 3

I woke up the next morning with the same unanswered questions. I had hardly slept at all. I'd lain awake most of the night watching the flashing red and blue police lights make shadows across my popcorn ceiling. This was a game that I had played many nights as a child. *Oh, look, Daddy, a fish!*

And now I was all grown up and my father had told me that he was guilty and belonged in prison. How could he say that? How could he say that he'd done it? I was so sure that my father was innocent that I hadn't paid much attention to the trial.

It must be some sort of depression, I told myself. And that was understandable, right? He was an innocent man, wrongfully convicted, so of course he was depressed.

That had to be it, because there was no way that my father could have been running an elaborate drug operation without me having a clue. We lived in the same house. We ate dinner together every night. There was just no way that I could believe that my father, who had been there for me my whole life, was not the man I thought he was. I couldn't believe it, even if the words were coming out of his mouth.

Those were the thoughts that swirled around in my head like the lights in a kaleidoscope—light, then shadow; a moment of clarity, then everything was blurry and out of focus again.

I finally mustered up enough strength to get out of bed. I felt emotionally drained. It took all of my strength to force myself out of bed. I felt like I was in a trance, like I was living someone else's nightmare. What I wouldn't give for that to be true. But as I passed myself in the mirror, there was no denying that it was me, my life, my nightmare.

I stared at myself. I remembered how my father would say that I had my mother's beautiful brown eyes, the eyes that were now red and swollen from crying. My face was stained with dried tears. My shoulder length hair was tangled and flattened on one side of my head.

Yesterday was horrible, but today is a new day, I told myself. "He didn't mean what he said. He didn't mean it," I said it to my reflection; it stared back at me unconvinced.

"Hey, sleepy head," my aunt said as she heard me walk into the kitchen. She was cooking something at the stove. The smell of burning food, which usually accompanied her cooking, perfumed the room.

When I didn't respond she turned around and looked at me. I knew exactly what she saw. The shower hadn't helped. I'd gotten in the shower hoping the hot water and steam would evaporate my problems and rinse them down the drain. But I got out with the same look on my face: equal parts confusion, fear, and anger. I could never be a poker player because everything that I was feeling was always apparent on my face.

I really wanted to believe that my father was innocent. He had to be. But that little seed of doubt he had planted in my head had started to sprout. It grew like a weed, choking the life out of everything good and beautiful around it, everything that I had thought was true.

"What is it? What's the matter?" she asked as she walked toward me with a sincere look of concern on her face. She held me and tried to comfort me as I began to cry again. How many tears can one person have? I buried my face in her shoulder and thought about turning back the clock, not just to the day before yesterday or even last year. Instead I imagined that I was four years old again and she was comforting me because I had fallen in the playground. It was true what they said; when you get older you don't heal as quickly. A kiss doesn't make it all better anymore.

She rubbed my back in a circular motion, like it was a genie's lamp and all she wanted to do was wish my pain away. That's what I wanted her to do too.

"Tell me what's the matter," she said after a long silence. She was giving me time to gather myself.

We sat at the kitchen table and I told her about my visit with Daddy. When I was done I waited for her to tell me that it wasn't true and put my fears to rest.

She didn't. She just sat there silent for what seemed like an eternity. Then she took a deep breath and began to speak. When she did, I realized I hadn't braced myself for what she was about to say.

"Your father loves you more than anything in this world," she said. My heart started pounding. If it wasn't true she would have just come out and said that. She reached across the table and grabbed my hand. "He always puts you first. He is a good father. But Brianna, your father is not perfect. He has made mistakes."

I snatched my hand away. "What are you talking about?" I shouted. "What mistakes?" My eyes desperately searched her face looking for an indication of what her answer meant. There was none. I had found the poker player in the family. I could tell she was reluctant to speak but I was starting to feel like I had been lied to enough. I needed someone to be straight with me, I needed answers.

I took the straightforward approach. The approach that no one else seemed to be taking. "Was he a drug dealer?"

She nodded slowly. That was all she could do. It was as if the words were stuck in her throat. Which was fine, because I didn't need her to say the words; with that slight movement of her head she had already told me everything that I needed to know. She grabbed my arm to stop me as I quickly moved to get up from the table.

I pulled away. "What?" I yelled. How could my father, my best friend, have been a drug dealer? "Please just tell me the truth," I pleaded. "Tell me what's going on."

I never in a million years thought I would be having this conversation about my father. Kids in the neighborhood, yes, but not my own father. It just didn't make any sense.

She started to speak slowly. "Your father and I grew up without a dad. I was still in diapers when he left us. Growing up, Keith always thought he was the man of the house. He didn't have much of a childhood. After school he would babysit me so that mom could work a second job to make ends meet. That was a lot for a young kid to deal with, but he didn't get angry or bitter like you might expect. Instead he was determined to figure out how to make things better for us. As soon as he was old enough he got a little weekend job to help out."

She felt the need to give me the backstory. To put my father's drug dealing in context, like that was even possible. I sat there and listened to her mainly because I was too stunned to move, but I was getting impatient.

"What does any of that have to do with right now? What does it have to do with him telling me that he's guilty and belongs in prison?"

"I'm getting there, Brie. I just need you to understand the full story so that you can see why he did what he did."

Well, that's a lost cause, I thought to myself. There was no way that I would ever understand why my father had become a drug dealer. But I sat silently and let her continue.

"Since your father is almost ten years older than me, he had some memories of our father. You know, like walking him to school, playing ball, just hanging out. That made it even more difficult for him to understand why he had left us and Keith hated him for that. He was determined not to be anything like our dad."

Too bad their dad wasn't a drug dealer. Maybe my father would have grown up being determined not to do that. He had probably turned out to be worse than his father had ever been. With every word she said, I was losing more and more respect for him, and her, too, for that matter.

"When I got old enough to stay home alone, your dad extended his weekend job to several weekdays after school. But he realized very quickly that the people in the neighborhood who seemed to always have money, nice cars, and nice clothes were the ones who were dealing drugs, stealing cars, or involved in some other illegal activity. When he was about fourteen he became a runner for one of the local dealers. He was observant and people trusted him. He didn't look like your typical drug dealer."

"Yeah, well, he sure had me fooled." Science fairs, open school nights. He was always there. I was torn between being angry and being extremely sad. But at that moment anger was winning by a landslide. My father had been living a double life: the caring father on one hand and the drug dealer on the other. But which one was the real him? I felt so stupid. Stupid. Stupid. Stupid. My snide remark got no reaction from Aunt Jackie, she just continued with her story, unfazed.

"He worked his way up and before long he was running his own block, and then another, and another, until he was practically running this whole neighborhood. He was bringing in a lot of money."

It made me sick the way she seemed to admire what he had done. Like we were talking about Bill Gates or somebody.

"That's when he started taking construction jobs here and there so that our mother wouldn't question him about the source of his income. I actually think she knew the truth all along. By that point she was just so drained, so physically and emotionally tired, that she didn't want to confront him or argue about it. She was just relieved to have some money coming in. I know that sounds bad but she really wasn't a bad mother. She wanted the best for us."

Yeah, mother of the year, I thought. *She deserves a freakin' medal.* I didn't know much about my grandmother. She died of a heart attack when I was about five years old. My aunt found her unconscious on the living room floor one night when she came home from work. She died in the hospital a few days later.

My aunt once told me that she blamed herself. She was at work taking care of old people, taking care of other people's mothers, when her own was at home alone. Beside that I knew absolutely nothing about my grandmother. But good mother or bad, good father or bad, there was still no excuse for what my father had done. There was only so much a person could blame on his parents. Despite everything that I had found out about my father, I would never use him as an excuse for the decisions I make in my life.

I wasn't in the mood to sit there and listen to my aunt make lame excuses for my father. *Just get to the point already. Can we speed up this little trip down memory lane?* I just sat there staring at her, not wasting energy trying to hide my impatience.

"Honestly," she continued. "I don't think it would have mattered at that point anyway because your dad had experienced what it was like not to struggle for once, not to be constantly worried about how we were going to pay our bills and keep food on the table. There was nothing that was going to make him give that up. He watched as other low-level dealers got caught by the cops or robbed by competitors, but instead of it scaring him straight, he learned from their mistakes. He treated it like a legitimate business."

The chair wobbled as I shifted my weight trying to find a more comfortable position. But there was nothing in the world that could make this conversation more comfortable.

"He wasn't flashy," she continued. "He paid himself like he would be paid at any other job. He never kept drugs or money in the house. That was his number one rule."

I remembered back to the night when the cops busted in and raided our apartment. They walked in like they owned the place, carelessly knocking things down and throwing our stuff around. My father was quickly arrested and hauled out of the apartment. Scared, I ran to Aunt Jackie's apartment to tell her what was happening.

I was out of breath and in a complete panic by the time I got to her. It was a Friday night, I remember, because she was dressed for the club, weave freshly done and hanging midway down her back. She was wearing a skirt in a size that looked more suitable for a toddler than a grown woman. She didn't seem at all concerned when I told her what was happening. She continued doing her makeup and told me not to worry that they wouldn't find anything. That made much more sense now considering my father's rule of never keeping money or drugs in the house.

When my aunt saw that my hysteria wasn't subsiding, she paused her Friday night transformation and walked me back over to the apartment so that we could assess the damage. There were two police dogs in the living room and yellow crime scene tape roping off the entry. Glass was all over the floor, the back had been taken off of the T.V., and the couch had been torn open and its white foam insides were visible. I could see the picture frame with the starfish lying on the floor. The picture inside was one of my favorites. Daddy and I were sitting on the sand at Rockaway Beach, building a sandcastle. I was about seven. I was missing one of my front teeth. But I was smiling so big, I was so happy. That picture found a new home on my bedside table in my aunt's apartment, in a new frame replacing the one that the cops had broken.

The cops refused to let us into the apartment. They said that it would take at least forty-eight hours to process the scene.

"The scene of what?" I asked. But I was just waived away. That was the beginning of this nightmare.

My aunt was still talking. "Like I said, he was observant. He knew which of the neighborhood cops were dirty and which weren't. The dirty cops had their own routes just like the dealers. He was determined to figure out a way to use this to his advantage.

"He figured that there was no real difference between him and the dirty cops. One day your father videotaped two cops pocketing drugs and money from a local dealer. He mailed a copy of the tape to the officers with a note stating that if anything happened to him, he had several more copies and had left instructions to mail them to high-ranking officers in the NYPD, internal affairs, and even the mayor.

"Now most other dealers would have simply paid off the cops. That would have been easy enough to do. But not your dad. The way he saw it paying them off gave them the upper hand because at any moment they could demand more money or decide to turn him in for their own benefit. Your father took a different approach. He got the dirt on them and used it to his advantage then he became the one with authority.

"From that time he had a silent partnership with those cops. They looked out for him, told him about scheduled raids and identified the snitches. That took care of the security issue. The only other problem left for him to solve was to figure out the best way to hide the large amounts of money he was making. Unlike other dealers, your father only spent what he had to. He was very low key. He could have moved us out of the projects, gotten a nice car, worn the fancy clothes and the jewels, carried around wads of cash. But he understood that the easiest way to get caught was to draw attention to himself. So even though his car was in the shop every other month he still drove that beat-up old Buick and we still lived in this three bedroom apartment.

"He read books about business and investing, also not typical of a dealer. He didn't see himself as a dealer, he saw himself as any other businessman with a product that was in demand."

Yeah and Madoff was just an investor, I thought. I looked up at her. I had broken off eye contact a while ago, disgusted by the words that were coming out of her mouth. But I looked at her then.

"Just stop," I said as I stood up and walked away from the table. I had heard enough, more than enough.

"Brianna"

I tried to stay calm but it was no use. "No, Aunt Jackie. No! I can't listen to this anymore! I know what I need to know. He lied to me my whole life, and you did too. You can call him a businessman, but he is nothing more than a drug dealer and a liar! And you may not have been dealing with him, but you were an accomplice to his lies. That's all I need to know!"

"You think your father is some horrible person? He is the same man that has been there for you your entire life. He is no different than the people on Wall Street. If you think they are not criminals, you're wrong. Everyone has a hustle, everyone. The cops, the politicians, doctors, lawyers, even the home-attendant agency that I work for. They pad invoices to state agencies. They are all criminals in one way or another, all trying to line their own pockets. Yes, it was wrong for him to lie to you, but he was just trying to protect you."

"He wouldn't have to protect me if he wasn't a criminal. He would not have had to lie if he wasn't doing something wrong. That started way before I was born so he can't use me as an excuse. He was trying to protect himself, his secret life, not me." My voice became more of a high-pitched shriek as I continued my well-deserved rant. "He thought he was doing me a favor by sticking around when I was born? I would have been better off if he'd left just like your father did. I would have been better off without a father than with a lying, drug dealing convict for a father."

I could tell that she thought my words were disrespectful. I was talking about her brother, the man who had helped raise her and her sons, too, for that matter. I didn't care. He had this whole secret life that was being revealed to me and there was no telling what else I didn't know. In my mind that outweighed all of the birthday parties and play dates.

If she wanted to only see the good in him, that was up to her. I had lived the lie for long enough. I didn't know what was worse: having doubts about my father's innocence after my conversation with him yesterday or having those doubts erased today.

Tired of screaming, and realizing that I had to give her some credit for finally telling me the truth, I took a deep breath, looked at her, and calmly said, "I can't handle any more of this right now. I'm going out."

I was already on the other side of the door when I heard her yell, "Be careful." She said that to me every time I left the house, but today it just seemed meaningless. I had lived with a criminal my entire life. What was there to be afraid of on the outside?

Chapter 4

A week passed and I still felt no need to finish the conversation with my aunt. Like I told her, I had all the information that I needed.

I woke up early, showered and dressed, making sure not to wear the bra with the underwire this time. I left my house on a mission. I wasn't in the mood to listen, but I did have things that I needed to say.

I picked a row of seats toward the middle of the bus and took the seat closest to the window. I stared aimlessly out of the window, looking at nothing in particular.

People say that hindsight is 20/20. Even if I scrutinized everything, there were no red flags. There was nothing to give me any indication that my father was dealing. Was I just seeing what I wanted to see? Having selective vision? Or was he really that good at hiding things from me? What else didn't I know about him?

I had never been to his job, but that wasn't unusual. He was a construction worker, after all. Sometimes driving in the car he would point to a building, and say, "I helped build that."

He never really invited anyone over to our apartment, but he never stopped me from having my friends over. So I didn't think much about that either.

Despite the lack of evidence, I knew that what Aunt Jackie had told me was true. And I had to confront him about it. The bus was scheduled to depart at 7:30. I still had a few minutes. I was anxious.

I had rehearsed what I wanted to say to my father, but none of the words seemed to effectively get across what I was feeling: confused, hurt, angry, betrayed. I knew that nothing I could say would effectively get these feelings across to him, but I also knew that even if I had the words, there was nothing that he could ever do to fix it.

I was distracted from my thoughts by the smell of men's cologne. I glanced toward the seats across the aisle from me and spotted him. I noticed his broad shoulders first. Then I worked my way down slowly, taking in every inch of him. Even though he was sitting, I could tell that he was tall, over six feet. He had an athletic build, not that of a football player, more like a basketball player or track star. He had a dark-skinned, smooth complexion; his hair was cut very low and he had a neatly shaped goatee, almond shaped brown eyes... The verdict was in—he looked even better than he smelled.

He looked slightly familiar to me. Maybe he just had one of those faces. I thought I was being discreet as I traced his body with my eyes, but when my glance made its way back up to his face, I noticed he was staring right at me. Smiling a little cocky smile, he arched his right eyebrow.

Even though I knew that there was no denying the fact that I had been checking him out, that didn't stop me from trying. I quickly turned my gaze back toward the window. I heard him laughing a little under his breath, no doubt laughing at me, but I didn't turn around to confirm.

The bus finally began to move and with it reality started to set in. With each mile I was getting closer to a confrontation with my father. With each minute I was getting closer to the most difficult conversation I would ever have. I had taken this bus ride many times before but I knew that this one would be my last.

I could feel his eyes staring at me from across the aisle. I still refused to turn around and make eye contact. I was too embarrassed. It was weird; I had so many things on my mind but for some reason I couldn't help but be intrigued by this guy.

I tried hard to make myself look busy. I pulled out the course cata-log for my nursing program and started to read through it for the hundredth time.

"That's where I recognize you from! I knew you looked familiar." His voice was deep, manly, sexy. It suited him perfectly.

"Excuse me?" I said.

He moved into the empty seat next to me. Uninvited. The close-ness made me uncomfortable.

"Yeah, I saw you at the school," he said pointing to my course cata-log. "Maybe about a week ago, you were registering for classes."

"Oh, yeah…yeah, um…that was me," I said, still staring down at the catalog. I had always been shy and awkward around guys. My aunt told me that it was something I would grow out of, but that obviously hadn't happened yet.

"My name is Demetrius."

"Brianna," I said, shaking his extended hand, "but you can call me Brie."

"How can I call you without your number?"

So corny, I thought, but it made me laugh. He was laughing too. I liked the sound of his laugh, full, deep, genuine. Was he flirting with me? I wasn't absolutely sure, maybe he was still laughing at me and the fact that he had caught me checking him out. The thought of that caused me to stop smiling abruptly. I didn't know what to think.

"Are you always so uptight, or is it the bus ride that's stressing you out? I know making this trip isn't easy, physically or emotionally. I guess I shouldn't assume it's the same for you, but that's generally how I feel when I get on this bus."

I didn't even know this guy, but he was talking to me like we went way back or something. He didn't know anything about me or my stress. I didn't appreciate him talking about things that I didn't want to think about and surely didn't want to talk about with a complete stranger. I turned away from him and looked out the window again, trying to ignore the fact that he was still next to me.

Ignoring him was not easy because he kept talking. "No offense or anything, you just look so serious. If you keep making your face like that, you're going to have frown lines before your time and that would be a shame."

I stared at my reflection in the glass of the window. He was right, I was making a face. There I went again letting everything I was thinking and feeling show right across my face. At the moment it was fear and anger. What I was feeling couldn't have been any clearer if I had spoken the words aloud.

I closed my eyes in an even more obvious attempt at ignoring him. Giving him a subtle hint hadn't seemed to work. My nerves had kept me awake the night before, so a moment with my eyes closed was all I needed to fall into a deep sleep.

I dreamed about my father. Even my subconscious wouldn't allow me to have a break from thoughts of him. Pictures of him flickered across my closed eyelids. *I'm sorry, Brianna.* Startled, I woke up, nearly jumping out of my seat.

I didn't know how long I slept, but when I woke Demetrius was still sitting next to me. Staring at me.

"You snore."

"I do not!" I couldn't help but laugh

"Your smile is just as beautiful as I thought it would be, I only got a fleeting glimpse of it before."

With that I was able to shake off the remnants of my unsettling dream and focus on what was in front of me. Don't ever believe that black people don't blush; my face felt like it was on fire. I hated the fact that I was so shy. I couldn't even look at him.

He saw fit to call me out on that too. "Why you acting so shy? It's not like I'm trying to get with you or anything. It was just a compliment."

Upset and more than a little disappointed, I said, "Well, you were the one staring at me while I slept. That doesn't sound to me like someone who is uninterested, unless you are one of those creepy stalker types."

"That's funny. It's good to know that you have sense of humor. It might help with the frown lines. But if anyone is the creepy stalker type, it's you. You have been eyeing me since I got on the bus, don't even front. Oh and FYI, I wasn't watching you sleep. I was trying to catch a nap myself, but your snoring stopped any possibility of that happening."

"Whatever."

"Oh, clever comeback."

We both laughed then, which broke some of the tension on my end. There was something extremely attractive and sexy about his confidence. It was borderline cocky, but I liked it.

"So this is what I will have to look forward to everyday once school starts?" I said, hoping the answer was yes.

"It depends. What's your major?"

"Nursing. And yours?

"EKG technician. So, unfortunately for you, we won't have any classes together. We will probably never even bump into each other. There are a lot of students there. Anyway, this is your first semester and I'm a senior so the chances of us seeing each other are even less."

"How do you know I'm a freshman?" I asked in an effort to mask my disappointment.

"Because only freshman read the course catalog." He laughed. "Anyway I have a feeling that you weren't really reading it, you were just trying to hide the fact that you were checking me out."

I didn't bother denying it. Instead I asked, "Why do you enjoy making me feel uncomfortable?"

"Because it's so easy. Don't get me wrong I actually think it's cute that you are shy and have this innocent quality. But you are an adult; people shouldn't be able to get under your skin that easily. I'm trying to help you. Besides you can't be all that innocent. You are riding this bus just like me, and it only goes one place. You have probably seen things in your life that have taken away your innocence."

"What did you say your major was? Because right now you are like some bootleg shrink. A Dr. Phil wannabe. You know what they say about people that assume things, right? And you got all of that from the fact that I am going to visit someone in prison?"

He shrugged. "I just call it how I see it. And from my experience people don't make this trip regularly unless it's to visit someone that they are dating or a close family member. You look like you have taken this trip before, so I put you in the category of a regular visitor.

"From the way you were checking me out, you are not going to visit a boyfriend. If I had to take a guess, I'd say you're visiting your brother, father, or maybe a close uncle, which means that you have been exposed to the system and everything that comes along with it. Thus my conclusion: you are not really all that innocent." He smiled, satisfied with himself.

I had only met him a couple of hours ago and he already thought he could sum me up in a neat little package. That annoyed me. It also annoyed me that I felt the need to defend myself to him.

"Just because I'm visiting someone in prison doesn't mean that I was aware of the life that they were living or the things they did to get sent there. For your information, until a few days ago I was living in a perfect little world believing that my father had been wrongfully convicted."

The words came out before I even knew what I was saying. Blurting that out to him of all people was not what I wanted to do, especially considering he had already formed judgments about me based on less information.

"What's he in for?"

"None of your business," I snapped, barely letting him get the question out.

"Okay. I didn't mean to upset you. I'm going to visit my brother. He's doing six years for armed robbery and assault."

"Did he do it?"

"Yeah."

"Then why do you go visit him?"

"Because he's my brother. He did something wrong and I make no excuses for him, but he is still my brother. Is the only reason you went to visit your father because you thought he was innocent?"

"I don't know." That was the honest truth. I didn't know if I could go visit him knowing the truth about who he was. It wasn't only that he was a drug dealer, it was that he'd lied to me for all of those years.

"So now that you know the truth about your dad, why are you making the trip today?"

That I did know the answer to. "Closure"

We were pulling through the large chain-linked fence that marked the entrance to the prison. The dreaded time had arrived.

Chapter 5

I had rehearsed over and over what I was going to say when I saw him. I would tell him that he was a liar, that he was everything he had warned me to stay away from. I would tell him that I hated him and that I never wanted to see him again, and then I would make my dramatic exit. I had imagined the relief that I would feel when it was all over.

But none of that happened. I can't believe he actually refused to see me. The possibility of that happening hadn't even crossed my mind. Maybe it should have.

I sat in the visitor's room as usual and searched for his face in the crowd. Once all the men had been seated across from their visitors, the chair in front of me was still empty. A guard came and politely told me that my father didn't want to see any visitors.

"Does he know it's me, his daughter?"

"Yes, I told him that... I'm sorry, he specifically said that he doesn't want to see you."

He was the one who had been doing wrong all these years, and he couldn't even look me in the eyes, and give me the chance to say what was on my mind. He owed me that much.

On the ride back to the city, traffic was backed up for miles. We would later find out that someone had hit a deer. That type of thing happens a lot on the roads of upstate New York. I could relate to what it felt like to be road kill. The news of my father's double life and his rejection of me had hit me like a Mack truck.

I didn't feel like talking, but Demetrius didn't give me much of a choice. He had this way of getting me to open up. By the time we arrived back in the city, I was starting to feel comfortable with him. When he asked me for my phone number, I surprised myself by making an attempt at flirtation.

"I thought you weren't interested in me?" I said, giving him a sly head tilt.

"I'm not interested in you. You're not my type, but we could be friends." He winked at me.

I didn't know what this feeling was that I was experiencing. It was unfamiliar to me, but I liked it. For a brief moment it allowed me to take my mind off of everything that had been going on lately. I jotted down my number and handed it to him. I walked away with a little extra swing in my hips, just in case he was watching.

Chapter 6

In the past two days, I'd been able to go no more than ten minutes without thinking about my father. I couldn't deny that it hurt me to the core when he'd refused to see me. But I couldn't force him to see me any more than I could force him to be the father that I thought he was all those years. All I could do was find a way to move on and live my own life.

I felt like I had come in on a movie that was already half-way over. I sat there struggling to figure out what I had missed. Everyone else was fully clued in on the plot, everyone but me.

What had I missed? That was the question that kept me awake night after night. And if I did fall asleep, that was the question that made me jolt upright in my bed five minutes later, my pillow drenched in a mixture of sweat and tears.

But he hadn't even made the effort to walk into the visitation room. Frustrated, I resolved not to waste any more time thinking about him. He seemed to have put me out of his mind easily enough, so why should I lose sleep over him? I thought.

I was excited when Demetrius called and invited me to "Do Lunch." It would give me a chance to occupy my mind with something other than my father and his double life.

I thought I did a fairly good job of hiding my excitement when I accepted his invitation. "Sure!"

I spent the whole afternoon with Demetrius. He told me to call him Dee. You know those people that have faces that just invite you to talk to them? Dee was like that, he really had a way of getting me to open up and talk to him. And that is exactly what we did, all afternoon, and then every night on the phone for the next two weeks.

He told me that his parents lived in Florida and that he wasn't really that close to them but he hoped to fix that over time. He told me that he had been in love before, with an older woman that had broken his heart. I felt a tinge of jealousy, not really sure why.

He told me I was beautiful, that he was attracted to me from the moment he saw me on the bus. He told me that he wanted to be with me, and had no intention of just being my friend. I told him I felt the same way.

Dee was a welcome distraction. But despite the distraction I still couldn't put aside all of the unanswered questions I had about my father. I wanted to hear the rest of what Aunt Jackie had to say.

Well, actually, it was more than that, I needed to hear the rest of it. I had to know the truth, even though there was nothing she could say that would change anything. I began to realize that before I could fully let go of any of this, I had to know the whole story. I told her that if she still wanted to tell me, I was ready to listen now.

Without hesitation she started where she had left off. "Keith had the security issues taken care of once he got the dirt on the cops. The only other thing he had to do was to figure out how to deal with the large sums of cash he was bringing in.

"He opened three different bank accounts at three different banks in three different boroughs. Each week he would make a small deposit in each account. He also opened a few CDs and he put the rest in a safety deposit box.

"When he went to open his account at Chase Bank, your mother was the representative that assisted him. They hit it off right away. They dated for about a year or so. He never told her anything about his dealing. He told her the same thing that he told you: he was a construction worker.

"He was so happy when they got married. Nine months later you came along. And you already know that your mother died in childbirth. Your father was devastated. The only thing that kept him going was you. He was really messed up for a while."

My father had told me his version of that part of the story, without references to the drug dealing, of course. He'd told me that they met in a bank and that it was love at first sight. It was for him, anyway. He'd said she'd played hard to get.

"It's always good for a woman to do that," he'd told me. "If you make a man work for you he will appreciate you more."

I'd laughed at that.

"It's the truth. You don't see that a lot these days. Girls are too easy. That's why they attract the wrong type of men. Men that will never respect them."

I thought about my father's words and realized that playing hard to get wasn't enough to keep my mother from attracting the wrong type of guy. She died before she knew the truth about him. Maybe that was a blessing.

My aunt was telling me that over the years my father had created an empire and with that came enemies. But ultimately it was his overwhelming sense of paranoia that caused his downfall. That, and the fact that he trusted the wrong people.

"By that point he was already the kingpin. He was running everything around here," she said. "He was at the top, but he was always looking over his shoulder. There were some young dealers that were trying to make a name for themselves. That wouldn't have been much of a problem but the cops that had been watching your father's back for all of those years were no longer in the picture.

"From what I heard, those two cops were involved in a shooting not too far from here. One was killed and the other was so badly injured that he was forced to take early retirement. Your father was paranoid. He thought that the crew of young dealers had taken the cops down because they knew he owned them.

"I warned your father to leave it alone but he was determined to find out if the young dealers were responsible for the shooting."

She warned him about the paranoia, but not the drug dealing? Way to go!

"He chose one of the guys that had been with him since the beginning, someone he thought was loyal to him. The plan was for this guy, I believe Terrence was his name, to infiltrate the young crew and find out the truth about the shooting."

Terrence? I knew Terrence. He was only a year older than I was. That was probably why my father was so afraid of me dating. The majority of the guys in the neighborhood probably worked for him in one capacity or another.

"Unfortunately, Terrence's loyalty was not as solid as your father had thought. He went to the other side for real. With the promise of higher status and a bigger percentage of profits, Terrence didn't have any problem turning on your father. Terrence made an anonymous call to the police leading them right to your father's stash house on the day he was their doing inventory. That's the problem with any illegal activity, knowing who to trust."

That was the problem? Out of all the things that were screwed up about this story and this whole situation, that was the problem?

"That's what it always comes down to," she said. "One wrong decision can cause you your life or your freedom. Loyalty doesn't exist, not really; it's like a commodity and it's always for sale to the highest bidder.

"Ninety-nine percent of the time it's not the cops alone that catch dealers, it's the snitch, the inside man. In this case, ironically enough, Terrance snitched on your father as a way to prove his loyalty to the young crew. Stupid move. He was a dead man walking before he ever picked up the phone to make that call. I mean how did he really expect anyone else to trust him after he turned on your father so easily?"

"Daddy killed him?"

"No, of course not. Your father's not a murderer."

"Don't say it like I should already know. I don't assume anything anymore."

She didn't bother to respond to that. "When the cops raided your father's stash house, his guard was totally down. There was nothing that he could do and he had nothing left to bargain with. He spotted them coming and was able to make a run for it, but they had found his drugs and he knew it was only a matter of time before they tracked him down. That's why he's in prison, for putting his trust in the wrong person. Now you know everything."

I was completely dumfounded. The story as a whole was outrageous to me but what was really crazy was that the moral she got from all of it was that you couldn't trust anyone, not that you shouldn't be a criminal.

Whatever. This wasn't an afterschool special and it wasn't my place to teach her anything. Like she said, I had the whole story now, there was no epiphany or *aha!* moment that made everything fall into place and make sense, but I doubted that I would every truly make sense of what he had done. The point was that now that I knew the truth, I would be able to put it behind me and move on.

I got up from the table with the intention of going to my room but I found myself walking out the front door instead. When I exited the building I was hit by the humid August air. The sun had gone down, but the temperature still lingered somewhere around ninety degrees. I sat on the bench outside my building and all kinds of thoughts were running through my head. I couldn't make sense of any of them.

Not even five minutes had passed when I was accosted by a guy walking past my building.

"Hey, baby. What you doing out here all alone on this beautiful summer night?"

Not now, I thought to myself. I was in no mood for this. He was wearing a wifebeater and jeans. His jeans were hanging so far below his butt that he might as well been wearing them as socks, and he had the nerve to have on a belt. And even in the darkness, I could see the cubic zirconias glistening, one in each ear. I had to turn away so that I didn't laugh in his face.

"I was just leaving," I said as I got up and began to walk away. I didn't want to sit anymore anyway. I'd been sitting for hours listening to my aunt admire her convict brother. I didn't slow down as the guy called after me.

"Hey, baby… boo… ma… stupid…" I tuned out the profanity that I knew was coming. Typical man, couldn't take rejection.

I took out my cell and gave Dee a call. Funny how natural that was starting to feel

He answered on the second ring. "Hey Brie, I was just thinking about you. What you wearing?"

I laughed. He had a way of making me do that even when I didn't want to. "Well considering I'm outside going for a walk, I'm fully clothed."

"Disappointing. Anyway, what are you doing outside so late? You know it's not safe."

"It's not safe inside my house either," I said.

"Don't be difficult. Where are you exactly? I will come and meet you."

I told him my location and he said he'd be there in ten minutes.

"Just stay put."

"Okay"

Chapter 7

Half hour later I was sitting in the passenger seat of Dee's Acura. It was a used car that he'd bought at auction two months ago.

He was renting a one bedroom apartment on Jarvis Avenue. It was my first time going to his place and I was nervous. But I felt so comfortable with him and I was so emotionally drained from the rest of the day that I decided not to over-think things. Instead I was going to just go with the flow.

He kept his apartment really clean, not what you might expect from a guy living alone. The apartment was small. I guess it was what a real estate agent would call cozy. In his living room he had a black leather couch, a coffee table, and a flat screen. He said that was all he needed, which was good because there wasn't room for anything else.

"Make yourself at home," he said, motioning toward the couch. The couch was comfortable, and as soon as I sat down I realized how tired I was. It had been a really long day.

"Something to drink?" he said.

I wiped my sweaty hands on my pant legs, annoyed that I was so nervous.

"I've got soda and iced tea."

"Iced tea, thanks."

He placed the cup on the coffee table in front of me, turned off the lights and started a movie. I guess he sensed my nervousness because he sat all the way at the other end of the sofa. My nervousness battled with my exhaustion. Exhaustion won. I didn't make it past the opening credits.

"So how did you like the movie?" The light from the TV flashed across his face just long enough for me to see he was smiling.

"It was good." I don't even know why I tried to play it off.

"Shut up!" He laughed that sexy laugh of his. "You slept through the whole thing."

"I..." Before I could get out my denial he had scooted down to my end of the couch. He grabbed me by the back of the neck and brought me to him. He kissed me, our first kiss.

It was so intense. His lips were so full and soft. His tongue danced a sultry tango with mine. He was using his hand to softly massage the back of my neck. I thought I would pass out when he let out a little moan. I didn't know how much more I could take. Then just as suddenly and unexpected as it started, it was over. He was in complete control the whole time.

"I'm tired. I'm gonna go take a shower and go to bed, unless you want me to drive you home."

"No its okay, I can take a cab."

"No, that's not what I'm saying. I was inviting you to stay. I want you to stay." He paused waiting for me to say something, but I didn't know what to say. So he continued, "I will take the couch and you can take the bed, but I want to wake up with you here with me in the morning."

"Okay." I said it quickly, before my logical thought process kicked in and made me change my mind. I didn't want to be logical and rational tonight. I just wanted to be with him.

He smiled at me, turned, and headed toward the bathroom.

Unfortunately, with him out of sight I had time to think. What was I getting myself into? We had just had our first kiss and now we were having a sleepover. I had known this guy for less than two months.

Despite all of that, I still couldn't help but think this felt right.

He came out of the shower with a white towel tied around his waist, beads of water still rolling down his chest. His body was as fit and defined as I'd imagined it would be. Besides the little trail of hair peeking out the top of the towel, he was completely hairless, smooth and glistening.

He noticed me looking, flexed, and made his chest muscles jump up and down in a sort of dance. I couldn't help but laugh. That's what he wanted, to get me to release some of my nervous tension. But that only lasted a second, because seemingly of their own accord, my eyes continued their exploration of his body.

When he caught me looking a second time, he didn't try to make me laugh. Instead, he eyed me and said, "You like what you see? Want me to lose the towel?" He went to undo the knot that was holding the towel on his waist.

"No!" It came out like a terrified shriek.

He was cracking up. "All right, Brie, all right. Take the bedroom and get off my couch so I can get some sleep. Here, you can put this on." He tossed me a T-shirt.

"I'm gonna take a shower too," I said, walking toward the bathroom.

"There's a towel already in there for you." He walked toward me, very casually kissed me on the lips, and said goodnight. Like we had been doing that for years, it was so comfortable. By the time I got out of the shower he was sound asleep. I didn't know whether I was relieved or disappointed.

His bed was comfortable. I thought about how the night before, he had been lying in this exact same spot. I slept well. I didn't think about how my father had lied to me, or how my life might have been different if my mother hadn't died. Instead I nestled myself in the part of the mattress that had formed to the contours of Dee's body and fell into a deep sleep.

The next morning I woke up feeling like the sun streaming through the window had given me sunburn on one side of my face. A few seconds later I heard Dee in the bathroom taking a leak. He didn't even bother to close the door. Had he forgotten I was here or was that just a guy thing?

He came into the bedroom and I closed my eyes pretending to be asleep. He got in the bed next to me.

"What are you doing?" My voice was panicky.

"I knew you weren't sleeping. It was too quiet, no snoring."

"You were the one snoring last night," I said. "It sounded like the MTA had a train running through your living room."

"Yeah, okay." His leg rubbed against my thigh as he stretched out in the bed, making himself comfortable "I got a crick in my neck sleeping on the couch. You don't mind if I lie in here for a while do you?"

"No, it's your bed. I was getting ready to get up anyway." I said it as I tossed my legs over the side of the bed and stood up. He grabbed the bottom of the T-shirt I was wearing.

"Stay."

"Okay, but stay on your side."

"Is this my side?" he said as he began to palm my butt.

"Not quite." I was nervous and it was apparent when my voice shook a little.

"How about this? Or this? How about right here?"

His touch was so erotic. I didn't know what he would do next, but the anticipation was part of the excitement. After a few more minutes of his playful teasing, I thought I would explode.

"Do you want to?" I could feel his breath on the back of my neck as he asked me. It was getting harder and harder... to say no.

"I've never..."

"I know babe. You don't have to. If you aren't ready that's okay. Just tell me what you want."

I didn't tell him. I touched him, showed him what I wanted, showed him I was ready. When it was over I had absolutely no regrets.

Chapter 8

I was on cloud nine. Up to that point, I think it may have been the happiest day of my entire life. I wanted to tell someone that I was in love, that I had this amazing guy. It was times like that when I wished my mother were still alive. This was something I would have wanted to share with her. Not the details of course, but the fact that I was in love.

I always imagined what my mother was like. She was beautiful, that much I knew from the pictures I'd seen: brown skin, thick brown shoulder-length hair, tall and slender.

As a kid I had imagined her baking cookies for my school bake sales and coming with me on school trips. I'd imagine telling her about my day as we sat on my bed and she combed my hair before tucking me in. She would always know what to say to make me feel better and she would give the best advice.

In my imagination she was a cross between Clair Huxtable and the father from *Full House*. In reality, I learned life's lessons without her. I used to talk to my aunt about certain things, but that was no longer an option because she was part of my father's cover-up.

I was determined not to let the fact that I had no one to talk to about it minimize what I was feeling. I was in love, and so what if it was my little secret?

Over the next few weeks I spent more and more time at Dee's apartment. The sight of my aunt was something that I couldn't deal with, not yet. I only stopped by the apartment when I knew she was at work and only to pick up fresh clothes or mail.

Before long, the semester was in full swing, and during most of the time that I spent with Dee, we were studying. We would sit at opposite ends of the couch with books in between us and highlighters in hand.

"Move in with me," he said one night out of the blue.

I looked up from my textbook for the first time in about three hours. "Huh?"

He'd caught me completely off guard. I was there every night anyway, I thought, but then the little voice in my head said, *officially moving in together is a big step, are you ready for that?*

"I'm with you, Brie, you know that. I'm not seeing anyone else and I don't want to."

That possibility hadn't even crossed my mind.

"You're here most of the time anyway." He nervously tapped his highlighter against his book. "I think you should just get all of your stuff from your aunt's place and bring it over here so you don't have to go back and forth so much."

"Oh, so it's a matter of convenience?"

"No, it's not a matter of convenience." He finally made eye contact. "I care about you and I hate to see you upset. Every time you come from over there you're upset. But honestly that is only part of the reason. I am a selfish guy and the real reason is that I want you here. I want to come home to you and I want to wake up next to you."

Well, that sold me on the idea. "Okay."

"Good. Once I find out my work schedule for next week we will figure out a time to go get your things."

I tried my hardest to hush that stupid little voice in my head, the one that made me doubt myself. The one that was telling me all of this was happening too fast, that there was still so much we didn't know about each other. Instead, I choose to follow my heart. The heart that beat faster every time he touched me, skipped a beat when he called me his girl, and at that moment it was telling me he was the one.

Chapter 9

It was six thirty in the morning and the halls of The Manhattan Institute were empty except for a janitor methodically cleaning in preparation for the onslaught of students that would be arriving in about an hour or so.

The school was quite peaceful at this time of day. It made me feel like I was getting a head start, an edge on the competition. And that's what it was, a competition.

It wasn't like other schools I had heard of, with cliques and people hanging together after class going to the club or the bar; it was not like that at all. It was a school where people were taking an intensive program to learn specific skills and there was no time for socializing. It was all about graduating and getting a job. No sororities or dorm parties. These were serious students. Everyone was trying to get the grades and make the connections that would allow them to land their dream job upon graduation.

But that morning I wasn't there to study. I had an appointment. The school had a counselor on staff, one of the many things I knew from reading the school's brochure. She wasn't an academic counselor. I guess she was more like a therapist that you could talk to about anything.

I had been feeling more and more guilty about how happy I was with Dee. Things had been going really well since I moved in with him.

It kind of felt like I was playing house or something. I wasn't much of a cook, but I started waking up early to make breakfast for him. Just like I had for Daddy those mornings he'd gone off to his imaginary construction job. Grits, eggs, sausage and toast—nothing fancy. But Dee liked to tease me about it.

"Nothing like waking up with a woman in the kitchen," he'd say. And I'd chase him and try to swat him with the dish towel. It was so perfect, too perfect, and that made me nervous.

I also felt like it was wrong for me to be happy considering my father was in prison, dealing with who knew what.

Then that guilt I felt would turn into anger. I mean, why should I have felt guilty? He was the one who had lied to me. He was the one who refused to see me. I deserved to be happy and move on with my life. And of course that thought made me feel guilty all over again. And so the cycle continued.

I needed someone to talk to. So I sat in the student lounge, waiting for my appointment. I found myself tapping my right foot a mile a minute. *There's really nothing wrong with me. There's not!* I said it over and over in my head. I was just about to get up and make a run for it when a woman appeared.

"Good morning. You must be Brianna," she said, extending her hand.

I could still say no. *Sorry you've got the wrong girl.* I guess I mulled over that possibility for a moment too long. "It's okay, Brianna, nothing to be nervous about. My name is Dr. Beekman. Why don't we go into my office?"

"Okay."

Her office was bright and spacious, yet I felt claustrophobic. There was a lot of early morning sunlight coming through the two large windows behind her desk. I noticed that one of her office walls was completely covered with degrees, certificates, and awards. Even though I was impressed by her accomplishments, I also thought the display was kind of obnoxious.

She directed me to take a seat. There was no comfy leather couch for me to lay down on as I poured out my deepest darkest secrets. In fact the chair was quite uncomfortable. But then again this whole situation was uncomfortable.

"So, Brianna, how are your classes going so far?"

I could tell she was starting me off with an easy question, trying to allow me to relax. Dr. Beekman was a petite woman with a friendly demeanor. She smiled a lot. The makeup on her fair skin looked as though it had been professionally done. Her dark brown hair, which was slightly gray at the roots, was the only indication of her age.

"It's only my first semester, but I think I'm managing pretty well." I was being modest. I was kicking butt. I predicted all As. "I'm starting to prepare for finals."

"That's good. You are getting an early start. Have you made any friends here yet?"

"Not really. I just go to class and then home. I'm just trying to stay focused."

She stared at me, tried to wait me out. What did she want me to say? It's not like I had been turning down social engagements. There was this one girl, Christina, who had approached me and made some polite conversation.

"Hi, Brianna, right?" she'd said.

"Yeah."

"My name is Christina."

"Hi."

"This class is tough huh?

"Yeah, he is moving through the material pretty quickly."

"And if that wasn't bad enough his accent doesn't help the situation."

I laughed. "Yeah, I know."

"By the way, your outfit is really cute."

I looked down, appraised myself, tried to figure out if she was serious, decided to play it cool. "Oh, thanks."

"Do you think we could go shopping together sometime? I have absolutely no fashion sense. If it wasn't for my mother I would probably wear polka dots and stripes every day."

I didn't consider myself a fashion guru or anything, but I reluctantly agreed.

"Oh, Brianna can you—"

"You can call me Brie."

"Oh, okay, Brie. I was absent last class. Do you think I could photocopy your notes?"

For my new friend? "Sure."

And that was the end of that. I saw her twice a week and she had never so much as said hello to me again.

Dr. Beekman was still talking. "...Social interaction is very important to the overall learning process. Don't you think you can do both, focus on your classes and make time for friends? I can tell you from experience that if you don't take some time out to enjoy yourself, you will burn yourself out pretty quickly. What do you do for fun?"

I was starting to feel a little defensive.

She continued. "You said you go to school and then straight home. What's home like?"

"Home is great. I just moved in with my boyfriend. He is also a student here." Calling him my boyfriend, my man, my boo... that never ceased to bring a smile to my face.

"So you talk to him about any problems you are having? He is your support system?"

"Definitely."

"Okay, that's good. So Brianna, what is it that you hope to get out of talking with me? Because listening to you I get the feeling that you think that everything is going great in your life."

The smile left my face. "Well, everything is going really well right now and that's the problem. The fact that things are good makes me nervous, because the last time I felt like everything was good, it all fell apart and I found out that everything I thought was true was actually a lie. I trust my boyfriend, I really do, I don't believe that he would lie to me. The thing that I don't trust is this happiness, it's the feeling itself that worries me."

I looked at her trying to gauge whether she understood what I was saying. She nodded for me to continue.

"And because I don't trust this happy feeling, I find myself trying to anticipate what is going to happen and brace myself for the next bad thing. I think that's what bothered me the most about finding out that my family had been lying to me, it's the fact that I had no clue and that I was caught so completely off guard.

"On the other hand I don't want to live my life with my guard constantly up. I don't want to always be nervous. I feel like it not only affects the way I think, it also affects my actions. I don't want to let this cause me to lose my boyfriend because he is the best thing I have in my life right now."

Dr. Beekman was giving me one of her comforting smiles. "Okay, Brianna. First, I'd like to say that you are way ahead of a lot of people simply because you are able to articulate quite clearly what you are feeling, and that puts you one step closer to learning how to deal with it.

"The thing that you need to realize is that like physical trauma, people react to emotional trauma in different ways. Now, we haven't gotten into what happened between you and your family. I hope that you will feel comfortable enough to tell me about that at some point, but from what you've said I can only imagine that it was emotionally traumatic for you."

I nodded.

"Your reaction is normal. Now it's about recovering from the trauma and moving on with your life. Let me give you an example. Let's say that there is a man who was in a car accident and has some broken bones. He has been lying in the hospital with minimal movement and

that allowed his bones to heal, but in order for him to regain full mo-
bility he needs physical therapy, the bones and muscles need exercise.

"In your case, time has passed and you have healed to some extent,
but now you need to do the exercise part of it to get to one hundred
percent. And one hundred percent is where you want to be, no fear of
happiness, no guilt for moving on with your life, and no trust issues.
That is what I am going to help you with."

That actually made perfect sense to me and I told her that. She said
she wanted to see me regularly, once a week. I wondered if she had
picked up on more issues than I realized I had. Once a week seemed
like overkill to me.

"Once a week for how long?"

"About forty-five minutes to an hour."

"No, I mean how many weeks? How many weeks will it take until
I'm fixed?"

"I'm not trying to fix you, really. Once you work through some
things, your thought process and the way you deal with situations will
change. I don't have a magic wand. It takes as long as it takes."

I didn't like the sound of that. It was a good thing these sessions
were free. I agreed to meet with her once a week.

"Good. So is next Thursday at this same time good for you?"

"Yeah I'll be here." I was optimistic about the possibility of her
actually helping me.

"It was really nice talking to you, Brianna."

I figured since I would be revealing my deepest darkest secrets,
"You can call me Brie."

Chapter 10

I was walking around in one of Dee's T-shirts when he came home that evening. I had been contemplating whether to tell him about my appointment with Dr. Beekman earlier that day. I didn't want him to think I was crazy or for him to start looking at me differently. But I also didn't want there to be secrets between us. Too many secrets is what started all of my problems in the first place.

"Hey, babe." I walked over to give him a kiss. "How was your day?"

He exhaled audibly, dropped his bag on the floor, and plopped down on the couch. "Dr. K's physiology class is killing me."

"Yeah, it's a very advanced class. But the semester will be over before you know it and you only have one more after that."

"But I have to pass this one first."

Okay, so this girlfriend thing was great, but it took a little getting used to. The comforting and nurturing thing didn't come that natural to me. I sat next to him on the couch and kissed him on the cheek. "I'm sure you will pass."

I had no clue as to whether or not he would pass. I knew he was always studying, but that could have just been because he was having a hard time understanding the material. It didn't matter whether I actually thought he would pass or not. I think the point was that I was being supportive. Fortunately for me, he just wanted to vent; he couldn't have cared less what I actually said.

"He says everything in the textbook is fair game for the final even if he doesn't cover it in class."

"That's crazy!" I said on cue.

"I know, right? He's insane. The hardest thing is trying to balance his class with my other classes and work. He acts like his class is the only one I'm taking. I have to pull another all nighter with this textbook tonight."

"I know it's tough, babe, but you will get through it and anything I can do to help, just let me know, I'm here for you." *Good job, Brie*, I thought to myself.

"You can stop walking around here looking so sexy in my T-shirt. It's distracting."

I laughed. "And I thought you didn't notice." I stood and gave him a little twirl so he could get the three hundred and sixty degree view.

"Oh, I noticed." He grabbed my waist and pulled me down into his lap. He kissed me, deep and passionate. I tilted my head slightly so I could take it all in.

When the kiss was over and I was still trying to catch my breath, he asked, "So what about you? How was your day?"

"Dizzy."

"Huh?"

Oh, did I say that out loud? That's how I felt, so dizzy, lightheaded. Even though I had never officially dated anyone before Dee, I'd been kissed before and it in no way compared to that. But I still had no intention of saying that out loud.

"Huh? Um, nothing," I stammered. "What did you ask me?"

He laughed. "How was your day?"

I got up off of his lap and walked in the kitchen to get some water. "I had an appointment with Dr. Beekman this morning."

"Why?" He coughed, cleared his throat. "You not feeling well?"

I saw the look of sheer terror on his face. I knew what he had to be thinking. *No, I'm not pregnant, just seeing a shrink.*

"No, she works in the counseling center at the school."

I watched as the tension left his face. "Is she your academic advisor?"

Okay, the moment of truth. "No she does personal counseling and therapy sessions, nothing to do with academics."

"Why do you need to talk to her? What's the matter?"

He looked concerned and that's when I realized that after my aunt had revealed my family secrets to me, I was so upset that I'd never really told him what happened. I'm sure I had mentioned bits and pieces, but he didn't know the whole story or how it was affecting me. Since I had moved in with him I had done my best to push all of it out of my mind.

I hadn't had much success with doing that so I figured it was as good a time as any to talk to him about it. I decided to use it as a trial run for what I would say to Dr. Beekman next week because I was sure it would be a topic of discussion.

I took a deep breath like the ones taught in Lamaze classes and I began. If I only knew then that there was so much left that I still didn't know, so much more that was yet to be revealed.

Chapter 11

Jackie woke up early as usual. But it was no ordinary day. It was her thirty-second birthday. She had already arranged for a sitter for the boys, and she was excited about treating herself to some well-deserved luxury.

Over the years her brother had been putting money into a bank account for her. It was small amounts at first, but the amount and frequency of the deposits had increased over time.

"And I deserve every penny of it," she told herself.

She had accumulated a nice little nest egg and today she was going to splurge. She thought about what her brother would say if he were here.

"You need to be more careful, Jackie. You can't just go out and spend like you're crazy and think it's not going to raise red flags."

Yeah, that was what he'd say. Keith had always been so cautious, always worried about what she would do. *And look who's the one on the inside*, she thought.

An hour later her car arrived. She had decided to hire a car service for the day, no MTA for her. After all, it was her birthday. She was excited, but she played it cool as she slid into the leather interior of the Mercedes S550.

From the backseat she told the driver her first destination. She did it casually, as though she had a personal driver every day. She should have one every day, she thought. What she wouldn't give to quit her job, take her money, and go start a new life somewhere. Luxury cars, beautiful houses, expensive vacations. *I hear St. Bart's is wonderful this time of year.* She laughed a little at the thought.

The truth of the matter was she had promised Keith that she would look after Brie, but now that she was seeing Brie less and less, she didn't feel obligated to stick around. It was her brother that was putting the brakes on her exit strategy. Of course, if he didn't even want her to treat herself every now and then, he would completely flip out if she emptied the account.

Jackie recalled the conversation when she'd tried to tell her brother what she wanted to do. He'd said, "If you touch the money, you will end up locked up or even worse, dead." She knew he was trying to scare her. Even though he was her brother, Jackie knew better than to trust him, or anyone else for that matter. Everyone has their own agenda. But she had to admit that she didn't feel as safe and comfortable in her hood as she used to when Keith was around.

The new crew that had taken over since Keith went away was young, violent, vengeful, and very well financed. They were moving serious weight. As far as organization, they had a long way to go but they were definitely paid.

Keith didn't hesitate to remind her about their vengefulness. "As soon as they even think you have some of my money, they will come after you." The thought made her laugh because, even though her brother had been kingpin, things were not always what they seemed.

She knew the truth. She knew that he wouldn't have been able to make anything happen without her. She had been the brains of his operation and there was no way she was going to get outsmarted by a bunch of youngins.

She glanced out the window as a patrol car sped past them. She wasn't afraid of the new crew, but the cops gave her pause. This whole NYC war against drugs wasn't simply a newspaper headline; it was having a real effect in the hood and she was not about to be added to the mayor's success rate.

So what is a girl to do, she wondered. She knew one thing for sure. Cleaning up after old people all day was not something she was going to tolerate much longer. Jackie hated taking care of old people. Feeding them and watching them gum down their food. Washing them, that was the worst. Seeing their loose skin hanging off their brittle, osteoporosis-infected bones. It all just made her want to throw up.

She knew she needed a plan. She decided that she was going to enjoy her day and push her worries out of her mind for now. She looked out of the window as the car made its way down the FDR and into Manhattan. She arrived at her appointment at the Peninsula Spa right on time. This was the life that she should be living every day, not only on her birthday, and she was going to do what needed to be done to make that happen.

Chapter 12

You never know how good you've got it until it's gone. That's what people say. Well, the opposite is true too. Walking into the projects, the place I had called home for so many years, it struck me how I had never realized how bad the place really was until I left there.

It was a cold and windy November day. Garbage, soda bottles, cigarette containers, paper bags, and who knows what else was circling above the ground like a tornado of litter. I tucked my face into the collar of my coat to protect it from the wind just as much as from the trash.

I ducked quickly into the building and was assaulted by the smell of piss in the hallway. Even if I were an Olympic swimmer, I couldn't hold my breath long enough to avoid the smell. The smell was even stronger in the tight confines of the elevator as I rode up to the tenth floor.

I used my key to unlock the door. The apartment was dark and there was a welcome silence. I didn't feel like seeing anyone. I grabbed the mail that Aunt Jackie had left for me by the front door and quickly made my way back to the elevator. That was the only reason I stopped by the apartment anymore, to pick up my mail. I felt bad because I missed the boys, but I just wasn't ready to see my aunt. I wasn't trying to cut her off or anything, I just needed time to get over the fact that all this time she had known about my father's secret and had never told me.

I had been away from the projects for too long, or maybe I was just distracted by thoughts of my aunt and the boys, I don't know. But for whatever reason I had my guard down. I didn't even hear the footsteps until it was too late.

Someone grabbed my hair tightly and pulled me backward. I stumbled and fell into him. I knew it was a man before he spoke because I could feel his hard chest against my back. He was taller than me but not by much. He smelled like cigarettes and spearmint gum. Reflexively I dropped my bag, thinking I was being robbed.

I was unable to force out a scream or a plea for help. Not that it would have mattered; the whole time there were people around, I could see them watching us. No one attempted to help me; they probably thought it was some type of domestic disturbance and didn't want to get involved. That might even have been giving them a little too much credit. The number one rule in the projects was to mind your own business and not get involved, and I could see that these people were sticking to that rule. I knew the same thing would happen if the police later came to question them; no one would have seen anything.

I tried to struggle free. He held me tighter.

Finally he spoke. "I don't wanna hurt you," he said. Which seemed to me like a stupid thing to say considering the circumstances.

Deep voice, husky thug accent.

I was trying to remember details. Maybe I had watched one too many cop shows. That was not how it worked in the hood, though.

"I want you to do me a favor. Give your father a message."

What? This was about my father? I wanted to say it out loud but my voice box was still out of service.

"Tell him that Jackie is playing a game, and she doesn't know the rules. She is aligning herself with some very dangerous people and she is going to get herself hurt."

He took out a knife and showed it to me. He rubbed it across my chest, which was heaving up and down with my rapid breaths.

"Let me give you a little advice," he said, still fondling me with the knife. "Daddy is not running anything anymore, so you are not untouchable. You are not protected. I wouldn't walk around here after dark if I were you. It's not safe." He grabbed my hair and in one quick motion cut off my ponytail.

"When you give your father the message, tell him it's from Atlantic."

Chapter 13

Iwas all the way back at the apartment before I fully caught my breath. On the bus ride home, someone asked me if I was okay and I couldn't even answer. I'm sure they just figured I was drunk or on drugs.

Inside the apartment I headed straight for the bathroom. I threw up, heaved uncontrollably. It was made more painful by the fact that I had no food in my stomach. I was finally able to make an audible sound, a moan, as a sick lightheaded feeling washed over me.

I wanted to call Dee. I needed him right now, but I knew that his phone would be turned off because he was in one of his night classes. I thought back to my conversation with Dr. Beekman and how she thought I needed to make friends. A friend would have been nice right then. I didn't want to be alone.

None of it seemed real. Maybe I was still in shock. From my classes I knew the symptoms that were usually associated with shock from a traumatic experience. I also knew that its lingering effects could last hours, weeks, or even years depending on the person.

I couldn't even grasp the fact that this had something to do with my father, and hadn't the guy mentioned my aunt too?

As I sat on the bathroom floor leaning against the side of the tub, I felt extremely tired. I could barely keep my eyes open. Sometimes people lose consciousness because it's the body's way of protecting itself, its way of dealing with pain. One of my professors had mentioned that in class not even a week before. I never thought I would experience it firsthand. So tired, so very, very tired. I closed my eyes, just for a minute.

Chapter 14

The baby was crying. I walked over to the crib covered with the yellow ducky bedding and looked down at a face identical to mine. She had a head full of curly black hair, chubby cheeks, and the most perfect brown complexion. I picked her up.

"It's okay, shhh." I tried to console her. I held her little body to my chest and gently bounced her up and down in an effort to hush her cries.

Someone was at the door. I propped the baby in the crook of my arm as I went to answer it. A man in a brown uniform stood at the threshold.

"I have a delivery for Ms. Roberts," the man said.

"That's me, but I don't remember ordering anything,"

He checked the electronic reader he was carrying. "It's from Babies R Us." He looked at the baby and then back at me. "It could be a gift for the little one. I don't see a card but I could take the package back to the warehouse and have someone look into that for you. It will probably take a few weeks for redelivery."

He seemed nice enough. "Don't bother, I'll sign for it." I signed scribbling illegible lines and swirls on the electronic screen.

"Where do you want it?"

"Oh, you can put it right here in the living room." I turned my back for only a split second to point to where he could put the box. That's when I heard the familiar click of the door being locked. Instinctively I held the baby tighter. When I turned around, there was a gun pointed at my head, a big gun.

What is it that people say? When they have near death experiences, they see their life flash before their eyes? Well, that didn't happen to me, all I saw was the gun and the tension in the finger wrapped around the trigger.

Could I make it to the bedroom? No, there was no lock on that door. How about the bathroom? Thoughts ran through my head faster than a Hunts Point hooker trying to outrun the cops.

I picked a dish up off the counter and threw it at him as hard as I could. I made a run for the bathroom, knowing all the while that there was no way I could outrun a bullet, no way that I would make it to the bathroom. But I had to try. I had to protect the baby.

In my mad dash for the bathroom, I knocked things down behind me, trying to slow down my assailant. I braced myself for the bullet, knowing that it would pierce my spine at any moment. Between the ringing in my own ears and the baby's crying, I couldn't tell how close behind me he was.

When I made it to the bathroom, I was out of breath and panting, but I was still in one piece. I quickly secured the lock behind me.

It was just a flimsy bathroom lock, and I knew it wasn't going to hold for long. I gently placed the baby in the tub and began to frantically look through the drawers and cabinets for some type of makeshift weapon. On my hands and knees, I looked under the sink. He was banging against the door. The force of his body was splintering the wood. I knew at any minute we would be face to face.

Toothpaste, mouthwash, Lysol, nothing that would slow him down for long. The frame of the door splintered more. It wasn't going to hold for much longer. I began to pace the length of the small bathroom.

"You're a fighter just like your mother," he said through the door. "This brings back such fond memories." Getting impatient, he fired through the bathroom door. The bullet flew past me missing by inches and shattering the glass of the medicine cabinet. I picked up a shard of broken glass and gripped it, ignoring my own blood as it poured from my hand and made a puddle on the floor.

He peaked at me through the hole the bullet had left in the door. Desperate, I screamed, cried. The baby joined in. "Help! Please! Somebody help me!"

Chapter 15

I woke up still screaming. Still sitting on the bathroom floor. Still listening to the frantic banging on the door. I was confused, not sure what was real and what were the leftover remnants of the nightmare.

"Brie?"

"Dee?"

"Yeah, it's me. Open the door...Open the door, Brianna."

I slowly picked myself up off the floor. My whole body hurt. I walked to the door and opened it. I was so relieved to see Dee standing there. My body was shaking uncontrollably.

"Okay, okay, take it easy."

I slumped against him, making sure that he was real, and that I hadn't drifted into another realm of unconsciousness. He wrapped his arms around me and held me tightly. I burst into tears.

"It's okay, Brie. Everything's okay. I got you." He stroked my hair as he held me, probably realizing for the first time that there was so much less of it.

"Don't cry Brie. Whatever it is, just tell me." I could tell he was nervous, but I couldn't talk, all I could get out of my throat were sobs. I cried until I was limp and exhausted.

After several more failed attempts at getting me to talk, Dee stepped away from me, put his hands on my shoulders and looked me directly in the eyes. "Brie, you were in the bathroom yelling for someone to help you. I need you to tell me what happened."

I didn't know it then, but my real nightmare was just getting started.

Chapter 16

I had never seen him so pissed. His hands were balled into fists, he was breathing heavily, and there was a row of sweat beads forming on his forehead. I knew that he was upset because he was scared, he was scared to think about what could have happened and this was his way of handling it.

"Move, Brie!"

"No!"

"Move!"

"No!"

I stood as a human barricade against the door. I had finally been able to compose myself enough to tell him what had happened and he immediately tried to leave the apartment to go find the person that was responsible. But I knew it was too dangerous and I stood with my back firmly against the door, staring him down. I was not about to move. He was pacing, mumbling, cursing under his breath.

He gestured emphatically with his hands. "You don't want me to call the police. You don't want me to go handle it myself. You know that people saw what happened. And you want me to just stay here... stay here and do nothing?"

I pleaded with him. "I want you to stay here with me. I don't want you to get hurt."

"Just because I don't have a rap sheet doesn't mean I don't know how to handle myself. I can handle myself, Brie."

"I didn't say you couldn't." He thought I was questioning his manhood. I would have to go about this a different way. "If something happens to you, then who do I have, who is going to be there for me?"

"Well, what's the sense of me being here if you don't let me protect you?" He made another attempt for the door. I stood my ground. We were in an old-fashioned standoff.

Tired of arguing he grabbed me by my waist, picked me up, and moved me out of his way. I balled my hands into fist and banged them against his chest.

"Haven't I been manhandled enough for one day?" I shouted.

He looked at me like he was ashamed and backed away. Taking advantage of the pause in his yelling I told him, "It's a no-win situation. If you go looking for a fight or something and get arrested, then what? Or if you go and get jumped, then what? I'm fine!" I said, patting myself down like I was doing an inspection. "See, I'm fine. As long as you stay here with me I will be fine."

"Yeah, you are fine this time, but what about next time?"

"There won't be a next time."

"How do you know, Brie? I've asked you a hundred times not to go there by yourself especially after dark. I told you how dangerous it is and that it's getting worse every day. Since your father went to prison, these new dealers are trying to make a name for themselves. People are getting killed and going missing every day.

"They're trying to send a message that they are in charge. Their guns are not for show, and this is not TV. They don't just flash them, they use them. It's serious out there right now, and…and I asked you not to go. But do you listen? Noooo , of course not.

"You do whatever you want, like you're invincible. You are not invincible. Do you think you're invincible, Brie? 'Cause you're not. Someone pulled a knife on you tonight. You could have lost a lot more than hair."

I wondered what our neighbors were thinking. I wished he would take it down a few octaves. He was turning it around on me, and that was okay, I would take it as long as it meant he wasn't blaming himself. He could vent all he wanted as long as he was doing it here with me, in the apartment and not in the street.

"You're right, Dee," I said, trying to defuse the situation and get him to calm down. "I shouldn't have gone there by myself, but I lived there all my life and I had no real reason to feel unsafe."

"Do you feel unsafe now?" he shouted, mocking me. "Is it real to you now?" He kept shaking his head like he couldn't believe how naïve I was. "I know I have never lived there, but I have been in enough projects to know that if you don't feel unsafe, then something is wrong. You should always realize you are not safe. That's what makes you cautious. That's your problem: you're not cautious." He was pacing again. I wanted him to hurry up and wear himself out.

"The reason you felt safe all of those years growing up there is because of your father. Even though you didn't know it, he was running everything. You might as well have been walking around with the secret service. You were untouchable, that's just how it works.

"Out of fear or respect for your father no one would mess with you. For you it was the safest place on earth. So your experience growing up there is not really what it's like. Now that he's gone and you don't have that protection you are getting your first real taste of what it's like. So you need to protect yourself which means being smart and not going there alone."

"Okay, okay," I said, putting up my hands in mock surrender. "I hear you, but you have to understand where I'm coming from, I want you to be cautious, too, and trying to go out there tonight is only looking for trouble. So stop pacing and try to calm down, neither one of us is going anywhere tonight."

Finally, he sat down. He rubbed his forehead with the palm of his hand, trying to rub away a headache I assumed. "I couldn't take it if something happened to you," he said. "When you were screaming in the bathroom earlier you sounded so scared. I didn't know what to do. I love you. I just want you to be safe."

He had never said that to me before. It was the worst day I'd had in a long time, but was it possible that it could also be the best? With the passage of time maybe the only thing I would remember about that day are those three perfect little words. I said them back to him.

Chapter 17

Between Dee tossing and turning all night and my own mind racing, I felt like I had slept a total of five minutes. Exhausted, I swatted at the alarm clock when it went off at seven.

"Babe, you only have one class today right?" Dee mumbled, still half asleep.

"Yeah"

"You should stay home today and rest. I'm sure that you can get the notes from someone."

It took no convincing for me to agree to that. "Okay."

Dee got out of bed and stumbled toward the bathroom. I stretched out.

When he got out of the shower and started to get dressed, he said, "I am going to call out from work, so I will be home right after my classes. I shouldn't be any later than five. Check and make sure there is nothing that you need because once I leave I want you to stay in the house until I get back. Promise me?"

"I don't need anything. I'll be here."

"Promise me, Brie." There was a slight hint of desperation in his voice. He was nervous about leaving me alone.

But I was telling the truth I wasn't going anywhere. "I promise."

Once Dee left, I went in the bathroom and for the first time fully inspected the damage to my hair. I'd always had long hair, now it barely reached the nape of my neck. I know some women would have been very upset about it, but I wasn't as upset about my hair as I was about the violation. The fact that someone had put their hands on me. That he had gotten that close. What scared me was that Dee was right, it could have been so much worse.

I went back to bed, but I couldn't sleep. I kept playing every detail of the day before over and over in my head. I squinted a little trying to put my memories into focus like the letters on an eye chart. I thought about the nightmare I'd had as I slept on the bathroom floor.

Gunman chasing me, running for my life, trying to protect my baby. What did it all mean? Maybe it meant nothing, maybe it was just my reaction to the traumatic experience. Maybe. But I felt like the nightmare was so detailed, so vivid. I'd never had a nightmare like that before.

Was my subconscious trying to tell me something? The gunman was using the weight of his body to try to break down the bathroom door. Pounding and pounding, the wood was splintering, giving into his force. What had he said to me?

"Think, Brie, think. What did he say?" I whispered to myself encouragingly.

I shot up in the bed and a chill ran down my spine as I finally re-membered. "You're a fighter, just like your mother."

I tried unsuccessfully to convince myself that it meant nothing, that it was just my body's way of dealing with the stress of yesterday.

There were many theories about dreams and their causes, a quick Internet search informed me of that. Since I had already scratched stress off the list, I pondered over the others. I scrolled through the website.

Okay, so the tricks your mind plays on you while you are in an unconscious state could be… a suppressed memory. That one seemed to jump off the computer screen and slap me in the face.

A suppressed memory. Something I had seen or heard as a child.

With that another disturbing thought came to mind. The thought that my family still had more secrets which had not yet been revealed to me. I turned off the computer. None of the billions of websites on the Internet could answer that question for me, or prepare me for what was to come.

Chapter 18

Instead of his usual cologne smell, when Dee came home that evening, he was accompanied by the smell of fried chicken and biscuits. He put down the bag from my favorite takeout restaurant and gave me a proper greeting. I loved the fact that he was so affectionate.

"So how was your day? Did you get any sleep?"

"Yeah, a little."

"That's good. Are you hungry?"

My stomach growled and answered for me; I just repeated what it said. "Starving." I couldn't even remember the last time I had eaten.

"Okay, let's eat."

But Dee didn't eat. He set out the food for the both of us but he just sat there without taking a single bite. I didn't notice this fact until I had completely devoured my food. I was licking my fingers, content with the fact that high cholesterol awaited me in the future.

"Dee what's up? You not hungry?"

He didn't answer. He just sat there rolling and unrolling the takeout menu. He had this intense expression on his face like he was deep in thought. I wondered if he was still upset about what had happened the day before. I wasn't over it myself, but having him around was helping. I knew that I would never go back to the projects by myself again, those days were over. But most importantly when I moved, no one, not even my aunt, knew my new address, and that gave me some much needed peace of mind.

"Babe, are you okay?" I asked. He looked at me like he was real-izing for the first time that I was sitting there next to him.

"Yeah. How's the food?"

I held up my empty plate as my answer. "You not gonna eat?"

"I need to talk to you about something, Brie."

I let out a nervous laugh. "You sound so serious."

"Brie, it is serious" He didn't crack a smile. I really wanted to see that sexy smile of his to ease my mounting nervousness. "It's about my brother."

"Did something happen? Is he okay? Is he..."

He held up his hand to halt my questions. "He's okay. Just give me a minute, okay? I need you to just listen. This is really hard for me to say. You have been through so much already. Just let me get it out, okay?"

I nodded. My heart began to beat a little faster.

He started again. "You know that my brother is in prison for armed robbery. You remember that's who I was going to visit the day we met on the bus."

I nodded.

"The armed robbery was a task given to him by a guy named Atlantic."

Atlantic? Atlantic? Where had I heard that name before?

"Atlantic is the kingpin of the new drug crew that has taken over the projects since your father went to prison. That drug crew is not new to the South Bronx, but because of the hold your father had on the projects, they had not been able to hit that market. They had been trying to force your father out for a while and they were starting to make some real progress.

"Anyway, Atlantic gave my brother this task. What most people don't know is that a drug cartel will give you a task to prove yourself when you are trying to get in, but also when you are trying to get out.

Jeff, that's my brother's name, he had been caught up with Atlantic for a while.

"He had always been a follower. Even as a little kid all he ever wanted to do was fit in with the crowd. He didn't hookup with them for the money, he did it for the friends. It took me a whole year to convince him that these people were not his real friends and that he was doing more and more things that were putting his life in danger."

He paused briefly. I didn't dare say anything.

"When my brother told Atlantic that he wanted out, Atlantic gave him the task of robbing a check cashing place. It was a nearly impossible task."

The message was from Atlantic; that's what the guy who had attacked me the night before had said.

"Brie, the reason I am telling you all of this is because my brother called warning me that people had seen us together and even though neither one of us was involved in either cartel, people, specifically Atlantic's crew, don't want us together.

"I'm not sure whether they are trying to get revenge on your father or my brother, but it really doesn't matter. The point is that we are not safe here even if we do avoid the projects like you've already agreed to do. I feel so guilty because I didn't tell you two days ago when I heard from my brother. Maybe the attack on you yesterday could have been avoided."

"What happened yesterday was about my aunt. At least that's what the guy said. He said that she was in over her head and getting involved in things that she shouldn't. But let me see if I understand what you are saying. Your brother was in Atlantic's crew. That crew and my father's were in a turf war and now when they see us together it's basically a slap in the face to them, even though neither one of us had anything to do with it."

"Exactly, Brie, it's always about our families and never about us. That's why I think we should move and start fresh somewhere else where we don't have to worry about who sees us together."

I guess I was a little slow because it took me a minute to really hear what he had said. I was on my own train of thought. "I think it's stupid that they're upset. I could see if you were also dealing for Atlantic and then started dating me, the daughter of the competition. That would make more sense, but it had nothing to do with you, it was your brother and he was trying to get out." My brain finally caught up to my ears "Move? Move to where?"

"Just so you know, since my brother didn't complete the task of robbing the check cashing place, he is still considered a full member of their crew even though he is locked up. But you're right, none of this has anything to do with us. We are just caught in the middle. And when you are surrounded by violent drug dealers, in the middle is not a good place to be. That is why moving is a good idea.

"Anyway, I think you're looking at it the wrong way. You are looking for logic or some reasonable explanation about why they don't want us to be together. These people don't operate based on logic, Brie. They operate based on hate, greed, and revenge.

"They hate your father because he planted a snitch in their crew which ultimately backfired on him. They know your father still has money stashed somewhere that the cops and the FBI have not found, at least that's the rumor. That's the greed part of the equation. And I guess my brother and your father both being in prison was not enough revenge, so they have to go after the people close to them, which leaves the two of us and your aunt. I have been trying to figure out what to do for a couple of days, and I think the best thing would be to go stay with my parents in Florida for a while until we can afford our own place."

"Florida? No. I thought you meant move from the Bronx to Brooklyn or Queens. I'm not moving to Florida. You really think running is the best solution?"

"Look, I don't know what kind of movies you have been watching, but this is real life, Brie. This is not like being a kid and wanting to prove that you are a fighter so that other people won't think you are a punk. You were worried about me going out yesterday after everything happened and now today you want to keep living here despite everything that I've just told you. I don't get you.

"When we first started talking you knew that I wasn't a dealer or a gang banger, you wouldn't have given me the time of day if you thought I was. I'd rather be smart about things. Because if I get myself into a situation where I don't have a choice but to use force, I know it's not going to end well and I will end up in prison or in the ground. So I think walking, not running, away is what we should do instead of waiting for things to escalate into something that we can't walk away from."

I really didn't know what to say. The first thing that popped into my head was, "What about school?"

"You just started. I'll probably have to make up a couple of classes, but it won't be an issue for us to transfer. There are schools in Florida."

"And my aunt?"

"Well from what you told me that guy said to you yesterday, it's hard to know if she is somehow involved in all of this mess or if he was just trying to scare you or get you to pass on some kind of cryptic message to your dad.

"Why don't we do this? We can go meet her somewhere outside of the projects and see what she has to say. I think we should feel her out a little before we tell her we are moving. We could probably make room for her to come with us if that would make you feel more comfortable."

My head was spinning. The thought of moving out of state was terrifying to me. "I still don't know. I have been in the Bronx my whole life."

I couldn't deny that Dee had a point when he said, "You told me just the other day that your whole life turned out to be based on a lie.

You have more bad memories here than good ones. All I'm asking is that you give us a chance to make some good memories together in a place where we can be out in the open with our relationship and not care who sees us. A place where we can be safe."

Despite the fact that everything he was saying was true, something was still making me hesitate. That little voice let me know what it was. *You just moved in together,* the voice said, a*nd now he wants you to move out of state. How well do you really even know him? It's all moving too fast.*

"This is a lot to take in," I said. "Can't we just wait and think about it a little more. Maybe there is some other option that we haven't thought of yet. Let's just finish out the semester and see how things are at that point."

Frustrated he got up and started to walk away from me.

"Babe?"

"Okay, Brie. You know how I feel about it. I don't want to force you to do anything you don't want to do. And I honestly don't want to leave you here by yourself, so I will give you until the end of the semester to think about it. But I am telling you now so there are no surprises, when the semester is over I'm leaving. I hope you come with me."

I never thought of that possibility. He would actually leave me here?

"You think that's messed up right? Well, I think it's messed up that you have nothing, absolutely nothing, worth staying here for and yet you won't move with me. I have been there for you since the day we met. I have given you no reason to question me, but you would rather stay here with knife-wielding maniacs sneaking up on you than to take a leap of faith with me. How is that supposed to make me feel? I told you I love you, asked you to move in, but that's not what you want. You want to stay here with the drug dealers and your dysfunctional, lying family. Yeah, I feel the love, Brie, I really do."

"Dee, please stop. I didn't say I wouldn't go…"

"That's exactly what you said."

"Okay, I just need some time to get use to the idea. I love you too. But this is my first relationship. You have to understand that things are just moving a little too fast for me. I just need a little time." I went over and put my arms around him. Stubbornly he didn't hug me back. "I know that we are going to be okay."

Chapter 19

Jackie told the boys to go play in the other room when she heard the knock at the door. The kids were driving her insane. She had enough on her mind without refereeing their constant fighting and roughhousing. She wondered what their father was doing at that very moment.

When she had first met their father, Rob, she was instantly attracted to him. He was gorgeous: tall, brown skin, broad shoulders. He was a bouncer at a club in the city. She was in line on a Friday night waiting to get into the club and shake her booty.

The DJ was on point, she remembered. She was already swaying to the beat as she waited in line. Rob pulled her out of the line and gave her the once over. He appraised her like he was trying to determine the value of a fine piece of art. Jackie didn't take offense because she was used to men checking her out. She thrived on the attention. Anyway, she was looking good, if she did say so herself. She was wearing something skin tight, showing off all of her pre-pregnancy curves.

She had dated enough men to know that Rob was different. He knew how to talk to her, how to make her feel special, he knew that she deserved the finer things in life. And most importantly he was not intimidated by her little arrangement with her brother. In fact Rob and Keith started to get pretty close after the kids were born. But instead of becoming part of the "family business," he became a customer.

At first it was just on the weekends, recreational. But it got out of hand really fast.

Keeping him around would have been like having a diabetic live in a gingerbread house. It would not have been good for anyone. It certainly wouldn't have been good for business. Jackie wasn't looking forward to being a single parent, but everyone had their priorities and no one—not her brother, not Rob, no one—was going to get in the way of her money. She knew that keeping him around for the boys would have been nice and even now she wouldn't deny that she'd loved him, but she'd done what she had to do.

It had been almost six years since she'd seen him. He used to call on the boy's birthdays, but even that was a thing of the past. She thought about Rob less and less as the years passed. But every now and then, usually when the boys were driving her crazy, she wondered what he was doing with himself.

The second knock at the door was a little harder than the first. She answered the door and, as Dee strolled into the apartment, Jackie had to admit to herself that Brie had good taste.

"Hi, Jackie, it's nice to finally meet you," he said, extending his hand.

She smiled and shook his hand. "You too. Come on in and have a seat."

"Thank you. I got your phone number from Brie's cell phone. She doesn't know that I'm here."

"It could be our little secret, if you like."

"Brie would say that all the secrets are why we are in this situation."

"And what situation would that be? You know what? Never mind. On the phone you said you wanted to talk to me about something important. Is Brie okay?"

"She's fine, but I don't know if you heard about what happened to her earlier this week."

"I've heard bits and pieces of information but you never know what to believe around here. It's like that telephone game that little kids play. You know, Stephanie likes Bobby, but by the time it gets to the end of the line Tiffany hikes for a hobby." She laughed. "So you never know. By the time I heard what happened it was probably a completely different story. But I've been worried about her. I called her a few times, but she doesn't answer my calls. I understand that she has been through a lot this past year and she's not ready to talk to me and I don't want to force it. That's why I was glad when you called. I really wanted to make sure that she was doing okay."

"She came here to pick up her mail and when she was leaving she was attacked by a guy with a knife. He didn't hurt her too badly, but he cut off her hair. She is actually handling it well, considering. She didn't see the guy's face but he gave her a message about you."

"About me? I can't imagine. What kind of message?"

"The guy said that Brie should tell her father that you are getting involved with the wrong people and you are going to get yourself hurt. Do you know a guy named Atlantic? The message was supposedly from him."

She shrugged her shoulders. "Well, obviously it's someone that knows how important my brother's family is to him. Sending him that message is a way to mess with his head. It would drive him crazy to feel like his family is in danger and he's helpless to do anything about it."

Jackie could tell that Dee wasn't completely convinced, but she didn't really care. He was irrelevant.

"Yeah, that helpless feeling is the worst," he said. "I felt that same way when I found out what happened to Brie."

He went on to tell her about his brother's warning and explain that he didn't think it was safe for them there anymore. "Even if the guy was just trying to get to your brother with that message, even if that is the case, these people would not hesitate to go after an innocent person or even a child," he said pointing in the direction of the sound of the boys playing, "if it would serve their purpose."

Jackie actually thought the possibility of someone coming after her was comical. *I have what they want. I have access to the cash. And you know what they say, money is power. Where did Brie find this guy anyway?* Sure, he was good looking, but that was about it. He wasn't holding no heat, no stacks, no jewels, nothing. He wouldn't last a day in the hood. But here he was venturing into the projects and trying to warn her, which she thought was sweet in a pathetic sort of way. Little did he know she was the one holding all the cards in this little game, she thought. She tried to put a concerned look on her face, but she couldn't help but laugh.

"What's so funny?" Dee asked, kind of annoyed that no one seemed to be taking him seriously.

"I'm sorry. I laugh when I'm nervous. I can't help it," she said. She deserved a pat on the back for actually trying to cover the fact that she thought he was a joke.

"What I think we should do is move out of state. I ran the idea past Brie and I think she would feel more comfortable with it if you and the boys came too. You know, if she had some family around. Florida is where I was thinking. My parents live there and we could stay with them until we get on our feet. I just want to get away from this mess before someone really gets hurt."

What a punk, Jackie thought to herself. It only took her as few seconds to put him in that category. That was one of her pet peeves, she couldn't stand punks. If it came down to it, she would rather a man take a beating like a man than run from a fight.

For all his flaws, Rob had been nobody's punk. If Rob was still around, the two of them would have gotten a good laugh at Dee's expense. Realizing he wasn't worth her time, she pretty much ignored Dee after that.

When he mentioned Florida she thought there was no way that was ever going to happen. She was going to leave the hood, but she was going to do it in her own time, on her own terms, and in style. No one was going to run her out of her own neighborhood, no one.

And Florida of all places. Wasn't that like the capital for old people? In her opinion the world would be a better place if they just floated the old people off on an iceberg like the Eskimos use to do. She wasn't even sure where she'd heard that, probably another fed up coworker. But it sounded like a viable idea to her. And this guy really thought that she was going to go live somewhere surrounded by them every day?

Not to mention that there was no public transportation down there, so everyone had to drive everywhere. On the road with a bunch of old people? How did anyone ever get anywhere? They probably drove so slow because they left the house and forgot where they wanted to go. They might as well have been driving backwards. Nope, nope, nope. Not going to happen.

She'd had enough of old people already. Day in and day out, cleaning up behind them, changing them, keeping track of their medications, enduring their crazy mood swings. There was no way she was moving to Florida to be surrounded by them.

Once he had stopped talking or once she'd gotten tired of pretending to listen—she wasn't sure which—she stood up and thanked him for stopping by, but she said, "I'm not moving and I can take care of myself."

"I can't believe this!" Dee said jumping up off the couch. "What is it with the women in this family? You are too stubborn for your own good. I'm trying to help you, can't you see that?"

"And I appreciate your concern," Jackie said keeping her cool. "But like I said I can take care of myself." To prove her point she lifted one of the couch cushions and exposed her arsenal. Two .22s, a 45mm, and a shot gun just for good measure.

Without anymore protest Dee showed himself out.

Jackie was sure that he'd had a rough childhood, she imagined him getting chased home from school. He had probably been running his whole life. "What a punk!" she said out loud and laughed.

Now that he was gone she could think in peace. Okay, so this so-called message for her brother was definitely an indication that her Plan A hadn't worked. A week ago she'd had a meeting with Atlantic, the head of the new drug cartel. He called himself Atlantic because he liked to brag that he made more deals and more money than the record label. There was no denying that he was running the neighborhood. But she tried to convince him that if he wanted to have a long-lasting empire like her brother, he might need to know her brother's secret weapon. That got his attention.

"And what secret weapon is that?'

"Me," Jackie answered with total confidence. "My brother would have been in jail a long time ago if it wasn't for me and he definitely wouldn't have had the know-how to expand the way he was able to do with my help." She bragged that she was the brains behind the operation, and she could offer her services to him now.

And that was the honest truth. Keith would have been absolutely lost without her, hanging on the corner selling nickel and dime bags. Even though she was younger than he was, she had always been the one to take charge of things. He had no ambition and no vision.

"But things are good the way they are now, Jackie," Keith would say whenever she brought up the subject of moving up in the crew. She told him that it could all be his one day. That he could be running everything. "But I don't need all of that." It was like talking to a two year old.

Over time she began to wear him down. She made her own connections and got her own suppliers. She would make regular runs to Baltimore and Virginia, pick up what she needed, and with their own suppliers, the two of them had no problem branching out on their own. She was hitting I-95 South regularly.

She even bought a minivan. Not only could she carry more product in it, but what cop would stop a female in a minivan, especially one traveling with two small kids. The "I am a proud parent of an honor roll student!" bumper sticker was what really sealed the deal.

Their product was better than what was already being sold, so of course they had more customers than they could handle. The laws of supply and demand were in full effect. Looking back Jackie shook her head thinking about the fact that the hardest part of the whole process had been getting Keith to go along with it.

Sitting on the couch, she replayed the conversation she'd had with Atlantic. She concluded that she was upfront, straight to the point, and very convincing, if she did say so herself. So what went wrong?

She had even told him, "With my help you will make more money than you could ever spend in a lifetime, and to prove my loyalty, I will even show you were my brother's hidden stash is."

That was it! She had come on too strong for him. She should have known better. Men were so easily intimidated by a powerful woman like her.

The message given to Brie was obviously a rejection of her offer to Atlantic. Okay, no biggie. She was up for a challenge. On to Plan B.

It was kind of annoying that she had to go through all of this just to safely move money that already belonged to her. She knew that she needed protection if she was going to move that kind of money, but she had never thought she would have to team up with the enemy.

She didn't even care if she had to split the money with him, because it would still leave her a pretty decent amount to make her exit. But unlike Brianna and Dee, Jackie was not afraid. There was nothing to fear when you had more to gain than you had to lose. In fact, that was probably the opposite of fear.

Chapter 20

"Ugh, where is it? Where is it?" This stupid bag has too many pockets. It's like the Bermuda Triangle; things go in and never come out.

I heard the train coming and I stood at the turn style frantically looking for my MetroCard. "Where is it?" Impatiently the person behind me shoved me out of the way. "Excuse you!" I said to the woman's back as she ran for the train. I thought about how funny it would be if she fell down the stairs. Then of course I felt guilty for having such a horrible thought. Maybe Dee was right, maybe we needed a change of location. New York definitely wasn't bringing out the best in me.

"Finally!" I had located my MetroCard. I swiped it and ran down the stairs yelling, "Hold the door! Someone hold the door please!" I got there just in time to see the conductor closing the doors. I could have sworn he was laughing at me. Sometimes I really hated New York.

I sat on a bench and tried to organize my bag while I waited for the next train to arrive. I noticed the mail that I'd gone to my aunt's house to pick up that dreadful night. It was still tucked in one of the pockets. With all that had happened I'd never gotten around to opening it. I had forgotten about it completely.

The first two pieces of mail were junk: a promotional gym membership and an automatic approval for a Visa card. I quickly tore them up. I almost did the same thing to the third piece too. It was from

Chase Bank. I didn't have an account there and it was about to be tossed when I noticed the official stamp on the envelope. It seemed important, so I opened it and gave it the once over. Then I read it again more carefully, and then a third time just to be sure.

The letter stated that on my nineteenth birthday, which was less than a month away, I would have full access to a trust that had been created for me by my father. My father's name and the word trust in the same sentence? I actually laughed out loud at the irony.

What was a trust anyway? "Okay, trust as in trust fund," I mumbled to myself as I looked over the letter again.

Wasn't that something that preppy rich kids had? Trust fund babies, wasn't that what they were called? The kids that were born with a silver spoon in their mouths? That had nannies and went to prestigious private schools and Ivy League universities and don't have a care in the world? Just sitting back and waiting for their checks to roll in? Well, that definitely wasn't me.

Fortunately, there was a glossary of terms on the back of the letter. Okay, so I had a trust fund. I couldn't help but laugh at the thought. People on the platform were starting to stare. But what did I care? I had a trust fund. I wouldn't have to care if the MTA was going my way. I laughed harder. And to think, all of this time I had been budgeting and living on my student loans and grant money.

When I glanced at the attached bank statement my laughter turned into a cough and then a desperate attempt to catch my breath. $986,823.68. The number looked more like a phone number than anything else.

"You have got to be kidding me!" There wasn't any doubt in my mind that it was drug money. What else could it be? Was this the money that my father had been able to hide from the FBI and police when he went to prison? The money that Atlantic was after? I had no idea. What was I suppose to do with it? I knew one thing: Dee had been worried about us being targeted before, but there was much more to be worried about now.

If anyone found out about this money we might as well be profiled on America's Most Wanted. People would come out of the woodwork trying to get their hands on it, and their most likely method of persuasion, I knew, would be force.

Even while I was thinking about all of this, I couldn't help but look at the glossary of terms that accompanied the letter and think how crazy it was that my father had done nothing but feed me lies my entire life, and the one thing he left me that was real and tangible was called a trust. At the other end of the platform I spotted the lady that had pushed me out of her way. She had missed the train too. I smiled. This must be my lucky day.

Chapter 21

I was worried about what would happen if anyone found out about the money. But Dee, he was pacing again. I could see the tension in the tightness of his clenched jaw. He took it to a whole new level, like the drug dealers in the hood were part of the psychic network.

"They will find out, Brie," he said. "They will know."

It wasn't like I was going to go around the hood doing the money dance, throwing money around.

Dee waived the bank statement around like it was all the evidence he needed. "Now you have to see!" he said. "You have to see how important it is that we get out of here. We have to move, we can't wait until the end of the semester. It's only a matter of time before Atlantic finds out that you are the one who has your father's money."

"You talk about them like they are the CIA. They don't know everything."

"I can't believe you right now! You are acting like a child… But why? But why? But why? I don't know how many other ways I can explain this to you."

I knew he was frustrated, but I had to let him know "I don't appreciate you talking to me like that. I might disagree with you, but I don't disrespect you, so I expect the same from you."

"Okay, fine," he said, waving me off but at the same time toning it down a little. "Let me put it to you this way. Your father used to run everything, he was the man. He did it from before you were born, and he was never arrested, so we must assume that he was good at it. Then Atlantic and his crew came along, and within a year your father is doing a bid upstate and Atlantic's running everything. These people are not stupid, can't you see that? They have eyes in more places than we could every really know. I'm telling you information about the money will get back to them faster than you think."

I didn't say anything so he continued.

"I know that you weren't thrilled about moving to Florida. Which is understandable, you don't want to move in with people you don't really know. Okay, fine. Now that you have the money we can move anywhere you want. Just pick a place and let's go."

"What are you talking about? I can't spend this money. It's drug money!" When I first saw the bank statement the thought of having that much money was funny to me. I let myself think about shopping sprees and fancy houses, but only for a moment. When the shock wore off and reality set in, I knew that spending the money was not an option. How could I be so upset with my father and then actually spend his drug money? That would make me no better than him.

"What am I talking about?" Dee was gesturing wildly with his hands. "No, what are you talking about? What do you mean you can't spend it? What do you propose we do with it? Turn it into the cops, or how about the FBI? Lets pay for a few of them to retire early. You know that is what will happen, right?"

I didn't like his sarcasm. I didn't like it one bit.

"It will never actually make it to evidence lock up," he continued. "And even if it did, the city officials would still spend it. The mayor will put it toward his new campaign or something. Why should they spend the drug money and not you? It was given to you. Okay, I know...I know what we should do. We should reimburse the crack heads. How about that, Brie? Does that make you feel all warm and fuzzy inside?"

People say that money gives you options, but I felt like my options were decreasing by the minute. I didn't know what I was going to do. "I guess you're right, Dee, but I don't feel comfortable spending it either."

"Well it's your money and your decision. I'm sure you will do what you feel is right. But whatever you decide, I hope you realize that because of this money we have even more reason to make our exit."

Chapter 22

I could hardly concentrate on my school work. Finals were quickly approaching and I couldn't focus on studying; all I could do was think about the money. Was I walking around with a bull's eye on my back?

I was becoming paranoid. Well, actually I was already there. Every time I got a look or even a fleeting glance from someone, I wondered if they somehow knew about the money. It was driving me crazy. I couldn't focus on anything. I would sit for hours with my open textbook in my lap, staring off into space.

I pictured myself being stuffed into the trunk of a car, driven somewhere deserted, and tortured until I gave up the bank account number. I wondered if this was how lottery winners felt, like someone was out to get them.

Life was so much easier when it was just the boogeyman under the bed that I had to worry about. The new monsters that I fear had real faces and real weapons.

And living with Dee was not helping the situation. He had made himself crystal clear on the issue. "Each day that we stay in the Bronx is a day closer to people finding out." His paranoia was definitely rubbing off on me, like a contagious virus I hadn't been vaccinated against.

In my last few meetings with Dr. Beekman, we had covered a lot of ground. We spent a lot of time talking about how I felt about my father betraying me.

As I waited patiently in the waiting room for our scheduled meeting, I wondered if today would be the day that I would confide in her about the money. I was reluctant. I knew that doctors weren't allowed to repeat things that their patients said to them, but I didn't know if there were any exceptions to that rule. It was drug money after all. I decided against telling her. There were a lot of other things left for us to talk about.

"Good morning, Brie. Come on in," she said with her usual pleasant demeanor.

I followed her into her office and she closed the door behind us.

"How are you doing?" she asked.

"Honestly, I really don't know."

"Well, that's not a good feeling, right? Why don't you tell me what's on your mind?"

I wasn't even in my seat yet when my words began to pour out. I felt like I really needed to talk. I hadn't been able to talk to Dee about it. His sarcasm and anger made it difficult to talk to him these days. "I have been having a hard time focusing on school lately and finals are around the corner," I said. "I'm getting nervous. I feel overwhelmed. I'll be moving out of state soon. I feel like everything is changing and I am just along for the ride."

"So you've made up your mind about moving?"

"Yeah, I think so. With everything that's going on, it seems like I will never be free of this mess that my father has created, and I don't want to constantly feel like I have to be looking over my shoulder. Just when I thought I knew all my family secrets something else comes to light."

"I can understand that. You shouldn't have to constantly be on guard, looking over your shoulder. And you should not feel like you have to pay for your father's mistakes. But that's not the real issue is it, Brie? If it were, your decision about moving would have been easy and you would have made it without hesitation. The question is whether or not you feel comfortable enough in your relationship with Dee to take the step of moving out of state with him. It's a big step," she said, mimicking that persistent little voice in my head.

"I have had time to think about it and he hasn't given me any reason not to be comfortable with him." I thought about our recent problems and no doubt we were going through a difficult time, but once we got away from all of this mess I was sure that things would improve.

"That's a good answer, Brie, it really is," she said, smiling. "That is what we have been working toward this whole time: finding a balance between learning from your past experiences with your family and not punishing other people for the fact that your family betrayed your trust. And that is exactly what you have done by saying that Dee hasn't given you a reason not to trust him. You are looking at your relationship with him, not your father or anyone else. You are judging Dee based on how he has treated you, and that is excellent progress."

"Thanks," I said, feeling quite proud of myself.

"So, what else is bothering you?"

"Well, do remember when I told you that I had the nightmare about someone trying to kill me?"

"Yes."

"And in the nightmare the guy made a comment about my mother?"

"Yes."

"I have been having more nightmares like that. And even when I'm awake I find myself daydreaming or thinking about my mother more and more."

"She died when you were a newborn, right? You never knew her?"

"Right."

"Did your father talk about her a lot?"

I thought about it before I answered her. I remembered my father answering specific questions that I had. I'd ask him what she was like, and he'd say, "She was smart and driven just like you, Brie." All of his answers were like that, full of adjectives you'd find in a Hallmark

Card. But it was a very rare occasion that he would recite memories of her without provocation.

I could tell by the look on his face when he talked about her that it was painful for him. So even though I wanted to know about my mother I eventually stopped asking questions. None of it would bring her back anyway.

Dr. Beekman was staring at me patiently waiting for my response. "He never really talked about her unless I brought it up first."

"Okay, so it's impossible that you are experiencing actual memories. But perhaps you are thinking about these things because of something you overheard or were told as a child."

"That's what I thought, too, but I've been racking my brain and I can't remember anything specific. I can't remember being told or overhearing anything."

She scribbled down some notes on her notepad. "That's normal," she said. "You can't access it when you are in a state of full alertness. That's why you may have a daydream or nightmare, but when you make a conscious effort to remember, you're not able to."

"So what should I do?'

"You want me to give you some homework?"

"Okay."

"Write a list of things that you remember about your mother. Keep in mind that you were too young to form actual memories, so everything on your list will be things that you were told by others. Bring the list with you next week and we will discuss it."

"Okay."

"Now, don't use this assignment as an excuse not to study for your finals."

"Okay, I won't. See you next week."

Chapter 23

I had mentally given up on studying, but I still went through the motions. I sat on the living room couch with my textbook in my lap, trying to keep up appearances even though I was the only one there. I flipped randomly through the pages of the textbook, closed it, glanced at the cover, reminded myself what I was supposed to be studying.

Anatomy—the study of the human body. "It's about how everything works together," the professor had told us. He was one of those professors who always looked disheveled, like he had so much on his mind that he didn't notice he had dripped soup down the front of his shirt during lunch. His fingers were permanently stained with the blue marker he used to write on the dry erase board.

Your knee bone's connected to your... That's what I was thinking as he spoke even on the very first day of class. So sitting on the couch months later knowing that there was no hope of salvaging the semester, I asked myself, "What's the point?" I closed the book and officially put studying and the semester behind me.

With that decision made, I pulled out my notebook and flipped past all of my class notes. Flipping through the notebook, I noticed the little doodles, flowers usually, that I'd made in the margins while sitting in class. They had slowly grown out of the margins. As the weeks passed they began to take over the whole page.

The last day that I actually went to school, the doodles outnumbered the words on the page. I would have loved for Little Miss "Oh I love your outfit, you look so nice" to ask to borrow these notes. The few words that were actually visible under my abstract artwork looked like hieroglyphics, like no language used in the modern world.

Near the back of the notebook, I found a blank page and wrote the word *mommy* with a question mark after it. I started to work on my list for Dr. Beekman. What did I know about my mother? She was married to my father; I jotted that down. She died giving birth to me.

I closed my eyes and tried to recall any other tidbits of information that I had stored in my memory. That's when I remembered that Aunt Jackie had told me that my father had met my mother while she was working at a bank.

I knew it was a long shot and I knew I wasn't Angela Lansbury or somebody but I decided to go to the bank where my trust fund was set up to see if just maybe that was the bank she had worked at. Maybe I would find someone who had known her. I hoped so, because my list was looking pretty pathetic. I couldn't even list five things that I knew about my own mother.

I needed to get out of the house anyway. I had been cooped up in there for days, too scared to go outside, scared that someone might have found out about the money. But I put all of that aside with the hope that I just might find out some valuable information about my mother.

When I walked into the Chase Bank on the corner of 7th Avenue and 23rd Street, I had no idea what I would find. All of the tellers looked to be around my age or only a few years older, so I knew they would be no help. I asked to speak to a manager. I sat for about five minutes, restlessly tapping my foot.

"Hello. My name is Ms. Fleming. How can I help you?"

She was a petite older woman. I couldn't tell her nationality but she was pale skinned with a brownish birthmark on her forehead in the shape of Florida. Maybe it was a sign, I thought, only half joking.

I stood and shook her hand. Not really knowing where to start, I said, "I received a letter in that mail about a trust fund. I wanted to get some more information about it because until this letter arrived, I had no idea it even existed."

"Well that must have been a nice surprise for you," she said smiling warmly. "Why don't we go back into my office so I can access the account information on my computer?"

As we walked down the corridor to her office, I tried to muster up enough courage to discuss the real purpose of my visit. I told myself that I couldn't possibly leave here with less information than I had come in with. I had nothing to lose.

She ushered me into a leather chair opposite her desk. The office was spacious, but it had no windows. I started to feel a slight tinge of claustrophobia.

Before I lost my nerve I blurted out, "I'm trying to find out some information about my mother."

"Excuse me?" she said, both startled and confused.

I cleared my throat, but the lump that was forming there didn't budge. "I think my mother used to work here," I said. "Her name was Alecia Roberts. Did you know her?"

I couldn't look at her, but I felt her searching my face, trying to figure out what to make of me.

I looked past her to the plaque hanging on her wall congratulating her on 25 years of service. I figured that if anyone in this place had known my mother, chances were it was Ms. Fleming.

I looked at her then. My eyes begging for her to break her silence, "Please," I said.

She shook her head reluctantly. "No. I don't know anyone by that name."

Discouraged, I realized that my mother had started working here before she married my father and I had no clue what her maiden name was. Maybe she worked at another bank that my father had used to hide his drug profits. I was thinking of other possible explanations when Ms. Fleming interrupted my train of thought.

"I knew an Alecia Nichols. She worked here a long time ago." She paused, looked me over again, and said, "you kind of look like her."

Yes! I thought. Now we were getting somewhere.

I shifted in my chair as she continued, "She died a long time ago in a car accident."

No, that can't be right, I thought. A car accident?

"It was so sad. She'd just had a baby." She paused and looked me over again. "Her poor husband was so completely distraught and on top of it all he was left with a newborn to care for. It was devastating."

She couldn't have died in a car accident. If that was how she died, why wouldn't my father have just told me that? Ms. Fleming had to be mistaken. She had to be. If she wasn't, it meant that my father had lied to me about something else, that he was hiding more than I ever thought possible. "A car accident? Are you sure?"

You know how people say that ignorance is bliss? Well, I didn't know it, but I was blissfully ignorant in that brief moment before Ms. Fleming answered my question and rocked my world to its very core.

"Yes. I'm quite sure," she said. "I shouldn't even be discussing this with you." She paused and I thought that was it. I thought that was all the information I was going to get. Perhaps it was the pleading in my eyes that kept her talking.

"...But I was not only Alecia's boss, we were friends. I remember her husband coming in and telling me what happened. A drunk driver. I didn't go to the funeral. I wanted to go and pay my respects, and so did everyone else that worked here. She was very well-liked. But I think the funeral was very small, family only. It was just so sad," she said. "She was so excited about having a baby, I remember; she really wanted to be a mother."

A sob formed inside of me, way down deep. When it made its way past my vocal cords, it was like no other sound I had ever heard. She handed me a tissue. "I'm sorry," I said.

She took a tissue for herself too. She dabbed her eyes, smeared her mascara. "She brought you here to visit once. I remember she was about to come back to work after her maternity leave and she stopped by one afternoon with this cute, chubby baby in the stroller. She was so happy, she was glowing. Then about a week later her husband stopped by and told us the news of her accident. We had just seen her. It seemed so unreal."

Unreal was a good way to explain this. I never considered the possibility that my little trip to the bank would make me have to cross something off my list, something that I had been told and believed my whole life.

I knew for a fact that my mother didn't die in a car accident—my father wouldn't feel the need to lie about that. But now I also knew that she didn't die giving birth to me.

I tried to hold onto some hope that what she was saying wasn't true…maybe we were talking about two different women. Maybe this Alecia Nichols wasn't my mother after all. It was a long shot, I knew, but I was grasping at straws. The way she told the story left little doubt that she was talking about my mother, but I had to be sure. Going to the bank was supposed to help me find out more about my mother, things that I could add to Dr. Beekman's list, but all it did was add to my list of questions.

"Do you have any pictures of her?"

"I really shouldn't be doing this but like I said, Alecia was a really good friend of mine." She paused for a moment and dabbed her eyes with the tissue. "You're right, let's not get ahead of ourselves, let's be absolutely sure. We probably still have the old employee files. I'll have to go to the record room. Give me a few minutes."

Alone in the room, my head started spinning. Even after I had found out that my father was a liar, it never once crossed my mind that he could have been lying about my mother's death. Maybe it should have.

I didn't know where this information would lead me, but there was no way I could turn away from it now. I had to find out the truth. I just hoped that with all the lies I had been told I would be able to identify the truth when I finally found it.

When my phone rang and Dee's name popped on the screen I immediately pressed ignore. I couldn't deal with him right then. He would be upset that I had left the house without telling him, but I was so close to getting information about my mother that I would just have to deal with him later.

Ms. Fleming walked back into her office holding a thin manila folder. She handed me a picture. The bold lettering said "1993 Employee of the Year," and below it was a picture of my mother smiling. It felt like she was looking right at me.

Tears formed in my eyes as I looked at the photo. We looked even more alike than I had realized. My father had shown me pictures of her and pointed out the resemblance. I'd noticed it, but never like in that picture.

Maybe I resembled her more now that I was older. She would never get any older, I thought, and I tried unsuccessfully to blink back a new wave of tears. I stared down at her smiling face, frozen forever in time by that Kodak moment. There was no denying that she was my mother, the woman that my father had told me was the love of his life.

I remembered the first time I asked my father why I didn't have a mommy. I guess I was about six or so. The kids at school were always talking about their mommies for one reason or another.

"My mommy is prettier than your mommy."

"My mommy is coming with me on the school trip."

And there were always kids crying for their mommies when they got hurt playing, or got in trouble or even at nap time. I cried a lot too. School was a new and scary place. But who was this mommy person that everyone was asking for?

I came home from school one day and asked my father, "Why don't I have a mommy?"

He didn't make up any stories for me to handle the news. He didn't tell me, *She is always with you or She is in a better place.* He told me like it was, or so I thought at the time.

"Brie, do you know what it means when someone dies?"

"Yeah. Like on T.V.?"

"No, Brie, remember I told you that T.V. is make believe? It's pretend, not real."

"Oh."

"In real life, not on T.V.," he'd explained, "sometimes people get sick or get hurt and their body stops working and if the doctors can't fix them, they die."

"Oh"

"So when you were a baby, your mommy was so happy, but her body stopped working and the doctors couldn't fix her. Do you understand?"

"Yes. Mommy died."

Back then I was only repeating what he was saying or what I thought he wanted me to say. I had no real understanding of death. I knew that everyone else had a mommy and I didn't. But I also knew that not many kids in my class had a daddy and I did, so it seemed okay.

As I got older and had more questions, my father always seemed to make a real effort to answer them. But as I sat in Ms. Fleming's office, I felt a close bond with that little girl, that younger version of myself. As I did then, I once again was feeling this overwhelming confusion, an overwhelming need to answer the question: why don't I have a mommy?

"You're sure that's her, that's your mother?" Ms. Fleming asked even though we both knew the answer.

I nodded. "But I was told that she died giving birth to me."

"Who told you that?"

"My father and my aunt."

"I don't know why they would tell you that. Like I said, your mother came into the bank with you to visit and you were already about a month old and you both looked perfectly healthy."

I looked away from her prying eyes and nodded.

"Well, obviously you suspected that they weren't telling you the truth and that is why you came here today."

She said it as a statement not a question but the truth was, "I never really questioned whether or not they had told me the truth. I never had a reason to. But I don't talk to my father anymore and I was hoping to find out more about her, maybe even something about her family. But I never thought this is what I would find out."

"This must be so difficult for you. Where is your father now?"

"In prison."

"For what?"

"I really don't want to talk about that."

"I'm so sorry. That's a very personal question. I shouldn't have asked you that."

"It's okay. Do you have any information on my mother's family? I know she started working here before she met my father, so who did she put down as her emergency contact?"

She opened my mother's employee folder, but quickly closed it again. "This is confidential information. I could get into a lot of trouble for telling you this."

"I understand. But I really need your help. I have no one else to ask and all I know for sure is that she worked here. That's all I know about my mother."

I thought about the fact that my mother had probably sat in the very seat that I was sitting in, talking to her boss about this and that. I couldn't walk out of there empty handed.

"You have no idea what it's like," I said. "To find out that everything you thought was true is actually a lie. Please, please help me." I wasn't too proud to beg. "I won't tell anyone where I got the information from."

She opened the folder again. "Her father, Richard Nichols, and her mother, Martine Nichols, lived in North Carolina." She picked up a yellow Post-It and wrote down their last known address. "That's all I can tell you."

"Thank you so much." I stood up to leave.

"So I guess you don't have a trust fund here after all, huh?" she said jokingly.

"Oh, actually, I do. I just have more important things to deal with first. This information," I said holding up the Post-It, "is the most valuable withdrawal I could ever make from this bank. Thanks again for all of your help."

She walked around the desk and hugged me, squeezed me tightly. "You're very welcome, sweetie. I hope you find some closure. If there is ever anything else that I can help you with, just let me know." She handed me her business card.

Closure. That was it. That was what I was looking for. I wasn't looking for a happily ever after. I had already given up on that. I was looking for answers so that I could move on with my life and finally put all of this behind me. Closure, that was what I needed.

Chapter 24

One of the many things my father taught me was how to defend myself. Perhaps at the time he had been preparing for the inevitable. The day when the double life he'd tried so hard to keep a secret would require me to use those skills. The day when his shady dealings would piss off his competition or a feinin crack head would act in a moment of desperation.

I wondered if my father's double life, his split personalities, were completely separate and distinct. I'd read about people that had multiple personality disorders and sometimes the individual personalities weren't aware of each other. Did my father know he was a drug dealer? Did the drug dealer know he was my father? That sounded like a question for my father's defense attorneys to ask. As for me, the verdict was in. He was guilty of way more than the jury had thought.

As much as I wanted to believe that my father was an unwilling participant—an innocent bystander—in all of this, I knew it wasn't true. It was my father who had sat across from me in the visitor's room and ratted out the drug dealer. The two of them were one and the same.

But either way, the person I knew was not a violent man. I had never even seen him lose his temper. So when he started giving me lessons about how to defend myself, he took time to stress the fact that I should always try to talk my way out of a confrontation.

"Your mind is stronger than your fists," he'd said. But he'd also stressed the fact that, in our neighborhood, knowing how to use your fists was important. He'd told me that there was no such thing as a clean fight and it was important for girls to know that, because they might not have as much physical strength as their opponent.

"Grab whatever you can," he'd instructed. "A bottle, a rock. Anything that you can reach is fair game. Go for the face, go for the private parts."

It seemed like he'd taught me that lesson right in the nick of time. When I was in junior high school, my school was closed down because it had asbestos and all of the students were bused over to the local high school. We were still separated in classes from the older kids, but because of the overcrowding we didn't have separate lunch periods.

Sharing the cafeteria with the high schoolers usually wasn't a problem. For the most part, they wanted nothing to do with us. But for some reason this one girl—Melanie, I remember her name was—didn't like me and thought she would take the opportunity to make that fact known. I didn't even know her, had never had any contact with her before that day. She claimed that I thought I was all that.

I couldn't help the fact that I was younger than she was and had hit puberty first. That's what I told her when she got in my face. "I can't help that you are embarrassed to change in the locker room. I would be too if I looked like you." I had a sharp tongue back then; maybe I still do.

That's when the crowd started forming around us. None of the adults in the room were paying us even the slightest bit of attention. She was both taller and heavier than me. While she was getting all in my face trying to make a scene, I was heeding my father's advice and taking the opportunity to survey my surroundings.

I saw a lunch tray nearby. *That'll work*, I thought. I waited patiently to see if she would attempt to hit me. I figured she was all bark and no bite, but with the crowd chanting her name, she got bold. When she swung at me I was ready.

I grabbed the tray and slapped her across the face with it. I still remember the sound it made when it made contact. Afterward everything was eerily quiet. The good thing about her being bigger than me was that she fell hard. I claimed self defense when I was sent to the principal's office. But he still suspended me, something about zero tolerance for violence.

Daddy wasn't mad. "Sometimes you have to make an example of people so others know not to mess with you. Never start a fight, Brie, but always...always finish it." During my three day vacation from school I hung out with my father and mastered a few new moves.

Unfortunately, leaving the bank that day, I wasn't able to put my father's advice to use. I was caught off guard yet again.

I was feeling good as I left Ms. Fleming's office. I felt like I had accomplished something. Mrs. Fleming walked me back to the lobby and gave me another quick squeeze. I told her I would stay in touch.

I fondled the little Post-It note some more before tucking it into my coat pocket for safe keeping and heading toward the door. I was almost out the front door when, out of the corner of my eye, I saw something rushing toward me. Before I could react, the force hit me like a Mack truck. I was on the floor, my face pressed against the cold tile, and it was on top of me, punching me, hard and fast, in the back of the head.

I was helpless, pinned underneath the weight of what I now knew was a woman on top of me. I was flailing around like a fish caught on a line. My sneakers made squeaking noises on the tile as I struggled to break free.

I reached back and tried to grab her. I clawed at skin, pulled hair, and did everything else I could to stop the onslaught of punches I was taking. I managed to get in a few good swings.

Somebody yelled for security. Finally the weight was off of me and I was helped to my feet. I tried to assess the damage. I had a scratch on the side of my face, my wrists hurt from trying to break my fall, and I was sure that at any minute swelling from the punches would cause a knot to form on the back of my head. The security guard was also giving me the once over; there was no denying it was a TKO.

Someone was yelling my name. I still had no idea who my assailant was. Security had dragged the person to the other side of the room. But there was that voice again, a familiar one, screaming my name. The security guard stood in front of the person, blocking their access to me but also blocking my view.

As she struggled to break free from the security guard and rush me again, trying to go for round two, I caught a glimpse of her face.

It was Aunt Jackie. "I want my money back, Brie! Did you think I wouldn't find out? I took care of you, and this is what you do? Steal from me! I'll kill you! Do you hear me? I'll kill you!"

I needed to get out of there. I didn't know what was pounding more, my head or my heart. Still a little wobbly, I made my second attempt for the exit. This time I was stopped by a security guard.

He was an older guy with powder white hair and kind eyes. The brass name tag pinned to his uniform informed me that he was Security Officer Lewis. All of the more intimidating members of the security team were still huddled around Aunt Jackie. Officer Lewis told me that I needed to stay and make a statement to the police.

"I don't want to talk to the police," I said. "I want to go home."

"Miss, she attacked you." His voice was gentle and so was his touch when he took my arm and walked me away from the door. "She threatened to kill you. You need to report it."

I looked over my shoulder, back toward the exit. There was another security officer standing there now. He looked like he popped steroids like Tic Tacs. There was no way that human wall was about to budge. I gave up, defeated for a second time.

I let Officer Lewis lead me to a nearby chair. "Just have a seat and try to relax," he said. "You are safe now and the police are on the way."

The police arrived quickly. They never responded like that in the hood. In the projects, I think the police take their time, hoping that the criminals will kill each other before they get there and save them the paperwork. But the official reason, the explanation that they would lead with on news broadcasts, was budget cuts.

When the police arrived all of the screaming that Aunt Jackie had been doing immediately stopped and she was completely silent. I didn't know if they assumed that they were responding to some type of robbery attempt, but the number of cop cars that showed up made it look like a NYPD parade was rolling down 7th Avenue.

The officers were very thorough. They took witness statements, interviewed all of the security staff and reviewed the tapes from the security cameras, which had caught the whole thing. Then it was my turn to give my statement. I didn't know what to write because I still wasn't sure exactly what had happened or why she had attacked me. I scribbled down a few sentences. I couldn't get done fast enough.

The officer who took my statement, Officer Stanley, was average height and physically fit by NYPD standards; his midsection only covered his belt a little. He asked me if I wanted to go to the hospital, if there was anyone that he could call. No and no. He read over my statement, took down my phone number and finally told me that I was free to go.

My third attempt at leaving the bank was successful. The cold wind made the scratch on the side of my face sting a little. I covered it with my hand. Aunt Jackie was sitting in the back of a patrol car parked out front. Despite the fact that the window was rolled up she tried to spit at me, letting me know how she really felt, as if the hate in her eyes and the beating that I had just taken didn't convey the message.

Chapter 25

I was multitasking, sitting at the kitchen table punching in numbers on my calculator, trying to solve for X. But I was only focused on that during the commercials. I was watching *The Real World*, an episode from one of the old seasons when the cast was actually interesting and the show was worth watching. I was also cooking dinner, I had a chicken in the oven.

I had timed it perfectly so that dinner would be reaching the table when Daddy walked in from work. He was working on a long term construction project out in Queens, or so I believed at the time. That was about a week before the cops busted into our apartment and took him away, and life as I knew it changed forever.

That was a normal day. I didn't know what normal was anymore. Getting beat up by my own aunt? Getting my hair chopped off? Finding out that my family had more secrets than the CIA?

The train ride back to the Bronx was a long one. It was rush hour and people were way too close for comfort. It was like a funky game of Twister. As I walked the few blocks from the train station to my apartment, I was multitasking again. As I walked, I tried to be keenly aware of my surroundings. After what had happened at the bank, I was more than a little on edge. My steps were swift and deliberate. But I was also deep in thought.

In my head, I was running through all of the things that I had found out. My father hadn't been wrongfully convicted. He was not only a drug dealer, he was a kingpin. My mother didn't die during childbirth. My aunt knew that I had the money and for some reason she thought it belonged to her. The more I thought about it, the more confused I became. Each step I took brought me closer to home, so I decided to focus on what was in front of me: Dee.

I knew a confrontation with him was unavoidable. I knew he didn't want me to leave the house by myself, especially without telling him, but at the same time I felt like going to the bank, even though it was a long shot, was just something that I had to do.

"Brianna! Brianna, is that you?'

I didn't turn around.

"Brianna! Hold up, girl."

Nope. I walked faster.

The person was persistent. "Brianna, it's me Claudia... from high school?"

Curious, I turned around and saw a pair of hot pink stretch pants speeding toward me. She was pushing a stroller. She was about a half block away from me and quickly closing the gap between us. I had a vision of this girl pulling a machine gun out of the stroller and taking me out in a hail of gunfire. Being caught off guard in the bank and attacked by Aunt Jackie was definitely taking a toll on me. My imagination was getting the best of me.

As she approached, I recognized her. We had been inseparable freshman year of high school. But I didn't care who she was, I still didn't appreciate her calling me out in the street a block from where I lived. Especially since I was trying to stay incognito.

I'd turned around to look at her mainly to get this person to stop screaming my name. She might as well have been a politician in one of those cars with the microphones rolling down the block.

"Hi. Claude. How have you been?" I asked trying to be polite. I slowed my pace but didn't come to a complete stop. A moving target is harder to hit than a stationary one, right? In a normal situation I might have actually cared how she was doing or what she had been up to since high school, but in that moment I was feeling vulnerable and exposed.

When I was in Manhattan rubbing shoulders with the massive crowds, I didn't feel as vulnerable. There was safety in numbers. But back in the Bronx, all of the people hanging in the streets seemed suspect. And there she was, screaming my name at the top of her lungs for everyone to hear.

"So you do remember me!" she said in an excited voice, way too loud, still drawing attention. My eyes darted around trying to see if anyone seemed to be paying too much attention to us.

"Yes. I remember you," I said, still putting one foot in front of the other. "How are you?"

She was dressed in a typical ghetto fabulous outfit, the whole purpose of which was to leave nothing to the imagination. Her outfit consisted of what I was pretty sure was supposed to be a shirt, but she was wearing it as a mini dress. Half of her butt was hanging out. Under it she wore hot pink spandex leggings, the staple of any ghetto fabulous outfit. Gold bangles on each wrist and large gold hoop earrings completed the look. Nothing you would ever see on the runways of Paris, but it was the hottest thing in my neighborhood.

"I've been great," she said while smacking on a piece of gum. "This is my son Justin, he's three. And this is little Ms. Alana." She gave her belly a pat.

"Aw, he's a cutie," I said, as I looked down at the smiling baby who was entertaining himself making spit bubbles. He really was cute, except for the fact that there was no excuse for a three year old to have a diamond stud in his ear. "So when are you due?"

"Another eight weeks. What about you? How many kids do you have?"

It was kind of funny, but I was use to that question. I was almost nineteen and had no kids. For a girl growing up in the projects of the South Bronx, that is probably some kind of record. So I always got the question *How many kids do you have?* instead of *Do you have any kids?*

"I don't have any kids."

"Oh."

It was a loaded response. She was probably thinking, *How do you take care of yourself?* Because just through my own personal observation, I noticed that a lot of women in my neighborhood had kids every few years so that they could keep their welfare benefits rolling in. Because once their child reached school age, the City of New York would force them to get some type of employment. They saw their kids as a source of income. That may or may not be true, but that had been my observation.

In high school Claudia was not one of the popular kids. She grew up in a two-parent household; that in itself set her apart. The fact that her father was a police officer didn't help her win any popularity contests either. She tried to be cool, but the kids didn't trust her; she might as well have been wearing the NYPD blues herself. But I liked her. She was smart, funny, and easy to talk to.

Unfortunately, my friendship was not enough for her. She wanted so much to run with the popular crowd. She hooked up with one of the most popular guys in school. I think his name was Devin. It wasn't a relationship or anything; she just slept with him in an effort to increase her cool factor. She spent more and more time trying to hang out with him, cutting classes, flunking classes. It got to the point where she thought she was too cool for school and dropped out. That was the last I'd seen of her.

I knew she'd had a baby though. I'd heard a rumor that she brought Devin on the Maury Show to prove that he was the father of her baby. But that was just a rumor.

"So are you still with Devin?" I asked, standing at the corner and waiting for the light to change.

"Nah, I haven't seen him since Justin turned one. I'm not thinking about him. I got me a real man now. He takes good care of me."

"Well, that's good."

"So what have you been up to, Brie? It's been forever since I've seen you."

"I'm in nursing school now."

"That's good."

We just stood and stared at each other for a moment. The light seemed to be taking forever. We no longer had anything in common.

"So do you live around here?"

That was confidential information. "No. I'm just going to visit someone. Take care of yourself, Claude, and good luck with the new baby." Green light.

"Thanks. Wait…wait!" She grabbed a piece of paper and a pen out of her bag. "Here take my number down. Maybe we can hang out sometime."

It was like one of those situations when you take a guy's number just to avoid the awkwardness of saying no, even though you have no intention of calling him.

I took the piece of paper and shoved it in my pocket. "Okay. Bye"

But running into her did remind me of one thing. Life can change so quickly. One decision can change it forever, set you on a completely different path. The decision that I had made that day to go to the bank was one I didn't regret. Sure I got into a knockdown, drag-out fight with my aunt of all people, and I had the bruises to remind me of that. But when those bruises went away, I would still have the most important thing: information about my mother. Possibly something that might even lead me to finding out more about her. So despite all of the drama, my trip to the bank had been a successful one. Who knows if I would have ever found out that information if I hadn't gone. I wasn't going to let Dee make me feel guilty about that.

Chapter 26

The couple who lived downstairs were making out in the hallway. The funny thing was that they were not "young whippersnappers anymore," as Mrs. Lily, the wife, liked to put it. Mrs. Lily and her husband were at the age where little blue pills were securely stored in their bedside table. There was something disturbing, but oddly sweet and heartwarming, about how in love and all over each other they were even after all the years they'd been married.

A few days before, I was going stir crazy in the house and had walked downstairs intending to stand outside and get a little fresh air. Their door was ajar, and when Mrs. Lily saw me she invited me in. Her apartment smelled like mothballs and talcum powder with a hint of Ben-gay.

"I love to talk to young people," she'd said. "You have the most interesting stories." *You don't even know the half of it*, I'd thought to myself. But Mrs. Lilly was the one who told the stories. She told me about how she had been a dance instructor, of beginners mostly. Despite the fact that age had made her less nimble, she still had a dancer's body: a tiny little waist and legs that went on forever.

She'd pulled out a scrapbook filled with pictures, dance recital programs, and newspaper clippings, all of which had yellowed with age. She ran her fingers over the pages as she reminisced. A few of her students had gone on to professional careers on Broadway, she'd told me.

As a Julliard alum and former member of the Alvin Ailey Dance Theater, her own career was nothing short of amazing. Her walls were covered with awards paying tribute to her professional dance career. Just as prominently placed were her family photos. But, with the exception of her husband, she didn't mention her family once. I figured I wasn't the only person in this building with family drama.

We'd sipped tea and munched on butter cookies as she told me about her husband. "It was love at first sight… for him," she'd joked. She told me they had recently celebrated their thirty-sixth wedding anniversary and she didn't know where the time had gone. I let myself imagine spending the next thirty years with Dee. I let myself think of names for our children.

I guess that's what pissed me off, made me fume a little as I stood on the other side of my apartment door. I had already made up my mind not to let Dee give me a guilt trip about leaving the apartment without telling him, but there I was standing there practicing, trying to figure out what to say to him.

It shouldn't be this hard, I told myself. I shouldn't have to think of a script just to get him to understand that I had to go to the bank. I had to at least try to find some answers.

Ms. Lily and her husband finally broke free of each other long enough to unlock their door and go into their apartment. I took a deep breath and went into mine.

Dee was sitting on the couch with a bouquet of flowers on the coffee table in front of him. He'd never bought me flowers before. No one ever had.

"Hey, babe. How was your day?" I said, ignoring the tense look on his face and the clinching of his jaw. I had become all too familiar with that look.

"Where were you?" he asked. He didn't yell, but I braced myself. I knew him well enough to know that there would be yelling. "I came home early figuring that you might be lonely stuck here in the apartment by yourself all day and to my surprise, you weren't here. I have been sitting here for hours worried about you. Do you know all of the things that were running through my head?"

"I'm sorry. I was expecting to be home the same time as you, if not earlier."

He glared. "Oh, so you thought you would go wherever and get home before me and I would never know?"

See, that's what I mean, our communication was off. I'm sure Mrs. Lily and her husband didn't have these types of issues. "No." I talked slowly, enunciating every syllable, partially out of anger and frustration and partially because I wanted him to understand me. "That's not what I said. I just didn't expect you to be home early and waiting so long for me. If I had expected that I would have called to tell you I would be late."

"Late!" He jumped off the couch. See, there it was: the yelling. "We agreed that you wouldn't go out by yourself. If you want to be going out and wandering around town, then we need to move and you can feel free and safe to do whatever. But here you can't do that, not anymore. I'm tired of having the same conversation with you over and over."

I matched his attitude, which wasn't hard for me to do considering now I was just as pissed off as he was. He wasn't even trying to see things from my perspective. "Good!' I said. "Because I don't want to have that conversation either. You think moving will solve all of our problems and it won't. I don't want to talk about moving."

He sat back down. "Okay, so what do you want to talk about? How about you tell me what was so important that you left the house without even letting me know! How about we have a conversation about that?"

I lowered my voice in hopes that he would follow my lead. I wasn't backing down; I knew I had just as much reason to be as upset as he did. I knew that my frustration was justified. It's just that the yelling and the conversation as a whole were giving me a headache. It wasn't the type of headache that was progressive, it was a full impact, pounding, throbbing headache. For a fleeting moment I wondered if I had a concussion. After all, I had taken several blows to the head.

I sat down next to him on the couch. Closed my eyes for a moment and rubbed my temples in a fruitless effort to alleviate the pain.

Despite the fact that he was pissed at me, he put his arm around my shoulder. "You okay?"

"Yeah, I'll be fine." That was the thing about Dee. He had a bit of a temper, but he was also very affectionate and caring. We never stayed mad at each other for too long. Maybe that was the key. Maybe that was what would allow us to make it to that thirty year mark.

"Okay, no more yelling." He lifted his hands in surrender. "You know the reason I get so upset is only because I worry about you, and for good reason."

"I know." He had more than good reason to worry and so did I, considering my own family was coming after me now.

Sitting next to him on the couch, he had a better view. "What happened to your face?"

I gave him the facts like a CNN reporter: no filler, no extra info. I didn't apologize for going to the bank, but I did apologize for not letting him know that I was going out and causing him to worry.

But unlike me, he didn't apologize. The words "I'm sorry" didn't seem to be part of his vocabulary. He didn't feel he had done anything wrong.

I tried to spell it out for him: he wasn't supportive. He didn't understand that I needed to know that truth about my family. He didn't get that all of my problems wouldn't be solved simply by moving. Wherever I go the questions will follow me, I told him. What questions? No, no, not just that my father was a dealer. I already knew that. But there were other things that I didn't know.

He sat there and listened, I'll give him that much, but I could tell that he didn't understand fully what I was saying. I really needed to figure out Mrs. Lily's secret.

After my conversation with Dee, the pain in my head had gotten worse. Sometimes talking to him was like hitting my head against a brick wall. I took a couple of extra strength pain relievers, but they were not as fast-acting as the bottle advertised. An hour later, my head-ache was still going and going like it was being fueled by the Energizer Bunny.

Maybe if I would have just let Dee hold me when he reached for me in bed that night—maybe if I wouldn't have turned away when he whispered "I love you"—maybe then some of what happened could have been avoided. Every decision, even the simple little ones, has consequences.

Chapter 27

I don't know what people did before the Internet. The next morning, after a less than restful sleep, I borrowed Dee's laptop. Within a few seconds I had a phone number to go with the address that Ms. Fleming had given me.

For a while I just sat there and stared at the number on the screen like it was some type of encrypted message. Like I should pull out my decoder ring and decipher its meaning.

When I was a kid, I really did have a decoder ring. Well, actually it was my father's, but he let me play with it. He took me to a Yankees game when I was about nine or ten and when I opened my box of Cracker Jacks there was some little flimsy prize inside. He laughed at my disappointment.

When I was a kid those things used to have the coolest prizes, he'd told me. He told me about his best prize ever, his decoder ring. He said he loved that thing as a kid. Then when we got home he went through all his old stuff on a hunt to find it. "I know it's here somewhere," I'd heard him mumble to himself. The next morning he presented it to me. And it was absolutely addictive. We would leave little secret messages to each other all over the apartment.

Unfortunately, he was hiding secrets that couldn't be interpreted by simply referring to my childhood toy. Knowing that there was only one way to decipher this mystery, I picked up the phone, held my breath, and dialed the number.

"Hello?" a female voice said on the second ring. A few rings too soon for my breathing to regulate itself.

I exhaled audibly. "Hello. My name is Brianna Roberts. Can I please speak to Mr. or Mrs. Nichols?" As I listened to myself say the words, I thought about how much I sounded like a telemarketer, or even worse, a bill collector. She was probably waiting for a recorded voice to tell her that the call would be monitored for quality assurance.

"I'm sorry, they no longer live here. I'm their daughter Marie Lambert. Can I help you?"

Their daughter? My mother's sister? The possibility of my mother having siblings never even crossed my mind. Why hadn't anyone ever tried to contact me?

"Yes. I'm trying to get in touch with my mother's parents and this was the name and address I was given. My mother's name was Alecia Nichols."

"Oh my goodness! I can't believe it's you!"

Then there was silence. Had we been disconnected? "Hello?'

She was crying. "I always hoped to meet you one day. I'm your Aunt Marie. You sound so grown up, how old are you now?"

She knew who I was and she sounded genuinely happy to hear from me. "Almost nineteen."

"How are you? Are you well?"

"I'm honestly not doing that well," I said, unsure of how much to reveal over the phone. Before I could say anymore she interrupted me and asked if I needed money. I know, I know, it was a reasonable question considering I was calling out of the blue, but it still stung a little.

"I'm calling," I clarified, "because I wanted to find out some information about my mother and it seems like I have a whole family that I don't know anything about."

"I'm sorry that you are having a difficult time," she said. "You don't even know me but if there is anything that I can do, I am more than willing to help you. From the sound of it, you could use someone to talk to. Maybe you would feel better talking in person. I know the family would love to meet you."

But if she wanted to meet me so badly why hadn't she looked for me?

"And you're right. You do have a whole family," she continued. "A big family. Your mother was the youngest of four."

"Wow. There's just so much that I don't know. I want to know everything, but I don't know where to start. I don't even know what to ask."

"Well, first the family tree. Your mother was the youngest, then there's me and Jason, we're twins, and then Lucas, he's the oldest. Even though we are all married with our own kids now, we are still a very close family. We all live within twenty minutes of each other."

"Wow." That was all that I could say as I tried to absorb all the information.

"We would really love to meet you. Do you live in New York?"

"Yes."

"Why don't you come down to see us? I know that my parents have been waiting for this for a long time. We all have. I could send you money for the trip fare."

"No, I have money to get there." I didn't want to be confrontational, but I knew if I didn't ask, the question would continue to eat at me. "If everyone would be excited to meet me, why didn't anyone every attempt to contact me before?"

"Aw, sweetie, it's way more complicated than you realize. I think that's something that we should all talk about in person. For now just know that this family has never stopped loving you and wanting to have a relationship with you. We want nothing more than to make you a true member of the family."

Before we got off the phone, I made arrangements to be in North Carolina within the next few days and I told her that I would call when my travel plans were finalized.

I had mixed feelings. She seemed like a genuine person, but I hadn't proven to be such a good judge of character. I heard Dr. Beekman's voice in my head reminding me that I shouldn't let my bad past experiences dictate how I act toward people, that I should judge people by their own actions, not the actions of others. I chanted that to myself, made it my mantra. *I will give them a chance. I will be open-minded.* Decoder ring or not, I knew that a lot of things would be revealed to me on that trip.

Chapter 28

Hindsight is twenty-twenty. What if we hadn't been arguing so much? What if I had let him hold me in bed that night? What if I hadn't seen Claudia in the street that day? All of these things separately might not have made a difference, but together...together they set the stage.

Dee agreed to go to the Laundromat to wash my clothes so that I could pack for my trip down south. He startled me when he came back less than twenty minutes later and slammed the door behind himself.

I rushed out of the bedroom. "What's the matter?"

He jabbed his finger in my direction, but the gesture, I'm sure, wasn't as forceful as he'd intended because I saw his hand trembling. "You're cheating on me!" he yelled.

At that moment, I didn't know what caused my reaction: all of the stuff with my father? My aunt? My pending trip to meet my family for the first time? I didn't know, but Dee's stupid accusation seemed like it wasn't worth my time. I told him as much by not saying a word. I just stood there and stared at him like he was stupid.

I mean, I had enough on my mind to deal with without Dee adding to my stress. He should've been comforting me, telling me that the trip would go well, that I was doing the right thing by meeting them. But instead he was coming at me with nonsense.

I had no reason to cheat on him. He usually treated me very well.

And even with his erratic behavior lately, I still wouldn't cheat on him because that's not my nature. I'm not a sneaky person. If this relationship wasn't working for me, I would have been upfront and told him that. I felt like I was getting pretty close to telling him just that.

For a long time neither one of us said a word. We just stood there, staring at each other. I could tell he was waiting for me to say something. I was inexperienced and I probably could have handled it better, taken his concerns more seriously, but surely he could have handled it better too.

He walked toward me, pushed me against the wall, and pressed his body against mine. He kissed me, hard and deep. I struggled against him, tried to jerk my head away. But my body betrayed me; I welcomed him, leaned into it.

When he stepped away from me the anger in his face somehow seemed even more intense. "Does he kiss you like that?" he snapped.

I responded to him then. "Who? What?" Where, when, and how, would be my follow up questions.

Instead of answering me, he walked to the kitchen counter, picked up the vase which held the flowers he had given me, and threw it in my direction. I took a step back and shiny shards of glass crunched under my shoes. I'd like to think that he wasn't aiming for me.

He'd lost his temper, but no, no of course he wasn't aiming for me. He would never hit a woman, he assured me later. That was later, after tempers had cooled, and the mess had been cleaned up, but in that moment, he was seeing red, and I didn't know what to think.

"Where else did you go yesterday besides the bank? Who were you with?"

"Nowhere! Nobody!"

"I thought you were different than the rest of the girls around here. I thought you were special. But you are even worse than them because at least they don't pretend to be something they're not." He paused for a moment to catch his breath then added, "You are a liar, just like your father."

Hit me where it hurts, why don't you? I thought. I had been a little scared at first, but now I was just confused. "What are you talking about?"

He pulled out the little piece of paper that Claude had written her number on. He must have found it in my pants pocket as he did the laundry. Okay, so I had the weirdest thought at that moment. I knew he was mad, but for some reason, I couldn't help but think about how this reminded me of the old episodes of *Three's Company* that I use to watch on Nick at Nite.

There was always some silly misunderstanding that caused havoc. Poor Janet, Jack, and Chrissy at least twenty-eight minutes of every half-hour show were spent in this clueless state. And it was always something really minor that caused all of the problems. I laughed a little as I thought about it. That set Dee off.

He went ballistic. "You're actually laughing! Oh, okay, I'm the idiot then. I'm the stupid one for trusting you. Get out of my apartment! Just go! Get out! You're already packing so it shouldn't take you too long."

A knock on the door interrupted us. Mrs. Lily must have overheard the commotion. Another quick wrap on the door. "Hello? Brianna... Brianna?" I tried to put on a calm face before I opened the door.

When I opened the door Mrs. Lily was standing there looking nervous and concerned. "Brianna are you okay?" She looked over my shoulder at Dee and gave him the evil eye. "Why don't you come down stairs with me for a while, I could use some company."

I told her that everything was fine. "I'm sorry we disturbed you. We will keep it down." I nodded and forced a smile, trying to reassure her. "Everything's okay."

She was skeptical. I could tell she was reluctant to leave. She glanced at Dee again. Then she squeezed my arm. "I'm right downstairs if you need anything."

"Thanks."

When I closed the door, Dee mumbled, "She needs to mind her own business."

"I'm surprised all of our neighbors haven't come knocking, or called the police, with the way you are acting."

I walked toward him. "Just so you know, I wasn't laughing at you before. It's just that this is crazy. I would never cheat on you."

Now he was the one with the skeptical look on his face. But he didn't respond and I could tell that he wanted me to convince him. That he wanted me to reassure him. For emphasis, I screamed, "I wouldn't cheat on you!"

He stared at me like I was a stranger. He was trying to read my face to see if I was lying. That should have been easy enough to do since everything was always written on my face. I walked closer to him. He tried to pull away initially, but then he gave in a little. He let me hold his hand. "Look me in the eye Dee. Look at me. Do you really think that I could cheat on you?"

He didn't answer me at first, but after a long silence, he said, "I don't know what to think. If you're not, then who is Claude?" There were tears forming in his eyes. I remember how he told me that he had been in love before and gotten his heart broken. Maybe this was just all too familiar for him. I squeezed his hand reassuringly.

"Babe, Claude is short for Claudia. She's a girl I use to know in high school who I ran into when I was coming home from the bank."

"So if I call this number a girl will answer?"

"How many guys do you know around here named Claude, be serious." By his expression I could tell he wasn't ready to joke about it yet. "Yes, a girl will answer."

"Are you sure? Because I might just call."

I started to get annoyed again. "Call! I don't even care! But I don't like the fact that you don't trust me. I have given you no reason not to trust me, but if you feel like you need to call, if that's what you need to prove that I am not lying, then go ahead."

I started to walk away, but before I made it back to the bedroom, he called me. I turned around and watched as he ripped up the small paper and threw it way. Then he got the broom and started sweeping up the broken glass. No apology.

Now, don't get me wrong, I loved the fact that he was self-assured, loved that cocky little attitude of his. But was the opposite side of the coin his inability to acknowledge that he could, possibly, by some slim chance, actually be wrong about something? That he could actually have a reason to say, "I'm sorry."

Later that afternoon, once both our tempers had settled he told me that when he saw that phone number he started thinking about the problems that we had been having lately. Little things like me not kissing him when he came home, or not letting him hold me as we slept, only saying, "I love you," if he said it first. He said when he saw the number all of those things started to add up and make sense. The only explanation in his mind was that I was cheating.

"You can't deny," he'd said, "that we aren't getting along the way we use to. I figured that the reason we weren't getting along is because you had already found someone else. I don't want to lose you. "

For the umpteenth time I tried to explain to him why we were having problems. That he saw everything in black and white and things weren't that simple. I told him that if he would try harder to keep his temper in check that I would try harder to communicate better with him.

I told him that I loved him but that he should have just asked me instead of accusing me of doing something. He should have given me a chance to explain. I also told him that the next time he tried to put me out he'd better be sure because once I left I wouldn't be coming back.

As I continued packing, I figured, a little distance between us wouldn't hurt. Maybe this trip would not only be good for me, but good for our relationship too.

Chapter 29

I have a fear of flying. I know it's an irrational fear since I've never actually been on a plane, but the idea of defying gravity just didn't sit well with me. So when making my plans for my trip down south, I knew taking a plane was out of the question. Besides, with everything that had been going on, I decided that it was not a good idea to tempt fate.

I was scheduled to leave on an 11 p.m. Greyhound bus that would arrive in Raleigh, North Carolina, the next morning at 11:30 a.m. Thankfully, on the Greyhound, there were no restrictions on electronic devices so I loaded up my iPod with a few new albums and figured I was good to go.

When Dee tore up and threw away the piece of paper with Claude's number on it, my anger didn't automatically go away. The worst part was that he had called me a liar and compared me to my father. That wasn't something that I couldn't easily just forgive and forget.

I know he sensed there was still some friction between us, because he started being extra nice to me. So nice in fact that it was getting annoying. *Can I get you anything? Do you need any help?* What I needed was space. I just wanted him to back off.

I told him he didn't have to, but Dee insisted on coming with me to Port Authority to help me carry my bags. At least he hadn't given me a hard time when I told him I was going. I think he was relieved to have me out of New York, if only for a few days.

"Make sure you call me when you get there, don't forget."

"Okay."

"Brie... the other day... I just got nervous. I didn't mean... I just... I don't want to lose you."

I didn't respond. I was stubborn. *It probably runs in my family*, I thought. I wondered what other things ran in my family. I would be finding that out soon enough. I was lost in my own train of thought when Dee said, "And if anything starts going wrong, or if you start to feel uncomfortable, let me know and I'll hop on a plane and be there in two hours."

"Okay."

He hugged me tightly and told me to have a safe trip.

As the bus exited the terminal, I thought the anticipation of meeting my new family or maybe my lingering anger over my argument with Dee would keep me awake. But my stress and anticipation was no match for the movement of the bus. I was asleep before we even got out of Manhattan.

Chapter 30

Jackie would have hired a personal shopper a long time ago if she wasn't so in love with the look on people's faces when she pulled out her black card. As a kid she had always been teased because her clothes were not name brand, or even worse, they were too small. She never got new clothes for school; instead her mother would get hand-me-downs from different charities or people she worked with. Times were hard. Jackie even remembered several occasions when she had to go to school in some of Keith's old clothes.

But those days were long gone. No one was laughing at her now, she thought as she stood in the line at Bloomingdales with an arm full of designer clothes—clothes worth more than what most people paid in rent for six months and that was just the first stop on her well-deserved shopping spree. She stepped up to the register and it only took a few seconds for her to come down off her shopping high.

"What the heck do you mean my card was declined? Have you ever seen a black card before? Black cards don't get declined. Run it again!"

"I'm sorry ma'am, but I have run the card twice already. It's been declined." The Bloomingdale's cashier tried her hardest to defuse the situation. "I can hold these items for you for twenty-four hours. That should give you a chance to go get this straightened out."

Jackie wanted so much to lunge across the counter at the girl. "Don't bother! You obviously don't want my business."

That's when the cashier forgot the golden rule of retail: the customer is always right. Upset because the loud obnoxious woman was making a scene and holding up her line she said, "Well, if you think we don't want your business because we won't give it to you for free, then yes, you're right."

"What? I know you're not talking to me."

"I don't have time for this. Step aside. You are holding up my line."

Jackie reached across the counter and missed the girl by only a few inches.

"Security!" The woman screamed, and security guards seemed to arrive in a swarm. They were uniformed and plain clothed.

"Ma'am, we are going to have to ask you to leave the store now."

Without a word Jackie made her way to the exit pushing people out of her way and knocking over merchandise as she went. She was having a bad day, but she had no idea how much worse it was about to get. It wouldn't be her last encounter with security that day.

From Bloomingdale's she made her way straight to the bank. While she waited to speak to a customer service representative, she tried to calm herself down. It was a lost cause; she was furious.

Julia, a young Hispanic woman, brought her over to her desk. After some needless pleasantries she got down to business.

"You know that although you have privileges on this account, it is not in your name?"

"Yes, I am aware of that," Jackie said, trying to keep her cool.

She knew that all too well. Keith had set up the account that way, supposedly in an effort to protect her.

"Jackie, it's the best way to handle it." Her brother had told her all those years ago. "You will have complete access to the account, it will be like your account and I will make regular deposits into it. Brie is just a baby, so if anything happens to either one of us they won't take money out of her account."

"That's the stupidest thing I've ever heard. Just because it's in her name doesn't mean if we get caught the cops wont seize that money. They will assume that it's drug money. There will be a record that you made the deposits. Did you ever think about that? There will always be a chance that someone will discover the money, but for now I would rather it be in my name."

"No. I am setting up the account the way I said. If that is not good enough for you, then I don't know what to tell you. I can set it up so that you don't have access at all."

When did Keith get a backbone? She remembered thinking to herself. But even as she asked herself the question, she knew the answer. It was his wife…Alecia. He never used to talk to Jackie like that, but more and more he'd been trying to flex his muscles. He'd actually said, "That's it… end of conversation."

Now eighteen years later, because of his stupidity, she had to deal with this. Maybe that had been his plan all along, to take care of his daughter if anything happened to him and to leave Jackie out in the cold. But it wasn't about to go down like that.

Julia continued, "Well, the way the account was set up, your privileges on the account were to be revoked as of a set date, which was two days ago. You should have gotten a letter to that effect."

"What?"

"You no longer have access to the account."

"So how can we fix it?"

"Unfortunately, Ms. Roberts, it's not something that can be fixed. It's not a mistake, that's just how the account was set up. It was set up in the name of a child and you were given privileges on the account until a set date. That date was thirty days prior to the child's nineteenth birthday. Once Ms. Brianna Roberts turns nineteen she will have full access to the balance of the account." She glanced at her computer screen. "Which is currently…"

"I know what the balance is!" So of course without the money in the bank, her black card was history.

"The only way to regain access is to be granted it by the account holder, Brianna Roberts."

Jackie was fuming. She felt a pounding in her ears. *This can't be happening*, she thought. She couldn't recall a time when she had been so mad. There had, no doubt, been a few tied for close second.

"I'm going to ask her to marry me," Keith had said as he showed Jackie a diamond ring.

She couldn't believe the words she was hearing. "What?"

"I love her, Jackie."

Quoting the words of Tina Turner, she'd asked "What's love got to do with it?" She was livid. Everything that she had worked for was at risk. "She won't understand. There is no way that she will marry you. She is a nice southern girl. She didn't come here to marry a drug dealer. Sometimes I don't think you realize what you really are. You're in denial."

"And what are you, Jackie?"

"Trust me I know who I am. I am the brains behind this whole thing, and as the smart one, I'm the one you should be listening to. Don't marry that girl."

"Stop calling her that girl. Her name is Alecia, and I am going to marry her. And you are the one in denial. You are not the smart one. You have been riding my coattails all these years. You're just afraid that if I get married, you will be out on your butt. It doesn't take a genius to figure that out."

That girl was bringing out a side of her brother that she had never seen before, and Jackie didn't like it one bit. She got in his face. "If you try to cut me out, you will be locked up before the honeymoon. You know you can't handle this on your own, so I am not even worried about that possibility at all."

"I really don't care what you're worried about. I'm going to marry her."

"It's easy to keep secrets from your girlfriend, but how are you going to hide the fact that you are a dealer from your wife? She's not stupid. Once she moves in and starts going through things, she will figure it out eventually."

"Maybe if you could actually keep a man, you wouldn't be so concerned with what I'm doing. What I do with Alecia is my business."

"You're right…you're absolutely right, it is your business. And as long as your business doesn't affect my business, we won't have a problem."

That conversation had given Jackie her first migraine. Now all these years later, as she felt another one coming on strong, she realized that her brother's decision on that day was what had set events in motion. Events that had led her to this very moment. Sitting there in the bank at a loss for what to do.

She figured this is what it must feel like to lose money in the stock market. One day it's there and the next it's gone. She needed to regroup. She walked away from Julia's desk without saying a word.

On her way out of the bank, when she saw Brianna, she thought it was a mirage. But from the way Brianna hit the floor when Jackie tackled her, Jackie could tell it was really her. Live and in the flesh.

Beat her like she stole something took on a very literal meaning. The security guard took an elbow to the jaw in the process of trying to break up the fight. It couldn't really even be called a fight; Brianna never really had a chance. Jackie knew that if it were not for the fast response of the security guards and the police, Brie might not have gotten up off that floor.

After the security guards came the police, the back of the squad car, and then central booking. All the while Jackie was thinking about the best way to get her money back. With her new financial situation, she was barely able to pay the five thousand dollar bail.

Now, three days later, sitting at home on her couch, reliving the experience brought back every ounce of anger and then some. She still couldn't believe that her own brother had done this to her, after all of the things she'd done for him.

He would still be selling nickel bags on the corner if it wasn't for her. She was the one with the vision, with the ambition. But there was no sense focusing on him right now. He was locked up and he had no control anymore. She was on her own, just the way she liked it.

Jackie told herself that if she was going to get her money back she had to be calm and she had to be smart. Despite her current situation, which she told herself was just a minor setback, she was confident that she would come out on top because she always did. She had a lot of experience with making something out of nothing. All she had to do was calm down enough to come up with her next plan; this one would be foolproof.

Chapter 31

They met me at the bus depot in Raleigh. I'd slept for most of the trip, and so had the woman sitting next to me, on my shoulder. When I got off the bus, and my eyes adjusted to the daylight, I recognized a woman searching the crowd. Well, of course I didn't actually recognize her since I'd never seen her before, but she did look like a light-skinned version of my mother. I could tell that, like myself, she was searching every face looking for familiar features. I waived at her and she came running, pushing her way through the crowd.

She hugged me so tightly I thought I might dislocate something. "I can't believe it's really you," she whispered with her arms still holding me tight. She kissed me on both cheeks, and her tears dampened my face. She shook me back and forth a few more times before finally letting go. "I'm your Aunt Marie."

The red and blue fabric of Marie's loosely-fitted dress flapped around wildly in the wind and made her look like a mythical creature. Maybe that was what this was—some perfect little story that I had dreamt up in an effort to escape my increasingly depressing reality. That's what I was thinking, I remember, as she took my hand and rushed me toward the rest of the welcoming committee: the family I hadn't let myself believe existed until that very moment.

She led me through the parking lot, and I awkwardly carried my bags with one hand, the hand that she hadn't confiscated. She was talking a mile a minute. Weren't things in the south supposed to be slower?

"Everyone is so excited to meet you! My parents, your grandparents, they just couldn't believe it when I told them that you were coming. Daddy cried."

She waived toward a van and people started climbing out of it like it was one of those clown cars in the circus. I thought the line of people would never end. At that point I realized that we were having an impromptu family reunion right in the parking lot of the bus station.

I have never been hugged so much in my life. With her southern charm spilling over, my grandmother hugged me and said, "I do declare, I never thought I'd see this day. I've prayed for it for so long."

It was all very touching, but completely overwhelming at the same time. Fortunately for me it was only fifty degrees, frigidly cold for the south, so everyone was in a rush to get back indoors. Otherwise it could have lasted all day.

Despite being overwhelmed, I must admit that it was love at first sight. I loved them all, their happy smiles and excited expressions. I felt like part of a family for the first time. I mean, I loved my father and growing up with him was great before I knew who he really was, but I had always felt like something was missing. And there in the parking lot of that bus depot, I felt whole for the first time.

But that stupid voice, it just wouldn't shut up. It wouldn't let me have my perfect happy moment. It asked, *why didn't they invite you into their lives sooner? Why didn't they come find you? Love you?* In the car as we drove to the house of my grandparents, who were lovingly called Gran and Pop, I pushed those questions out of my head, at least for the moment.

Once we arrived at the house, I was introduced to even more family. I felt like I needed a mnemonic device—or better yet name tags—to keep track of all their names.

Okay, so the grandparents were easy enough to keep track of. They were just too cute, like one of the old couples you might see walking down the street holding hands. Even when they were fussing with each other, it was adorable. The whole ride from the bus station, they argued about whether the heat in the car was too high or too low. "Woman, you are too old to be having hot flashes," Pop said. And at the next red light, Gran had promptly proceeded to slap him upside the head.

They kind of reminded me of Mrs. Lily and her husband. That sort of thing always made me smile. When we arrived at the house, Pop walked around the side of the van and opened the door for her. How cute is that?

Gran was the shortest member of the clan at only about 5'5" and she had a healthy plumpness to her. Pop was slim but by no means frail. He told me later that it was all of the yard work that kept him fit. He bragged that he had the best vegetable garden in the neighborhood. "The key is to stay active," he'd told me. "Idle hands are the devil's tools, not to mention what sitting around all day will do to the midsection." He laughed and Gran shook her head.

Okay, so Gran and Pop, check. Then there were their children, my aunts and uncles. There was Marie, whom I had spoken to on the phone, and her twin brother Jason. And Lucas, their older brother. Marie's husband was Irish and both of their beautiful children had his green eyes and freckled cheeks. There was one that looked to be around eleven or twelve. She was friendly but kind of shy. I told her not to take it personally, that I was just really bad with names. She was tall for her age. We all seemed to have the height thing in common. She was very light skinned, almost pale and had light brown hair with natural blond highlights.

Then there was her sister Karen, Kelly, something with a K. My plan was to just smile and be polite and figure out the names later. Anyway, her sister was about seven or so. Jason also had two kids, a twelve-year-old son and a sixteen-year-old daughter. Lucas' daughter was about thirteen and she was the spitting image of me at that age. There was no denying I was a part of this family. And no one tried to deny it. That's what made it so hard for me to understand why they had never tried to contact me.

Chapter 32

They brought out the good china. No mismatched cups and plates. The table looked like it was set for a Thanksgiving feast. Even the table cloth was fancy, with its white lace detail. Martha Stewart would be proud.

The women helped bring the food out of the kitchen. I wanted to help. It was awkward sitting there with the men. "No, you just have a seat. You're our guest," Gran said, waving me back into my chair.

"I didn't know what kind of food you liked," she said. "So I made a little bit of everything."

She wasn't kidding. I don't know how many trips she made into the kitchen, but each time she came out carrying another platter of food, followed by a new savory smell that made my mouth water. Every time she went into the kitchen, I thought it had to be her last trip, that there couldn't possibly be anymore food in there. Then she would do an about face and head back into the kitchen.

Once the food was being passed around the table, people began to discreetly unbutton their pants to make room. Southern cooking is no joke. I couldn't remember the last time I had a home-cooked meal that was so good. Maybe never.

Aunt Jackie wasn't much of a cook. She tended to rely on take out and frozen foods or things from a can. Her specialty was hot dogs with mac and cheese. Her favorite kitchen appliance was the microwave.

She had a really bad habit of standing in front of it while she was heating stuff up. *Doing that will give you cancer*, I used to tell her. I didn't know if that was true, but I'd heard it somewhere. What was the point anyway? Standing there watching the dish spin around wasn't like stirring a pot on a stove or doing some actual cooking.

Anyway, it was hard to imagine, but she was a chef compared to my father. He would send me over to her apartment for dinner. When I got older, I started teaching myself some of the basics, but I was still a work in progress. So needless to say, this type of home cooking was new to me.

Maybe no one wanted to spoil their meal and that is why the conversation was kept so light and casual. It was like no one wanted to talk about what was really on everyone's mind. No one wanted to tackle the big issues.

But soon enough, dinner was over, the kids were in the family room watching a movie and the rest of us were sitting at the now cleared dining room table. I could tell by the looks on everyone's face that there would be no more talk of sports and weather. It was time to get down to business.

Gran sat with her hands folded on the table. Her short, low-maintenance haircut framed her face, which suddenly looked very sad. I thought I saw her hands shake a little. I could tell she was trying to figure out where to start. *Let's start with why you never looked for me*, I thought to myself.

As if she had heard what I was thinking, she looked at me and gave me a nervous smile. The chandelier cast a warm light over the room and I noticed that her eyes were glistening with tears. *This is going to be tough*, I thought.

After a few moments of awkward silence, Gran mustered up enough strength to start the conversation. This conversation was no doubt years in the making, and I could tell that I was not the only one suffering from the feeling of nervous anticipation.

Everyone else knew the story, so Gran focused on me. I knew that this was going tough on all of us but at least I would finally know the truth.

As a senior in high school my mother had excitedly told her parents that her straight As had landed her scholarships to two different out-of-state schools. They didn't share her excitement. Maybe she was being selfish, Gran told me, but my mother was her baby and she just wasn't ready to let her go so far away from home. After some compromise, my mother had reluctantly agreed to stay in North Carolina for college. But those four years seemed to fly by, and before Gran knew it, they were having the same conversation again. "It was like this town just couldn't contain her anymore. She was ready to head off to the big city."

Gran realized she was fighting a losing battle. My mother packed her bags and headed off to New York.

"Everyone else stayed here in North Carolina, but Alecia was always the adventurous one," Lucas said.

For a while everything seemed to be going okay. She got an apartment and a job she loved. "The job at that bank seemed perfect for Alecia," Gran said. "She liked dealing with finance, but what really kept her going was that she felt like she was really helping people. People came to her when they wanted to buy their first home or start a new business. She really loved helping people." Gran used the back of her hand to wipe her damp eyes.

I couldn't help but think that as happy as we were to finally be together as a family, for them this reunion also meant having to relive what had happened to my mother.

Gran's voice cracked when she told me how much she missed my mother when she moved to New York. "She was good about calling regularly, but it just wasn't the same. During one of our phone conversations, in between telling me about some award that she had gotten at work and wanting to go back to school to get her master's degree, she casually mentioned that she was engaged."

Of course Gran and Pop were absolutely shocked by this news. How could she be engaged, she hadn't even told them she was dating anyone? They weren't prudes; they knew she was a grown woman, and they expected her to date, but they also expected her to tell them if she was in a serious relationship.

Pop took it pretty personally. "Like Gran said, she and Alecia were very close but I made it a point to be close with my children also. I grew up with a father that thought his only job was to bring home the paycheck and take care of us financially. But there is so much more to parenting than that. I made sure that all of my children knew that I was there for them and wanted to be involved in their lives. So Alecia not telling either one of us until after she was already engaged, well that hurt. It wasn't like her. And that was the problem. I felt like whoever this guy was, he was having an effect on her that I didn't like. Making her keep secrets from her family."

Yeah, I thought. I could see her picking up that character trait from him. He definitely knew how to be secretive.

"It all seemed to be happening too fast," Gran said. "She told us that she'd met him at the bank. He was a customer. He owned some type of large architecture and construction firm."

My father was very successful in his fictional life.

"I guess I am kind of old school," Pop said. "But if some guy is going to marry my daughter, he should ask me first. And if that was too much to ask, then I should have at least met him, gotten to know him a little before he proposed to her. It was a matter of respect. I told her to bring him down for a weekend so that we could all meet him."

When they arrived, the family had mixed feelings about him. My mother was like his shadow. They didn't have much of a chance to talk to either one of them alone.

James said he'd gotten a bad vibe from my father right away. "It was like he was hiding something."

I wished that I'd had his intuition. I could have saved myself a lot of heartache and disappointment.

James said he couldn't put his finger on what it was that bothered him about my father. But it made him uncomfortable enough to bring it up to my mother. "Alecia was pretty patronizing when I mentioned it to her. She basically wrote me off as being the typical overprotective older brother."

Marie, who had been quiet up to that point, told me that James was always observant about things like that, but she didn't see anything wrong initially. She was happy for her sister. To her, my father was handsome, polite and charismatic.

It wasn't until she had a few minutes alone with Alecia that she started to notice something was wrong. "It may sound stupid," she said. "But when Alecia and I were younger, we could spend hours dreaming about what our wedding day would be like. We would even cut pictures out of magazines. I knew my sister very well, so when I asked her about her wedding plans and she shrugged and said it didn't matter to her, I knew she was lying. She said Keith didn't want a big production. They would probably just go to the justice of the peace. I knew that was not what she wanted."

Marie said she started paying closer attention then. And when she looked beyond my father's smile and charisma she didn't like what she saw. "Every time I asked Alecia something the answer was always, 'Keith wants...' or 'Keith thinks...' It was never what Alecia wanted. I never heard her opinion on things anymore. And that worried me."

This was turning into the meeting of the We Don't Trust Keith Roberts Club, the WDTKRC. We could have T-shirts made up. I elected myself president.

Like James, Marie told her sister about her concerns. "Part of me is sorry that I ever confronted her about it. I feel like it pushed her away from me and made her reluctant to confide in me about things."

After they got married the phone calls came less and less often.

They were lucky to hear from her every other month. When they did talk, it seemed more like a courtesy call than anything else. It was nothing like the heart-to-hearts they use to have. Then months went by and there was no word from her at all.

"We called everyday and all we got was the answering machine. Then, finally," Gran said, "I was able to get her work number from Chase's corporate office. That was no easy task. There must be a Chase Bank on every corner in New York. I didn't know if she took Keith's last name or not. Needless to say I listened to a lot of smooth jazz while I was on hold during this process. But finally they were able to track her down." She corrected herself. "They tracked down her phone number."

When Gran called my mother's office, she was informed that my mother was out on maternity leave. "Those words broke my heart," she said. "It hurt worse than the news of her engagement. She hadn't even told us she was pregnant."

Pop said that was when the red flags turned into flashing neon danger signs. Something was very wrong. They immediately caught a flight to New York. It was far from what they thought their first trip to New York would be like. "All we had to go on was the postmark on a Mother's Day card she'd sent me," Gran said. "On the plane I kept thinking, *What if the address is wrong? What if we can't find her?*"

But they were lucky. They didn't have to look for my mother too hard. When they got out of the cab in front of the building, they spotted her walking down the block. Pop said, "I remember she was pushing a cart with groceries and she had you strapped to her chest. She looked beautiful. My fear and anger melted away, for a moment at least. All I could do was look at her. My baby had a baby of her own."

Not that I ever doubted it, but it looked like Ms. Fleming from the bank was right. My mother hadn't died giving birth to me. Another lie that my father had told me. I wasn't shocked. I had become numb to that emotion. I just shook my head. "I was told that she died giving birth to me."

Jason sprung out of his chair like a Jack in the Box. This whole time I could tell he was fuming. He wasn't sad and hurt like everyone else. This discussion had brought out something different in him. He was furious. Gran flinched when he banged his fists on the table. "That lying bastard! He killed her, I know he did. Everyone at this table knows it."

"What?" I said. "That's what you think? You think my father killed my mother?" Okay, so maybe I shouldn't have been so surprised. For a fleeting moment, sitting in Ms. Fleming's office in the bank, I'd had the same thought. But it just didn't make sense. My father was not a violent man.

The conclusion I'd come to was that my mother's death was somehow related to his drug operation, and revealing the truth would mean that he would have to admit the drug dealing too. Was I in denial? Sure, I had rarely seen him lose his temper, but I'd never seen him deal drugs and that didn't make it any less true.

"Jason...Jason, please sit down," Gran said.

Ignoring her he leaned forward toward me. He was the only one who decided to answer my question. *Did they really think my father killed my mother?* It wasn't meant to be a rhetorical question. I needed an answer.

"We don't think it. We know it. We just haven't been able to prove it. Think about it. Why would he have lied to you about something like that if he didn't kill her?"

Pop gave Jason a quick look that put him back in his seat. "If you cannot handle this you can leave and come back tomorrow after you've calmed down. Is that what you want?"

"No, sir."

"So stay in that seat and be quiet!"

"Everything that came out of that man's mouth was a lie," Pop said. "That much we can agree on now."

When Gran talked about how much happiness my mother had

brought into their lives, she didn't look at me. She was staring down at the tablecloth, fingering its intricate detail. But she looked me directly in the eyes when she said, "Parents are not suppose to outlive their children. It's just not suppose to happen like that."

Pop grabbed her hand and kissed it. "If we would have known when we went to visit Alecia in New York that it would be the last time we saw her, we would have done things a lot differently."

When they saw my mother walking down the block, she looked beautiful, but that was only from a distance. Up close, she looked nervous, sick even.

"She looked weak," Pop said. "I don't know how to explain it. She just didn't look like herself."

They found out later that my mother was in fact sick on that day. But as her parents hugged her outside of her building and saw how weak she looked, they'd just brushed it off as exhaustion. She'd just had a baby after all.

They figured it wasn't a good idea to start off the visit by putting her on the defensive. Not if they wanted to get answers. They needed to find out why she had stopped calling. To figure out whether Keith was treating her okay.

But when they followed her up to her apartment Gran said she didn't want to be rude, but she couldn't hold her tongue. "Why," Gran wanted to know, "were they living in the projects when they both had good paying jobs?"

"Keith has an emotional attachment to this place because he grew up here," my mother had told them.

Gran knew that explanation was bogus. She had no doubt that her daughter, who was young and naïve, believed it, but Gran knew better. Growing up in poverty is not something to be sentimental about. Gran said she knew this first hand.

Gran explained that she had grown up in a trailer park about an hour south of where she lived now. When she was very young, her father was injured working on a tractor. After that he wasn't able to work and all of the financial responsibility fell to her mother. "My mother cleaned houses and cared for people's children just so she could keep food on the table. I think about it every day, even now, because it keeps me humble and makes me thankful for everything that I have. But there is no way that I would have wanted to raise my own family in that environment if I had other options."

Pop said that their living situation surprised him, too, but he was more concerned with how jumpy and nervous my mother seemed. He said he was starting to think the worst.

Pop had planned to confront my father when he saw him but he didn't have the chance. During the three days they spent with my mother in New York, my father never made an appearance.

"What do you mean he's out of town?" they'd asked her. Gran said she knew how difficult it was to care for an infant, so she was even more concerned when she'd found out that Alecia was spending so much time home alone.

"Keith's sister is only five minutes away, if I need help," my mother had assured them.

They were reluctant to end their visit but they made plans to visit again in a month. They would get to the bottom of everything then, they'd thought.

Pop groaned. "I should have never left her there. My gut told me something was wrong... I shouldn't have left her."

Jason comforted his father. "It's not your fault, Pop. It's his fault not ours."

About a week after they got back to North Carolina, my father called and told them that my mother was missing. That she'd run away and left me with him.

My father had gotten better with his lying over the years. That's what I was thinking while I listened to Gran and Pop. At least with me his lies had been consistent. This was his third explanation for my mother's absence. She had died during child birth, in a car accident, and now she had supposedly just run away. I didn't know what to believe. So I asked for proof. "Besides your gut feelings, do you have any real evidence that she didn't just run away? I mean you said she wasn't happy that last time you saw her, right?"

They told me that I was their proof. "You never had a chance to really know her," Marie said. "But if you had you would know that she would never abandon her child. Brianna, she would have never left you behind… something horrible happened to her."

They had tried to get the police involved but they weren't any help. "It was obvious," James said, "that a missing black girl in the projects of the South Bronx wasn't going to register high on their radar." He had a point.

The police's nonchalant attitude toward my mother's disappearance wasn't their only obstacle. The story my father was telling would seem plausible to anyone who didn't know my mother. To hear him tell it, my mother was a young new mother who was overwhelmed because her husband traveled a lot for work. She was depressed, maybe even suffering from post-partum depression. And so she ran out on him, leaving him to take care of a newborn. He was the victim in the story, not her.

"But for that story to be believable," Lucas said, "you couldn't have known Alecia. To us, it was clearly a lie. She might have left him, but like Marie said, she would have never in a million years willingly left you behind."

Gran and Pop rented an apartment in New York so they could stay on top of the investigation. They spent their days getting updates from the police, putting up flyers, and posting ads in the local newspapers. All of that and for months there wasn't even a single lead.

Then one day, when my mother had been missing for about eight months, they got a phone call from a lady claiming to have seen something.

"There was a man," the voice on the other end of the phone told them. "He was medium height, dark skinned, and slightly overweight. He went into the apartment with a key but it wasn't her husband. I'm sure of that. The husband is much taller. A few seconds later I heard a gunshot."

Gran said that the woman refused to give any information about herself. As I listened to Gran, I couldn't help but think that I was surprised the woman had given them any information at all. I mean, it was the projects. Now a days, there were these signs all over the city, especially in the subway, telling people if you see something, say something. But in the projects, the cardinal rule was the exact opposite.

Gran said that she and Pop had cashed in a couple of investments so they could set a fifty thousand dollar reward for information. And she figured the caller was just after the money. But the woman, Gran remembered, was adamant about the fact that she didn't care about the reward.

She'd seen their ad in the paper day after day and she couldn't stop thinking about how horrible what they were going through must be. She told them she'd called against her better judgment.

"But now you know what I saw," the caller had told them. "I'm sorry about what happened to your daughter, but I will not give you any information about me. I will tell you this though. Her husband was a bad man. He's into a lot of bad things: drugs, guns, and who knows what else. And you are never going to get any real help from the police because he pays them off."

I guess this was before he started videotaping and blackmailing them instead.

Before that phone call they had been holding on to hope that my mother was still alive, but after that anonymous tip they were forced to admit to themselves that she was gone. Pop was already on an extended leave of absence from his job. He said he kept telling himself that he couldn't go back home until he found out the truth about what happened to his daughter.

They knew that my father was responsible, despite what the anonymous caller had told them. The most important thing that they could do for their daughter now was to make sure that I was safe. Pop said, "When we thought things couldn't get any worse, the court turned us down when we petitioned for custody of you. They said that we had no proof that Keith was a danger to you or that he had anything to do with Alecia's disappearance."

They had tried to get custody of me?

They were on a mission to find proof. Pop called in a favor from a childhood friend who worked for the FBI. "Keith was smart," Pop said. "I found out that he never actually had an architecture firm. I wondered if Alecia had found out his secret and he'd killed her because of it."

Which secret? I thought. He had so many.

Even though the business was fake, they figured that the money must be real because he was one of my mother's customers at the bank. Pop's friend used some of his contacts to find out that the police in New York were very well aware that Keith was dealing drugs, in fact he was a pretty high level dealer. But they'd never had enough evidence to charge him.

Gran said, "If what our anonymous caller had said was true, it wasn't that they didn't have enough information to charge him, it was that the police were also getting something out of the deal."

They were becoming more and more frustrated with the process. They felt like they had let their daughter down a second time. After living in New York for over a year, they went back to home to North Carolina, feeling empty and defeated.

The fact that they had tried to get custody of me when I was a baby made me feel less bitter about the situation but they could have tried harder, especially once I got older. "Why didn't you ever try to contact me?"

"We did!" Gran and Pop said in unison

"We wrote you letters," Pop said. "We wrote to you all the time. But the letters were always returned unopened. We called the only number we had and your father refused to let us talk to you. We still called regularly in the hopes that one day you would be the one to pick up the phone. We never stopped thinking about you. That's why we were so happy when you reached out to us."

The room was silent. I took that as my cue to talk. I told them about my father and prison, my aunt and the fight, the money and how I had tracked them down. I told them about the threats to me and Dee, about the man who had cut my hair. I told them everything. It sounded so crazy, saying everything out loud and all at once like that. From the looks on their faces, it sounded crazy to them too.

"Well the good news is that he is in jail and we are finally together as a family," Gran said. "The rest of it can be dealt with. Everything will be fine now that we are all together as a family."

Once everything was finally out on the table, there were a lot of tearful hugs and kisses. It's funny, I used to feel like I hadn't really missed out on much by not having a mother. I mean, I never got to know her, so I didn't really miss her. But after that conversation, for the first time I actually mourned for my mother. Not the imaginary, Clair Huxtable mother I use to dream about as a kid, but my real mother, Alecia Roberts. The one that loved to smile and brought such happiness to her family.

Chapter 33

After that conversation, I thought that I would have trouble sleeping. But within a few minutes of putting my head on the pillow I was already dozing. I fell asleep with Gran's happy but nervous smile flickering across the insides of my eyelids. That look she had given me pretty much summed up what I was feeling: happy to finally have them in my life, but nervous that what they'd told me about my father was true.

If it was true, he'd gotten off easy. I'd lost count of how many more months he had left on his sentence. Well, not so much lost count, as stopped counting. But if he had anything to do with my mother's death, I hoped he would never walk out of there.

In the short time that I'd been there I learned so much about my family and knowing how much heartache they'd been through made me protective of them. If it came down to me choosing between them and my father, that decision was a no brainer.

Besides learning about my family, I'd also taken notice of a few things about Raleigh, the place that three generations had called home. I was thinking about calling it home too.

The city of Raleigh wasn't much of a city at all. I had to agree with my mother about that. It was charming in its own way, but it was definitely nothing like New York. It wasn't just the size and the pace of things, it was the people too. For one thing, if you walked past someone without saying hello they'd look at you like you were strange. In New York the exact opposite was true. In New York if you spoke to someone that you didn't know they would look at you like you had two heads. I guess in the south parents skipped over the "don't talk to strangers" lesson.

One thing I did love was the architecture: big beautiful houses with manicured lawns. Pop had pointed out one of the projects to me and even they looked like houses.

As for Gran and Pop, they said they had downsized when they bought their current house. If that was downsizing, I would be curious to see what their old house looked like. A mansion? Aunt Marie and her family lived in that house now, the house that my mother had grown up in.

Gran and Pop's current house was really spacious. The guest room that I slept in had a queen-sized bed and there was still plenty of space left for a dresser and a nice seating area. The room was decorated in very neutral colors. The only thing that exuded any personality was Gran's very extensive doll collection. Those dolls were on every surface. Some were even enclosed in a special glass cabinet.

Despite the prying eyes of the dolls, I'd slept deep and peaceful. There were still the lingering questions about my father's involvement in my mother's death. I still didn't know the whole story, but at least I had the same amount of information as everyone else. Maybe I would finally be able to move on and put it all behind me.

I felt good when I woke up. It was the first night in a long time that I'd slept with no nightmares. I allowed myself to wake up naturally, no alarm clock. The next morning—well, afternoon—when I got out of bed it took me a moment to recognize where I was. I heard muffled voices coming from downstairs. The family had reassembled for day two of this long overdue reunion.

I sat on the side of the bed and for some reason I started to think about Dr. Beekman's assignment: writing the list of things I knew about my mother. Neither one of us could have known that assignment would lead to this discovery. But now that it had, I'd send her a thank-you letter and let her know I wouldn't need her services anymore.

Had I called Dee? I couldn't remember. After my arrival at the bus terminal, everything happened so fast. I must have, I thought, otherwise he would have called by now. My coat was hanging on the back of the door. I reached into the pocket and grabbed my cell phone. No missed calls. I dialed his number, excited to hear his voice. And I did, when his voicemail picked up. His voice told me to leave a message at the beep.

"Dee, call me back. I got here safely and everything is going well. Just wanted to talk."

I looked at the clock. It was already one. He was probably in the library studying for finals. It was only a few weeks ago that I was studying right along with him, burning the midnight oil, highlighter in hand. But it seemed like a lifetime ago. So much had happened since then.

I made my way downstairs a half hour later. Gran was sitting on the living room sofa dressed in a grey velour jogging suit. She had a crossword book in her lap. "Hi, Brianna. Did you sleep well?"

"Yeah."

Aunt Marie came out of the kitchen. "No, you can't call a baby-sitter," she said into her phone. She made eye contact with me and waved. "Late. I will be home late." She disconnected the call.

Hanging up on someone is never as dramatic when you do it on a cell phone. Back when people used landlines you could slam down the phone and get your message across more effectively.

Marie's caller didn't get the message. "No, we didn't get disconnected, Charles. I don't want to talk to you."

Well, there was no miscommunication there, I thought to myself. Marie hung up her phone a second time and said, "Hi, Brianna. How are you doing?"

"Uh, um, I'm okay."

They offered to take me to the mall. Really, it was the last thing I wanted to do. I hated shopping, and still do, especially at the mall. Too many people pushing and shoving. And it was the start of the holiday season, so I could only imagine what it would be like.

I was about to tell them about my hatred of shopping when Gran said that it would give us time to hang out away from the men and the kids. "Just the women, you know, getting to know each other." How could I say no to that?

"Where is everyone else?" I asked.

"The boys and Pop are in the backyard. Getting into something messy, I'm sure," Marie said.

"As long as they don't track anything into my house, they can get as messy as they want. Come on, let's get out of here before they notice," Gran said, getting up off the couch and grabbing her coat. I laughed.

The mall was packed just as I knew it would be. I bought a Raleigh, North Carolina, T-shirt for myself and a matching one for Dee.

We ate lunch in the food court. Seeing Marie and Gran together showed me what a close mother- daughter relationship was supposed to be like. Up to that point, all I had to go on were the T.V. shows I'd watched as a kid.

"But Mom," she whined. "He's never home. And when he is, he's always too tired to do anything fun with the kids. It's like I'm a single parent." I got sad for a brief moment thinking about how many mother-daughter conversations I'd missed out on.

"Brie, what's the matter?" Gran asked turning her attention away from Marie. I hadn't even noticed the tears rolling down my face.

"I'm okay," I said, wiping my face. "It's just that seeing the two of you together makes me—"

"Want to throw up?" Gran said jokingly, trying to lighten the mood.

"I guess I just miss my mother," I told her. "I feel like I missed out on so much."

Gran stroked my hand. "There's nothing I can do to bring your mother back. Believe me, I would give anything to do that. But you're not alone anymore. You have all of us now and we have to make up for lost time. Trust me, you will be sick of us soon enough."

"That will never happen," I said confidently.

Turning the attention back to herself, Marie put her head in her hands and said, "We argue all the time."

Gran looked at me and rolled her eyes. I shook my head and smiled. "You think your father and I don't argue?" Gran asked Marie.

No Response.

"You probably do, don't you? Well, we've had our share of arguments, every couple does. But we make a point, even now, not to argue in front of our children. My advice is that you do the same. No matter what type of problems you two might be having, discuss it in private, away from the kids. Now, I'm not telling you not to voice your concerns to him. That will only make you resent each other. Are you listening to me Marie?"

It seemed as though Marie was frustrated that Gran wasn't simply telling her she was right. I didn't know her well, but it seemed to me like she didn't really want advice, she was looking for validation.

Marie picked her head up and looked at Gran. "Yeah I hear you, Ma. But it's not my fault. He doesn't even try. I mean the kids are growing up so fast, they need their father. He needs to be around more."

"If you want him to have a better relationship with them, talking about him or criticizing him in front of the kids is not going to help you accomplish that. Men have a lot of ego. You have to talk to him without making him feel inadequate because that's just going to make him defensive." I made a mental note of that for future reference.

In the car ride home Gran continued to address what Marie had been complaining about all day: her husband. I continued to listen, hoping to glean some more insight on how to improve my relationship with Dee. It felt good that they were comfortable enough to have such a private conversation in my presence. I sat silently in the back seat, knowing I didn't have enough experience to contribute anything.

"No marriage is perfect," Gran told Marie for the hundredth time. "You need to be realistic about your expectations and choose your battles wisely. He owns three Holiday Inns. He works hard. You need to work on supporting him instead of constantly nagging him."

"I know that, Ma! You don't have to tell me that! He's a good man," Marie admitted. "I just want his kids to know him as a good father too."

Gran told Marie that she needed to figure out a way to talk to her husband without putting him on the defensive. "Otherwise it will be the kids that get the short end of the stick."

I felt like a fly on the wall as I sat in the darkness of the back seat listening to their conversation. But it wasn't these types of conversations that taught me the most about the dynamics of my family. It was all those letters that Gran and Pop had written to me over the years, the ones I'd never received.

Later, around Mother's Day if I recall correctly, Gran put those letters in a box, gift wrapped them with pink and green paper, and hand delivered them to me. In those letters, one of the many things that Gran revealed was that Marie, her only surviving daughter, was the neediest of her children. According to Gran, it was Marie's way of keeping her busy, keeping her from dwelling on my mother's death.

Marie had taken on that impossible task, Gran told me in those letters, because she was the type of person that took on other people's suffering and pain as her own. Marie had figured that the only way she could get her mother to finally come out of her depression was to show her how much the rest of the family still needed her. So Marie started looking to her mother for help with even the simplest decisions. In her own annoying way, Marie was trying to show her mother how much she loved her. But in the car that night without the benefit of this background information, I couldn't help but find them amusing.

Marie turned around to face me. "Why are you so quiet back there?"

"No reason."

"It's been an interesting couple of days, huh?"

"It's been an interesting year," I said. "I've found out a lot about my father, and my aunt, and even myself. But I feel like now I can finally pick up the pieces and move forward."

"That's great, Brie," Gran said. "Have you thought anymore about your decision to move out of New York?" She eyed me in the rearview mirror.

That's one of the things that I had mentioned to them the night before, when it was my turn to tell my story. They all agreed that getting away from New York would be a good thing for me.

"I think you guys are right, getting out of New York is the best thing. I mean, I already knew that. It's just that before I was feeling like I was running away from my problems and that they'd just follow me wherever I went. But I don't feel like that anymore. Now I feel like I'm moving toward something."

"What do you mean?" Gran asked as we pulled into the driveway.

"Well, I was thinking, if it's okay with you, instead of moving to Florida to live with Dee's family—"

Gran's shrieking cut me off mid sentence. "Yes! Yes! Absolutely, yes!"

I had planned to sit Gran and Pop down together later that evening and make my proposal. But since she'd asked, I figured I might as well test the waters on the issue.

It was a good thing that Gran had already pulled into the driveway and cut the engine, because to go along with her screaming she pumped her fists in the air and did a little dance in her seat.

"I've been dying to ask you that all day!" she said. "I didn't want to be pushy of course. I wanted to let you make the decision yourself. I'm so happy! Wait until I tell Pop. All last night he kept talking about how we need to get you to stay here with us. Do you think your boyfriend will go for the idea?"

I loved how happy she was, and I wasn't worried about Dee, I knew he'd be happy too as long as we were out of New York. That's pretty much what I told Gran.

"So then it's settled. You and your boyfriend will come live here with us."

That should have been the end of the story. That should have been followed by: and they lived happily ever after. But this is my life we're talking about and nothing was every that simple for me.

As we took the bags out of the trunk, Marie said, "Speaking of your boyfriend, what's he like? Got any pictures?"

"No, not on me. But Dee's great, he's smart and kind and he treats me well." Except for when he's having one of his temper tantrums, I thought.

Marie gave me a sly look. "But what does he look like? Is he hot?"

I thought Gran was about to jump in, but she just looked at me inquiringly. I had to laugh. "Oh, he's hot!"

We were still laughing when we made our way through the front door. I hate to think about how clueless I was at that moment. Still so blissfully ignorant.

"Did you leave anything in the store?" Pop wanted to know.

"There was a sale," Gran said.

"There's always a sale. I think they call in extra workers when they see you coming."

At some point between getting out of the car and walking through the front door, Marie had forgotten all of the advice that Gran had given her. Marie's husband, Charles, and the rest of the men were sitting in the living room watching T.V. and drinking beer. Typical. The younger kids were at the dining room table making a mess with rainbow glitter.

Marie lit into him. Right there in the living room in front of everyone, right in the middle of ESPN's top plays of the day. "What are you doing here! You were suppose to take the kids out."

"I did. We just came here afterward."

"Taking them out doesn't mean taking them to the car and driving them over here. You can't even handle your own kids alone for a few hours! How long have you been here?"

He started to answer, but she held up her hand. She turned to the rest of the men. "How long has he been here?"

Silence.

Frustrated, Marie turned back to her husband. "You're pathetic." Like a child that had just been scolded, Charles' pale complexion turned beet red. "And then you leave them in the dining room," she said pointing at the kids, "unsupervised with glitter and glue. Do you know how many years that table has been in my family?"

Charles wasn't the only one that was embarrassed, all of the men in the room were. They tried to ignore the scene, but Marie was making that impossible.

"And I know those are not cookies they're eating at this time of night. You never—"

Gran cut Marie's rant short. She pinched her. Hard. I was certain that Marie's arm would be a color similar to her husband's face. "You get more with honey than vinegar," Gran whispered.

My phone buzzed in my pocket. Missed call. I guessed the service in Raleigh was a little spotty. I didn't recognize the number. "Excuse me. I'll be right back," I said, but no one noticed as they watched the now silent staring match between Marie and her poor husband.

I walked upstairs to my room. My room…my new home…my family. It all sounded very comfortable to me.

Chapter 34

Confused, I replayed the voicemail messaged for a third time, leaned against the wall in an effort to keep the room from spinning and listened to Dee's shaky voice in my ear. "You know me, Brie. I didn't do this."

I dropped the phone, and it broke into several pieces. Somehow I managed to stay on my feet but I felt like I was falling to pieces too. The floor seemed to shift beneath me.

No! No! No! I hadn't screamed like that since that night I fell asleep on the bathroom floor. This time it was Gran, not Dee, who came knocking on the door.

"Brie?"

I couldn't catch my breath, so answering her was impossible. She walked into the room and instinctively wrapped her arms around me.

"Brie, what's the matter?"

I felt lightheaded. She sat me down on the side of the bed and sat down beside me. Her voice seemed muffled and far away. "You know me, Brie. I didn't do this." Those were the only words that I could hear clearly.

When I was finally able to speak again the only word I could say was "No." And I kept saying it over and over, trying to convince myself that this wasn't happening, that this couldn't be happening.

Gran held my hand as I muttered irrationally and replayed Dee's voicemail message in my head.

He'd told me that he was in jail. That he'd been arrested. Attempted sexual assault. He said he'd never seen the girl before in his life. That it must have been a case of mistaken identity. But there had been a lineup and the girl had pointed him out. She was a hundred percent sure, the cops had told him.

I could hear the fear in his voice. And why shouldn't he be afraid? There are too many innocent men sitting in prison for him not to be afraid.

He'd said he'd be seeing the judge in the morning, but he wanted me to come with his checkbook so that he could post bail. He didn't think he could spend another night in there. "You know me, Brie," he'd said. "You know me. I didn't do this."

I jumped up off the bed. Finally in control of my faculties again and realizing I had no time to waste. "I have to go," I heard myself say. "I have to go home."

"Brie, what's going on? Tell me what happened."

No time for twenty questions. "I have to go."

"Is it something we did? I know it's been difficult... I thought we had a good day today."

I was packing, throwing stuff back into my bag. I told her it was nothing like that, that I'd be in touch soon, but right now, "I need to go."

Gran told me that she was a good listener. Maybe I'd feel better if I just talked about what was bothering me.

Are you a good driver, I wanted to ask, *because that's what I need.*

Not taking the hint, Gran said she was going to make us some tea and then we'd sit and talk.

"No!" I screamed, louder than I should have. I didn't mean to make her scurry from the room like that.

And what was that annoying noise? I looked around but I couldn't figure it out until I caught my reflection in the mirror. It was me, whimpering.

I put aside my fear of flying and called every airline trying to get a flight back to New York. There were none. It was the start of the holiday season.

I said apologetic goodbyes and within an hour I was in the car with Pop on my way to the bus station.

"Brie, I know that you don't know us well yet, but I need you to be honest with me about something." He said as he pulled into the parking lot. My bus wasn't scheduled to leave for another twenty minutes.

"I regret not asking your mother more questions. Maybe I could have…" He didn't finish his thought. He just let the words linger. "Are you in any kind of trouble? Is that why you are leaving like this?"

Seeing the pain in his face, I reluctantly told him what was going on. He asked me whether I was sure about "that guy." I told him I knew that he wasn't capable of doing anything like that.

"I can tell that you're very independent, Brie. You get that from your mother. But… you… everybody needs help sometimes. You don't have to deal with everything by yourself. We're here for you, whatever you need. I want you to tell me if there is anything… anything at all that we can do to help you. And make sure you call when you get back to New York. You hear me?"

"Okay."

On the bus I found a window seat near the middle. I looked across the aisle and imagined it was Dee sitting there, just like the day we first met.

Chapter 35

Underestimate me at your own risk, Jackie thought to herself. It had taken her a while, but she had finally figured it out and was about to set her master plan into action. She was going to get her money back. Confidently, she walked through the door and sat directly across from Atlantic.

Their first meeting hadn't gone well, but she'd learned from that and she was going to approach it differently this time. Instead of explaining what she could do for him, she would approach it as a fragile female in need of help from the big strong man. That would stroke his ego, even if it did make Jackie sick to her stomach. Once he realized that he would get something out of the deal, he wouldn't be able to say no.

But he tried to play stupid. "Do I know you?"

Of course he knew who she was; they had already met together once, and even without that meeting her reputation preceded her. But whatever, she chose to stay cool. "Not as well as you should." Despite it being the dead of winter, Jackie had risked frost bite and pneumonia and made sure to wear something revealing, just to up the ante a little. She caught him taking in the eye candy.

"You've got my attention, but I've been told that I have ADD so make it quick."

Jackie had planned to do just that. Time was of the essence. "You were responsible for getting my brother locked up. At least partially responsible."

"So what do you want? An apology?"

"No. You outsmarted him. I admire that. I'm not concerned about Keith. He had a good run, but I know he's not getting out anytime soon. That's why I have to make sure that my kids and I are taken care of. But I need your help."

"What's that got to do with me? I'm not your baby daddy. That sounds like a personal problem."

"No, it has nothing to do with you. I understand that. The point is that I know where my brother's money is. The money that the Feds didn't find. I'm sure you've heard the rumors."

He raised his eyebrow. "Why are you telling me this?"

"Because I need your help. I'm willing to split the cash with you once I get it."

"And why can't you do this by yourself? Get to the point. What's the problem that you want taken care of?"

"Well, I used to have control of the money. Because, like I told you last time, I was pretty much in control of everything. But recently the account was transferred to my niece and I need you to help me persuade her to give it back to me."

He laughed. "By persuade you mean blackmail, right?"

"Exactly."

"Well what do you have on her?"

"She's squeaky clean. It is more about getting to someone she cares about. Her boyfriend, Demetrius. From what I understand your crew already has some connection with his family."

He smiled. "What do you want me to do exactly?"

She went on to describe her plan in detail. Atlantic agreed when she showed him her last bank statement before the account was transferred. When he saw the amount of money involved he jumped at the opportunity. As Jackie knew he would.

"When do you want to do this?" Atlantic asked.

"As soon as possible."

"I already have someone in mind. I'll contact you when it's a go."

Two days later Jackie was in a good mood. She wondered if she had gone into the wrong line of work. She was a good actress and if this all panned out the way she expected, her performance would be Oscar-worthy.

She picked up the phone and dialed Dee's number. He answered on the third ring. To prevent him from hanging up once he realized it was her, she opened with, "Brie's in danger." Yeah, that worked. He had a million questions. She followed up by telling him how sorry she was for everything that had gone down in the bank. She never meant to hurt Brie and she would never be able to forgive herself if anything happened to her.

She played him like a fiddle. "Maybe I was too quick to judge the last time we spoke, but if your offer to move out of state is still open… I know you don't trust me. I don't blame you. But I don't have anyone else to call. I just want Brie and my boys to be safe." Jackie couldn't believe how convincing she sounded, especially considering she was channel surfing the whole time. Dee must have thought she was convincing, too, because he agreed to come over to her apartment within the hour to discuss their move. In fact, coming over had been his idea.

It was his paranoia that made things easy. "We shouldn't be talking about this over the phone," he'd said.

"Why don't I come over so we can work out the details and figure out how to get Brie on board with the move?"

Satisfied, she'd gotten off the phone, unmuted the T.V., and relaxed while she waited for him to arrive. Things were moving along nicely.

Chapter 36

Jackie's eyes were damp. She wiped them more than necessary, to make sure he noticed. As soon as Dee crossed the threshold of her apartment she hugged him. She let her voice crack a little when she spoke.

"I'm so sorry about everything that happened. I hope that one day you and Brie can forgive me." She inhaled sharply. "But for now it means so much that you even came here to talk to me."

She could tell he didn't really know how to react to her show of emotion. It was a big departure from what he'd encountered the last time he was there. But as she expected, he was more concerned with getting Brie out of New York than anything else.

Don't let your enemies know your weaknesses. She recalled trying to teach that lesson, unsuccessfully, to her brother. And here she was using it to her advantage. If she didn't know how much Dee cared for Brie, what she had to do might be a little more difficult. But the way things stood, she was going to use that bit of information and milk it for everything it was worth. In her mind that was close to a million dollars.

"So what kind of danger is Brie in?" he asked, right on schedule.

"Well, the word around here is that people know that she has her father's money and there is a plan to get it from her."

"I knew it! This is exactly what I was worried about. She thought I was being paranoid. I told her that she wouldn't be able to keep something like that a secret. She's so stubborn sometimes. Where did you here this from? The rumors, I mean. Who's coming after her?"

"I can't really say. At this point the word is out, so it could be anyone. You know, first come, first served. It's not going to end well if we don't get her out of here. I don't want to think of what could happen."

"I'm not going to let anything happen to her."

"I know you won't. I'm glad she has someone like you looking out for her. The safety of Brie and my children is what is important. Because you never know. They could try to come after me to get to her. I didn't even let the kids go to school today. They have been begging me all day to go outside and play in the snow. But I said no. I'm so nervous to let them out of my sight. I don't even care where we go. All I know is we've got to get out of here. Florida would have not been my first choice of places to live, but beggars can't be choosers, right? Where we live doesn't matter anymore. By the way, where is Brie?"

He obviously wasn't too bright, Jackie thought to herself when Dee told her that Brie was down south visiting family. She had just attacked Brie not even a week ago, and here he was telling her where Brie was. Stupid.

Then another thought came to mind. Maybe he's not stupid, maybe he's just way too trusting. It didn't really matter, Jackie considered both to be major character flaws. It was survival of the fittest, that was, like, a commandment or the golden rule or something. Of course someone higher up in the food chain was gonna take him out. It was only natural. If it wasn't Jackie, it would be someone else.

He was talking about having an intervention. Sitting Brie down and scaring her into moving out of state.

"I'm okay with doing that. Anything I can do to help."

"Okay, I will call you when she gets back so we can schedule a time to get together." He looked at his watch and got up off the couch. He was running late for his night class, he told her. He walked to the door and thanked Jackie for reconsidering his offer to move, but told her that she would have to work really hard to gain Brie's trust again.

Did her really just thank her? Jackie smiled. "I will do my best."

They said their goodbyes. Jackie made a quick phone call and then glanced at the old bank statement that she carried around with her. *It won't be long now,* she thought.

Chapter 37

Dee glanced at his watch again. He walked out of the building and the sheer force of the howling wind made it hard to walk, let alone run. But that's what he did. He was making a quick sprint back to his car. The wind was picking up the flakes from yesterday's snowfall and making it hard to see. Snow crunched under his Tims and his lungs burned as he picked up the pace a little.

The wind was what prevented him from hearing the feet gaining ground behind him. It only took a second for him to be face down on the ground with a knee in his back and snow in his nostrils. He tried to fight back, but he was outnumbered. There were two of them. He still kept fighting, until he felt the handcuffs. Beyond the howling wind, the police officers' cursing and the ringing in his ears, a woman was screaming, "That's him! That's the man!"

Chapter 38

He's not capable of what they are accusing him of. That's what I had told Pop only a few hours before. But as I sat on that bus, the voice came back. The voice that I had tuned out over and over again. The one that kept telling me things were moving too fast between Dee and me. I didn't know him well enough.

I thought about how I had met Dee not even six months before, on a bus not unlike the Greyhound bus I was sitting on. I thought about how I had been instantly attracted to him. Had I let that attraction blur the warning signs? Could he have actually done what they were accusing him of? Attempted sexual assault? He did have a bit of a temper, that much I could attest to, but I still found it hard to believe.

What really gave me pause was the fact that I had found my father's guilt hard to believe, too, and I was dead wrong about that one. Aren't those that don't learn from the past doomed to repeat it?

What would Dr. Beekman say? I was letting my past experiences with my father affect my relationship with Dee. I had trust issues. I should give Dee the benefit of the doubt.

There was one good thing though. The bus driver's foot was heavy on the gas pedal. We were actually making really good time. Hopefully, once I got to New York and was able to talk to Dee face-to-face, I could hush that voice in my head and put my doubts to rest.

Chapter 39

It started off as that pretty white snow, the little flakes that make you feel like you're inside a snow globe, but in the few minutes that I was in the apartment picking up Dee's checkbook, the snow had become heavy and wet and the wind had picked up. I made my way back to the train station to head to the precinct. I speed walked partially because I was in a rush to see Dee and partially because the weather was brutal.

I passed a store that had a T.V. in the window. As I walked by, I caught a NY1 reporter announcing a list of homeless shelters and advising the homeless to find someplace indoors to stay because hypothermia was a real danger.

When I reached the train station I found out where all of the homeless had decided to go to protect themselves from the elements. They were sprawled out on every possible surface. They wore layers of tattered clothing, and what they couldn't wear, they carried with them in plastic bags.

When my train arrived I saw that they had taken it over too. It was the smell that hit me first, musty and sour, warning me to find another train car. I heeded that warning. I ran a little down the platform, and got in the next car.

I barely made it. The doors closed, catching my bag. The train doors opened and closed quickly several times, never really quite giving me a chance to pull my bag free. When I finally did it was bruised, its contents crushed. I found a seat and collapsed into it. I tried to brace myself as the train started to move me toward Dee.

Chapter 40

His eyes were red and swollen and he had a dark bruise on his chin commemorating his encounter with the NYPD. We looked at each other and before a single word was said, I had the confirmation I needed. What I'd told Pop was true. Dee wasn't capable of what they'd accused him of.

Dee was not my father. They were nothing alike. I focused on the man in front of me and I knew that he wasn't a criminal. He was the guy who had tried to get his brother to live a straight life. He was the one that had tried to protect me by getting me to move. He didn't do this. I only had to see his face to know that was true.

With that little voice in my head finally silenced, I could focus on what I had to do: prove his innocence. I made this silent commitment to myself and him before either one of us had said a word.

"Babe, I'm so sorry about this. It's some kind of huge mistake."

"I know." And I did.

He started to tell me what happened and I had a bad feeling right away, deep in the pit of my stomach.

"I was rushing to school after meeting with your aunt and—"

"What? Why were you meeting with her? Wait. Let's not talk about this here. Let's get you out of here first. Have you met with the judge already?"

"Yeah, the judge set bail early this morning. Since I have no record, she set it at forty-five hundred. Because of what I'm being charged with, the prosecutor wanted the bail to be much higher but fortunately the public defender that they gave me was pretty good and got it reduced. If it was much higher than that, I might be stuck in here."

"That wouldn't happen. Money is not an issue." At that moment I couldn't think of a better reason to dip into my trust fund. I had never even considered touching that money, but like I said, for him I was willing to do whatever I had to do. "Let's get this taken care of. I have your checkbook, so I will post the bail and meet you out front."

"Okay, but it might take a while. The cops in here are so slow. It took forever for them to let me make my phone call."

An hour later I was still waiting for Dee to be released. I sat in the waiting room, feeling guilty, knowing that none of this would have happened if I hadn't been so reluctant to move when Dee had first suggested it.

But worse than the guilt was the feeling that something just wasn't right, something was still missing. And the missing link was my aunt. Dee getting arrested leaving her apartment? That wasn't a coincidence.

For the last year I'd felt like I'd been putting together a jigsaw puzzle without the benefit of having the puzzle box to know what the picture was supposed to look like. Every time I thought the picture was coming into focus I realized that I'd had it all wrong.

But one thing I was sure of: Aunt Jackie somehow fit into the equation. She was looking more and more like the common denominator.

A man startled me from my thoughts when he asked me to move my bag so he could sit down. When I did, I noticed how much damage the train door had done to it. I was kind of like that bag, I thought. Beat up, struggling to get free and every time I thought I had, every time I was almost free something came and slammed into me again, crushed me a little more.

I was anxious to get out of there and I was sure Dee was too. I glanced at the digital clock above the front desk. The date and time rolled by slowly in red letters. Happy birthday to me, I thought.

Chapter 41

I hadn't been able to sleep since Dee's release. Every time I closed my eyes, I would start thinking about how things just weren't adding up. I was missing something. That feeling that I'd had the first time while I was sitting in the waiting room of the police precinct? No matter how much I'd tried, I hadn't been able to shake it.

I needed to talk to Dr. Beekman. Fortunately for me, I hadn't officially withdrawn from school and was still able to get an appointment. There was so much that I needed to talk to her about. Maybe she could help me get to the bottom of things. But I would have to tell her everything. I would have to finally tell her about the money.

Dee wasn't his normal self. He was distracted and preoccupied so when I told him I was going to see Dr. Beekman, he told me to be careful, but didn't give me too much grief about going out by myself.

I didn't think that I'd be seeing Dr. Beekman again, and from the look on her face she wasn't exactly happy to see me either. She didn't have her normal welcoming smile. She was cordial when she led me into her office and told me to have a seat, but she seemed upset, too, maybe even a little annoyed.

She didn't keep me guessing for long. She got right to the point. "You missed your last appointment," she said. "I checked your attendance record and you haven't been to class either. I called you several times and got no answer." She counted each of my transgressions on her fingers as she spoke.

I apologized, said it to my shoes really, not wanting to look her in the eyes.

"Okay. Let's put all of that aside," she said, taking pity on me, or so I thought. But I was about to find out that this would be our most difficult session yet. "You look like you haven't slept."

Was it that obvious?

"What's going on? How are you?"

Why did I always get stumped by the simple questions? "I don't know," I said.

"Okay. Let's see if we can figure it out together." She grabbed her trusty notepad from of her desk drawer. "First, why haven't you been attending class?"

"So much has been going on." I told her that I hoped to start back school as soon as everything was resolved.

"I'm sure you will, Brianna."

Was she patronizing me? I didn't need this crap. School was the last thing on my mind. I couldn't think about grades or studying, I had real problems.

Her attitude turned me off a little, but still I didn't get up to leave. She'd helped me in the past. I thought maybe if I could get through this, there would be some light at the end of the tunnel.

"You say that so much has been going on? Why don't we talk about that? The last time we met, which was what?" She referred to her appointment book. "Ah yes, nearly three weeks ago. During our last meeting... I gave you an assignment, right? To make a list of things you know about your mother. How did that go?"

Was she trying to upset me or was I just on edge? I couldn't tell. I ignored her passive-aggressive comments and I told her about my trip down south to meet my family. I told her about the bank and the fight with Aunt Jackie, I told her about Dee's arrest, and with some reluctance, I told her about the money.

When I finished, I looked at Dr. Beekman. Her face was expressionless. She was shaking her hand, flexing it, no doubt on the verge of getting carpel tunnel syndrome from writing everything in that notepad of hers.

When it was all said and done I'd gone way over my one hour time slot. I guess Dr. Beekman finally started to see my desperation, and short of writing me a prescription, she told me to sit tight for a minute and she'd see if she could get us some more time.

I'd spent most of the first hour talking about my family. It was obvious they were the root of my problems. "Be thankful, Brie. Some people don't have any family at all. And some people have very large families, but they're really more like strangers than anything else. You know?"

No, I didn't know. I had no clue what she was talking about. It wasn't Dr. Beekman who had told me that; I guess she knew better. Those were the words of my fourth grade teacher. Why had she said that to me? Well, I'd spent days on my living room floor with my father, a glue gun, green and brown markers, and a big sheet of oak tag paper. My assignment was to draw my family tree.

In an effort to make my tree look less pitiful, I'd drawn the branches extra large to try to fill up the paper. One girl, I remembered, had drawn her tree big and colorful, its branches reaching up to the sky. She had written the year and place of birth for each of her family members.

When I went to hand in my assignment I rolled up that paper so tight and held it close to my chest hoping that none of the other kids would see it. It felt like everyone was laughing at me. When I reached the teacher's desk at the front of the class I was nearly in tears. That's when she'd whispered those words to me.

In the last few days I'd been able to add plenty of names to my family tree, but the two main branches on that original tree had in fact turned out to be strangers.

My teacher's words were just as irrelevant in this situation as they were all those years ago. I hoped that Dr. Beekman would be able to help me figure out some way to handle everything.

In the hallway, I heard Dr. Beekman ask the student who was waiting if he could reschedule his appointment for later that afternoon. He agreed and Dr. Beekman came back into the room with a reassuring smile.

"Okay, we've got another hour," she said as she plopped back into her seat. "So you've found out a lot of information about your family in the last few weeks. But you said you feel like there are still parts of the story missing. That could be paranoia or it could be intuition. Let's figure out which."

"Yes, let's."

"Let's start with your aunt, okay? Why do you think she…uh, attacked you?"

"She used to have control of my father's money and she was angry that the account was transferred to me. I didn't even know about any of that until I checked with the bank later. She just kept screaming that I'd stolen from her. So I know that's what it was about."

"And why do you think that your father put her in control of such a large sum of money in the first place?"

"Because… well, the obvious reason is that he was probably trying to spread it out, hide it in different places so that if he ever got caught, the cops wouldn't be able to find all of the money and trace it back to him. And I guess his plan worked."

"And the not so obvious reason?"

"Huh?"

"You said that was the obvious reason your father put her in charge of the money, so what's the not so obvious reason?"

I shrugged. "Because he wanted her taken care of if anything happened to him."

"I can tell that you've already given this a lot of thought. But maybe you are over-thinking things," she said, leaning back in her chair. "For the questions I'm about to ask you, I just want you to give me the first answer that you think of... say the first thing that pops into your head, okay?"

I nodded.

"Don't you think that it was risky for him—your father, that is— to put that kind of money under someone else's control?"

"Maybe... I guess so... but it was his sister, you know? Maybe he didn't think it was risky. My aunt told me that my father was too trusting."

"Hmm, interesting."

"What? What are you thinking?"

"You came here today for me to say out loud what you already know. But I am not going to do that for you." She reached into her desk drawer and pulled out a pack of M&Ms, offered it to me. I shook my head. How did she expect me to eat at a time like this? That didn't stop her. She tore open that package and tossed a couple in her mouth.

"I was also thinking," she said, still munching. "That your nightmares and your sleepless nights? They are not the result of trying to put the pieces together, but rather the result of not wanting to admit to yourself what you're really thinking.

"You're afraid that you did it again, right? That you trusted the wrong person. I told you before, and I will tell you again and again...I will tell you as many times as it takes until you start to believe me. When someone...anyone betrays your trust, it's not you that has the problem. It's not a reflection on you at all. It's the other person... the other people that have the problem."

She told me that in my situation that was probably difficult to understand because the people who betrayed me were my family.

"And of course in a perfect world you would be able to trust your family members, but you probably know better than most that we don't live in a perfect world. I am going to ask you again. Be honest with yourself. Why do you think your father put your aunt in charge of his money?"

What was the answer she was looking for? She'd been asking me the same question for the last half hour and I still didn't know what she was getting at. She just sat there, staring at me, waiting.

"I don't know! I don't know! I don't know!" At that point I'd realized why therapists usually had couches in their offices. I really needed to lie down. Instead, I began pacing the length of her office.

"It's all right here," she said, shaking her notepad at me. "You already answered the question. I am not going to put it together for you, Brie. You have to do the work. It's just me, you are safe here, just say it."

"It was her!" I blurted out. Those words were the hardest. After they were out I sat back down, stared at Dr. Beekman, blinked away a few tears and let the rest of the words come.

"My father was the one that got sent to prison and it's not like I think he's innocent. I know better than that now. It's just that I don't think she told me the whole story. I could tell when she was telling me about my father's dealing that something wasn't right. When she told me, it was like… she seemed proud of him… like she admired what he'd done. I don't know. It just didn't seem right."

I couldn't stop now, the words were pouring out of me like a damn had broken.

"I pushed it aside for a while, you know? I didn't want to think she was part of it. I had already lost my father. She was the only family I had. I didn't want to be alone, with no one. So I was angry with her, but I was angry because she lied to me. I didn't let myself think any deeper than that. I told myself that maybe she just loves her brother to the point where she's decided to overlook the fact that he was dealing. You know? Only seeing the good in him. But then, when I was attacked by the guy with the knife, and he mentioned her, all of the doubts and questions flooded back.

"And when she attacked me in the bank? At first I thought she was just jealous, but then I found out the money used to be hers... And you're right, my father probably put it in her name like that because they were partners or something. I don't know that for sure, but it would make sense, right?

"Then on top of everything else, Dee was arrested when he was leaving her apartment. Her apartment!"

I could feel beads of sweat rolling down my back. My fists were clenched so tightly that I had nail imprints on my palms.

"I just don't believe that all of this is a coincidence. At the very least she knows more... she's more involved than she made it seem when she was telling me about my father."

"Good job, Brie!" she said, a bit too excited considering what I'd just told her. "You were finally able to say out loud what has been bothering you all of this time. That's an excellent first step."

First step? I was already so exhausted. If she'd noticed that I looked tired on my way in to her office, I could only imagine what I'd look like on my way out.

"Now what are you going to do about it?"

"Get away from it! That's what I'm going to do! I don't want to fight with her or anyone else. I'm tired. I just want to move down south and get to know my new family. I should have moved a long time ago when Dee... I can't even do that now," I said remembering Dee's criminal charges. It was not like he was free to leave the state. *We're stuck here*, I thought, *all because of my stupid stubbornness*. "I should have listened to Dee and moved when he first brought it up months ago."

"We are making such good progress. Let's not get caught up in regret." She was being way too calm, way too clinical, way too rational. I wanted to scream and cry and throw things, and she was sitting there with her hands folded on her desk talking to me with absolutely no emotion. I noticed that her nails were freshly done. Had she noticed that mine were chewed down to nubs?

I know it was her job, and she was not supposed to get emotionally involved or whatever. But I resented her sitting there like she didn't have a care in the world when I felt like everything was crumbling around me.

She told me that regret wasn't productive, that it was a waste of time. "And isn't that part of what you're upset about. That you've wasted time being stubborn, and now you can't get that time back? Well, why would you want to waste more time on something that's just as useless. Why don't we focus on what you can do right now?"

"I need to figure out a way to prove that Dee didn't do what they are accusing him of."

"Well, with everything that we have talked about today, it seems like finding out if and how your aunt was involved would be a good place to start. I don't think I need to tell you this, but you are dealing with very dangerous people, Brie. I know you want to prove Dee's innocence but you don't want to get yourself hurt in the process."

"Yeah, I know, but if my aunt is involved, and I'm pretty sure she is, I can't let my family ruin Dee's life the way they have tried to ruin mine."

"And I'm not asking you to. All I want is for you to be careful. Try going to the police and giving them the information you have, and let them follow up with it."

Dr. Beekman knew as well as I did that I wasn't going to the police. My father had blackmailed the police when he was dealing; who was to say that he hadn't gotten that idea from my aunt in the first place. No. Going to the police was out of the question.

Maybe Dr. Beekman had just made that suggestion because of some type of professional obligation. You know, don't advise your patient to do something that might put them in danger? So to absolve her of any guilt, I told her what she needed to hear. "Yeah, okay, I'll go to the police."

I left Dr. Beekman's office with a new determination and clarity, but I was still lacking a plan. I knew that my aunt had no interest in Dee; she was using him to get to me, and she was trying to get to me, to get to the money. That much I'd figured out. I didn't care about the money, but there was no way I was going to let her get away with hurting Dee. She'd definitely crossed the line.

Chapter 42

After my marathon session with Dr. Beekman, I thought long and hard about everything that we had discussed. She was right. On some level, I had known all along that my aunt was somehow involved in my father's drug dealing. But exactly how much of a stake she had in it, I didn't know.

Back at home, I tried to figure out my next step. I thought about going to talk to my aunt face-to-face, but considering what had happened the last time, I scratched that option pretty much immediately.

My newly replaced cell phone started ringing and startled me.

"Will you accept the charges?" I knew right away who was calling. I agreed to accept the charges before I could stop myself.

My father's voice came on the line, urgent and shaky. "Brie, I don't have much time. Jackie was just here visiting me."

It didn't surprise me that he'd decided to walk into the visitor's room for her. Yeah, I was still bitter about him ignoring me the last time I'd gone to see him. He knew how far I'd come. I'd been on a bus for six hours and he couldn't even walk into the visitors room. But, whatever, it made no difference now anyway.

He said that since Jackie had never come to visit him before, he'd gotten nervous and started thinking the worst, that something had happened to me. "Brie, I couldn't take that. I'm so sorry for everything. Getting you mixed up with this… putting you in the middle.

That was never my intention. All I ever wanted to do was protect you. I know you don't trust me, but I really need you to listen to me now. Your aunt is a very dangerous woman."

That much I already knew.

"More dangerous than you realize," he said. "She told me that she had your boyfriend arrested by getting someone in Atlantic's crew to set him up. All she cares about is the money. That's all she wants, Brie. I shouldn't have given it to you, but I didn't think... please, Brie. Please just transfer the money back to her so all of this can go away. Please... I don't want anyone else to get hurt. There's already been too much pain."

He didn't want anyone else to get hurt? I heard Gran's voice in my head. Was it true what they'd said? Was he admitting that my mother's death had something to do with his drug operation?

The phone disconnected. During the whole conversation I hadn't said a word. I guess that was a good thing because even when I got off the phone I didn't know what to think, I was still speechless. One thing was for certain: my suspicions had been confirmed. Jackie was not after Dee, she was after me. She was after the money.

The problem was that for some reason I just couldn't bring myself to turn over the money to her. Maybe I was being selfish, or childish even; it's not like I wanted or needed the money for myself. It was just that I couldn't let her win.

Maybe I should have been thinking more about Dee and how he was an innocent bystander in all of this. But instead of heeding my father's advice, I went back to brainstorming. For any of this to make sense I couldn't let her ride off into the sunset rich and happy. I knew that it would be her greed that would bring about her downfall. I just had to figure out a way to make that happen sooner rather than later. I knew I couldn't do it by myself, I needed reinforcements.

Chapter 43

Since he was Pop's childhood friend, I knew James Clarkson couldn't have been as young as he looked. But when I first met him, I couldn't help but think that his baby face, dimples and all, made him look more suitable to be a kindergarten teacher than an FBI agent.

For the past couple of weeks, living with Dee had been almost unbearable. He was completely losing it. Muttering to himself, walking around in his pajamas all day, not showering. He'd used up all of his vacation time from work and had blown off his finals after working so hard all semester.

On the rare occasions that he'd actually calm down long enough to fall asleep, he would even talk in his sleep. His incoherent ramblings were usually no more comprehensible when he was awake than when he was sleeping.

There was absolutely no consoling him. But that didn't stop me from trying.

"Dee, now that we know that my aunt is behind all of this, if it comes down to it, I will give her the money. You are not going to prison. I won't let that happen."

Ignoring me, he'd ask, "Do you know how many innocent people are in prison right now?"

Maybe that was why, when James wrapped his arms around me the first time we met and told me with such confidence that everything was going to be okay, those words, even coming from a stranger, were so comforting to me.

I knew that Dee would be completely inconsolable until the charges against him were dropped, and to make sure that happened, I needed to figure out a way to deal with Aunt Jackie. After racking my brain for weeks, I kept coming up empty. That's when I decided to give Pop a call. It felt really good to have that option. Without hesitation he told me that him and his 'old FBI buddy' would be in NY in two days.

When I hung up the phone, I was feeling better already. Just knowing that I wouldn't be alone, that I had backup on the way, made me breathe a sigh of relief.

I had planned to meet James and Pop at the airport, but they arrived early and came knocking on my apartment door. James took control right from the start. He already had our so-called victim's name. The police report identified her as Sandra Carter. He told me his search didn't turn up any connections with Atlantic's crew.

"There has to be a connection," I said. "My father told me that my aunt had used someone in Atlantic's crew to set Dee up. There has to be a connection."

Pop made a good point. "If the connection was obvious the police might not have given her story much credibility."

So the connection wasn't obvious, that just meant that we'd have to work a little harder to find it.

In preparation for their arrival, I'd gone to Krispy Kreme and bought half a dozen donuts. I made coffee to go with them. I thought that would be an appropriate snack considering the situation. But there would be no old-fashioned stakeouts, no pounding the pavement trying to ferret out witnesses. Those techniques wouldn't work.

But thankfully I'd finally come up with a plan. Once I'd called Pop and I knew the two of them were on their way, I'd been able to calm down and think straight. And now that I had my reinforcements, I was ready to put that plan into action. I ran my idea past Pop and James.

Pop brushed some crumbs off the front of his shirt and simply said, "Sounds good to me."

James was a little more inquisitive. He wanted to know how I'd come up with the idea.

"It was something that my aunt had told me once."

"Well," James said, "if it works out it will solve everything at once."

"Exactly. And it will work out. It has to. The beauty of it is that I think that my aunt will pick up on the irony."

After our team meeting, I walked them to their rental car. They would be staying at a hotel near JFK airport.

On the way to the car James pulled me aside. "Brianna, I need to tell you something."

"Yeah?"

"I just want to let you know that when your grandparents came to me about your mother…" I took a deep breath when the conversation turned to her, as I usually did. "I was just a rookie," he said. "I'd been on the job for less than a year. There were no solid leads."

Looking at the ground, he confessed that not being able to find out the truth about what happened to my mother had haunted him for his entire career.

"Technically," he said, "I am not on the job right now, but I want you to know that I take this very seriously, and I will make sure that everything works out. You have my word on that. I owe it to you and your family."

He hugged me, held me for several moments, and whispered in my ear. I believed him when he told me that everything was going to be okay.

Chapter 44

Bright and early the very next morning, James walked into the projects wearing a bulletproof vest and an FBI-issued windbreaker. Although I was two blocks away, safely seated in the back of his rental car, I could imagine the looks that he was getting from people. Even without the letters on his back it would've still been obvious that he didn't belong there. But as out of place as he was, he walked like he owned the neighborhood. He had a confidence about him that was undeniable.

I was nervous. My fingers fidgeted with the antennae of the two way radio I was holding. Up on the eighth floor, James knocked on the apartment of Sandra Carter, our so-called victim. Pop was humming in the front seat and I shushed him so that I could hear the conversation through the radio.

She answered the door. Later, I'd find out that she was pretty, slim yet curvy. Just the type of girl most guys in the hood would be attracted to. Maybe it was her looks that made her sexual assault claim more believable.

"Sandra Carter? Come with me please." I heard James say in a cool and even voice.

"What? No! What did I do? What did I do?" I smiled as I imagined a look of panic on her face.

"You filed a false police report," James said. "That's a crime."

"Please…No. Please don't do this."

James paused for a second, made it seem like he was thinking things over.

"Please." Saundra continued to beg,

"Okay," James said. "Maybe we can work something out. Let's go somewhere and talk. If you fully cooperate with me, I won't charge you."

"Really?"

"I said maybe," James reminded her. "It will take some convincing on your part. It all depends on how cooperative you are."

"But if I talk to you, he will kill me."

"I understand that you are afraid, but if you work with me I can protect you."

Reluctant, Sandra asked, "Isn't there any other option?"

James laughed. He had a mean streak, I remember thinking. But it wasn't exactly an evil laugh it was more of a nonchalant little chuckle. And that was the same tone he used when he answered her question. "Sure there is, sweetie. You always have options."

In my head I pictured him leaning casually against her doorframe, flashing his smile and those dimples, right before he clobbered her. "Let's see," he said. "You can talk to me or you can go to prison. Yeah, I know, I know, not the best options. But they're options, right? You choose."

I almost felt sorry for her. Almost. She was crying and sniffling. But James's strategy was effective. She agreed to talk to him. Having achieved his goal he turned back into his normal self.

Acting like they were old buddies, he said, "Okay, I'm hungry. How about I treat you to breakfast?"

Even Pop had to admit, "He's good."

"Yeah," I agreed.

Step one… check, I thought to myself.

In a second rental car, James drove Sandra to a popular diner in

Brooklyn. We had all agreed the day before that she would be more likely to open up and tell us what we needed to know if we got her out of the Bronx.

Pop and I discreetly followed their car. Pop lost James in traffic a few times, but we didn't have to follow that closely because we already knew where they were headed. As long as we stayed in reception range for the two-way radio everything would be fine. I didn't want to miss a word.

"How old are you?" I heard James ask.

"Eighteen," Sandra said. By the tone in her voice I could tell that she was really scared. It just wasn't adding up. I hadn't even really met her, but I was thinking that she didn't seem like the type of girl that would be hanging around a drug dealer. Then again my father was one and I was clueless to that fact, so I decided not to make any assumptions.

"How do you know Jackie Roberts?"

"I don't."

There must be static on the radio, I thought to myself.

"You don't know anyone by that name?"

"I know of her. But I don't know her personally."

"She's lying," I said. This time Pop shushed me.

"So how did you get involved in this whole set up of Demetrius Wright?" James asked.

I turned up the volume because I couldn't make out what she was saying. Then I heard the faint sound of someone praying. She was praying.

The fear, the praying, something was really wrong with this picture, I thought.

James didn't interrupt her. He pulled into a parking space right in front of the diner. When she was done, he said, "Look Sandra, you are going to be okay. You made the right decision by talking to me and I will protect you. No one is going to hurt you."

"It's not me that I'm worried about."

"Then who?"

"My sister!" She burst into tears. She cried so hard, she started to cough and wheeze. She was struggling to catch her breath. From where Pop had parked I could see inside James's car; he was rubbing her back. She pulled out an inhaler, took a couple of puffs, and took a deep breath.

"Are you okay? Whatever it is I am sure that we can figure out a way to work it out. You just have to trust me. Let's go get some breakfast and see what we can come up with, okay? You ready to go inside?"

She didn't answer him but a few seconds later they were both getting out of the car and heading inside. Pop and I stayed in our car, on the edge of our seats.

Once James got inside, he took a table by the window, like we'd planned. He didn't waste any time resuming the conversation.

"So, Sandra, what's going on with your sister? Why are you so worried about her?"

I could see that she wasn't looking at him. She stared down at the table, folding and unfolding the napkin in front of her. A waitress came over to the table to take their order. James ordered for the both of them. Finally when the waitress was out of earshot, Sandra began to speak.

"My sister's name is Toni. She's sixteen. I became her legal guardian eight months ago when I turned eighteen."

"What happened to your parents?"

"My father was never in the picture and when a judge sent my mother to a residential drug treatment center, my sister and I were put into foster care. I begged our social worker not to separate us. Even before my mother went away, she was pretty messed up. All Toni and I ever had was each other. I told the social worker that, but she just blew me off. Told me how busy she was and how many open files she had. That was the problem; to her, we were just open files."

I saw James shaking his head as he listened to her.

"She didn't even give me a real answer," Toni said. "She didn't even try to keep us together."

"So you went to two separate foster homes?"

"Yeah. We were able to visit each other twice a month. We'd never been apart like that before. When we did see each other, I started to notice that she was different."

"Different how?"

"I don't know. She was just real quiet and she wouldn't talk to me about what was going on. All she kept saying was that she wanted to go home. I had nightmares about all of the awful things that could be happening to her. But to this day she has never told me what happened. She started doing drugs while she was there. She hid it really well. I didn't even know until after I had been granted guardianship of her."

The waitress came back balancing their order on a tray. James shook his head when she asked if there was anything else they needed.

"When the guardianship order finally came through I was so happy. I thought I could get her home and everything would be back to normal." She took a quick sip from her cup. "The social worker made arrangements for us to get our old project apartment back, the one we'd shared with our mother. But when Toni came home, it was like invasion of the body snatchers or something. That girl was not my sister. She had mood swings and an uncontrollable temper and she'd go out and not come home for days. There was nothing I could do to control her."

Pop looked over his shoulder from the front seat of the car and said, "It seems like this girl may be as much of an innocent bystander in this whole thing as your boyfriend."

I nodded because I had been thinking the same thing.

I turned my attention back to what Sandra was saying. She was telling James that it had taken her less than a week to figure out that her sister was on drugs. "I couldn't believe it. After everything we had been through with our mother, how could she get caught up in the same thing?"

"And she got her drugs from Atlantic?"

Sandra nodded. "Before long she had racked up a serious debt with Atlantic's crew that she couldn't pay."

"Did you tell your social worker about any of this?" James asked.

"No. Maybe I should have. But after the guardianship came through, we didn't see much of the social worker anymore. I got the feeling that we were pretty much on our own. Plus, I was afraid that if I told some-one they would just take her away again."

Neither one of them had touched their food, which no doubt was now ice cold. The waitress came over and offered to reheat it for them, but James shooed her away.

"My sister was young and beautiful," Sandra said. "So I could only imagine what she was doing to pay off her debt to Atlantic. I actually saw her a few weeks ago. I barely recognized her. She was so skinny. Her hair was falling out. She didn't speak to me. It was like she didn't recognize me either." She looked directly at James like she was plead-ing with him to understand. "I had to do something. She's my sister!"

"So what'd you do?" he asked, even though that was the one ques-tion we already knew the answer to.

"I went to see Atlantic. I was so nervous. I had no clue of what I was going to say I just wanted my sister back. I wanted to get her some help."

"And what did he say when you met with him?"

Atlantic had told Sandra that she could trade places with her sister. That she could become responsible for paying her sister's debt. And despite what that might mean for her, she'd always been her sister's protector, so she'd agreed.

"I asked him what I would have to do and he said that he would let me know when he figured that out. Weeks went by and I heard nothing from him. I thought he'd forgotten about me. Then out of the blue he sends one of his men to come get me. He takes me to some apartment and tells me that I have to file a police report against some guy. That's when I met Jackie. She was there too."

"What was Jackie doing?"

"She was the one that spelled everything out for me. Told me exactly what I had to do. I didn't want to do it, but I kept thinking about my sister and how I didn't want her to end up like my mother. I had to do something, so I agreed. I did what they wanted me to do. I pointed him out to the police when he came out of Jackie's building. I felt so guilty; my heart broke when I saw the confused and terrified look on the guy's face."

Yeah, I thought. My heart brakes a little more every time I see that look on Dee's face. What made her drug addicted sister more important than Dee? Why should he be the collateral damage?

"So where is your sister now?"

"She's still with Atlantic. After I filled out the police report, I went back to Atlantic and told him I had done my part and that I wanted my sister. He told me that I had done a good job, but that I had to wait because if he gave me back my sister I could go back to the police and tell them that I had picked out the wrong guy. And he was right, because that is exactly what I'd planned to do. I'd saved up some money and I was going to take my sister and get out of town."

I guess I wasn't the only one looking to run for the hills, I thought.

"Atlantic told me that once the situation was resolved he would let Toni come home. I asked him how long that would take and he said it wouldn't be long."

Jackie and Atlantic were obviously confident that I would simply give them the money and this whole thing would blow over. But that was not going to happen. I had to admit that I found it hard to hate her. She was backed against a wall and she did what she felt she had to do. But James didn't hesitate to remind her that what she'd done was wrong.

"I can understand that you were in a difficult situation, but you could have ruined an innocent person's life. Sent him to jail for something he didn't do."

"I know." She started to cry again. "I just tried to focus on my sister. I was responsible for her."

Sandra's story complicated my plan. I honestly didn't know what I was going to do. Sandra and I had one thing in common; she felt like she would do anything to protect her sister and I felt the same way about proving Dee's innocence.

I would do what I came there to do. And if I couldn't figure out a better way, I would see this plan through to the end, whatever that may be.

I rolled down the car window, pressed the zoom button on my camera, and made sure that I could clearly see her face as well as the bright yellow letters on James' jacket. I pressed the button.

Chapter 45

Between Dee and I, Dee was the neat freak. But with everything that he had on his mind, keeping the apartment clean wasn't on the top of his to-do list. Hey, I could have used the same excuse, right? I was still embarrassed when Pop and I walked into the apartment. It looked like it had been hit by a tornado. I moved aside some papers on the couch so Pop could have a seat. In the kitchen there were dishes in the sink and food wrappers all over the counter.

I offered Pop something to drink, but he declined. I didn't blame him. I wouldn't want to eat or drink anything in there either. Somewhere on the counter underneath all of the wrappers was a note from Dee, letting me know that he was going to be working an extra shift.

His boss had called two days ago, a week after his vacation days and sick leave had run out, and he'd demanded that Dee come back to work or lose his job. After his first day back at work, I guess he realized that keeping busy was better than sulking around the apartment all day. He had been pulling double shifts ever since.

I was relieved that he wasn't there because he didn't know the details of my plan. I had decided that the less he knew about it the better, considering he wasn't exactly thinking straight and I didn't want anyone, not even him, to jeopardize my plan. Unfortunately, I hadn't factored in Sandra.

James dropped her off in a room at the same hotel that he and Pop were staying at and met us back at the apartment so that we could brainstorm.

When James arrived, Pop was the one who said what we'd all been thinking on some level. "I feel sorry for the girl."

She'd had a rough childhood, there was no doubt about that. A mother addicted to drugs, no father to speak of, and now she had taken on the responsibility of a sister with a drug problem. I might admire her strength if she hadn't pointed the finger at Dee for something he was clearly innocent of. Still, Pop was right it was hard not to feel sorry for her.

Stubbornly, I tried my best to shake off that thought. I refused to let it linger too long because it was dangerous territory. The sorrier I felt for her and her situation the less effective I would be in helping Dee which was my ultimate goal. I had to stay focused.

I was trying to hate her for what she'd done and I was doing the same exact thing: looking at the situation with tunnel vision, focusing on one person, and not caring who else got screwed in the process. But I felt completely justified and I let James and Pop know it.

"She did what she felt that she had to do to protect her sister," I said. "And I have to do what I have to do to protect Dee, and that puts us on opposite sides, so I refuse to let myself get caught up in feeling sorry for her."

James tried to play mediator. "You don't have to look at it like that, Brie," he said. "Sandra is not the enemy. You and Sandra are not on opposing sides. Really, you two have both been hurt by your aunt and Atlantic that should put you on the same side."

I wasn't trying to hear that. "Really?" I said. "Is that right?" I felt myself losing control. No one was trying to understand things from my perspective. So I took the volume up a few octaves.

"She accuses my boyfriend of sexual assault! Has him spend the weekend in jail! And we're on the same side? I don't think so!"

Pop was giving me a look. He seemed to be contemplating wheth-er or not we were close enough yet for him to tell me that my behavior was out of line. It reminded me that they were there to help and that I was taking out my frustration on the wrong people. His look said it all.

But I still couldn't stop. They just sat there and watched me. Allowed me to go on and on until I'd exhausted myself.

When I was finally out of steam James said, "You feel better now?" I rolled my eyes at him. "We could go find a shooting range if you want." I know those dimples got him far in life. I smiled too.

Maybe my outburst was just me trying to save face. I'd felt defen-sive, like James was trying to call me out with that *Sandra's not the en-emy* comment. I really didn't have an excuse. Deep down I knew James was right. We were all victims, Dee, Toni, Sandra, and me. We were all Aunt Jackie's and Atlantic's victims.

Originally I thought I'd take the pictures and mail them to Jackie. The same way my father had used pictures to blackmail those police officers Aunt Jackie had told me about. The plan was that I would mail her the pictures of Sandra talking to the FBI agent, and blackmail her to get the charges dropped. So what if something bad happened to our so-called victim? She deserved it. Bad things happen to bad people, right? And she was a bad person.

But then Sandra had told her story and it was impossible for me to fit her squarely into the 'bad person' category. I mean, if we were go-ing to compare sob stories I was pretty sure I had her beat, but I didn't want to add to her problems just to solve my own.

And that little revelation complicated things. Not to mention there was still her sister to consider. Toni was still with Atlantic and I didn't want to do anything that could cause her to get hurt any more than she already had been. I was out of ideas.

"We just have to regroup." Pop said. "We need to figure out a way to get the sister away from this Atlantic guy before we move forward with anything else."

James said, "I could take this information and contact my supervisor and start an official investigation. The problem is that with an official investigation also comes all of the bureaucracy involved in going through formal channels and that will definitely slow down the process."

I was finally calm. I knew what we had to do: protect not only Dee, but Sandra and Toni too. Ashamed by the way I'd spazzed out, I was reluctant to rejoin the conversation. But I did. "We still have some leverage," I reminded them. "I still have the money, which is what they really want, and we also have the element of surprise because they don't know that we have spoken to Sandra."

I remembered that Dee had once told me that these types of people operate on greed, not logic. And with that thought in mind the ideas started to flow.

Chapter 46

James and I stood side by side in my bedroom. That was the only place in the apartment that we had a full length mirror. James thought a mirror might be helpful.

"This is the safety," he said as he demonstrated how to use the gun. He handed it to me. It was heavier than I expected. "Put your hands like this... Hold it securely. Okay...but not too tight. Spread out your fingers a little. Good... that's good"

I stood there staring at myself in the mirror. I pointed the gun at my reflection. *Say hello to my little friend.* What in the world was I doing? What was I getting myself into?

"So once your grip is right it's pretty simple," James was saying. "Just point and shoot."

A lot of people in my neighborhood have guns. I'd seen guns before, I'd seen someone get shot before, too, but not up close. I'd seen it from my apartment window, but I never thought I'd be in a situation where I might have to use one myself. That thought sent a very visible shiver threw me.

"You okay?" James wanted to know.

"Yeah," I lied.

"You nervous?"

"A little."

I shook my head when James asked me if I wanted to reconsider the plan. So he went back to showing me how to conceal the gun in my clothing. "It's not likely that they will frisk you, but if they do and they find it, don't worry. I'll be there with you and there is no way that they will find everything that I will have on me."

"Okay." *Please let them find it*, I thought. *At least then I won't have to worry about the possibility of having to actually use it.*

"Did you make all of the arrangements with the bank?"

"Yes."

"Where is your boyfriend? Did you talk to him about all of this?"

"No, I didn't tell him," I said. James gave me a disappointed look. "His reaction would have been even worse than Pop's."

When I had suggested this plan, Pop was completely against it. He'd said it was too dangerous and he didn't want anything to do with it. "This is not the wild wild west," he'd said.

He basically forbade me from going through with it. But I told him there were no other options. "It's not as bad as it sounds," I said. He walked out.

James said not to worry about Pop, that he'd come around. "Just give him a little time. He's worried about you."

"I know."

"But I think the least you can do is tell your boyfriend what's going on. He deserves to know."

"No! Dee has enough on his mind without me adding this to it. A lot of this is my fault, you know? I should have just moved when he originally suggested it. If I would have, none of this would be happening."

When I met Dee I couldn't have imagined how much I would grow to love him in such a short period of time. He had changed my life for the better, but unfortunately all of my drama had the opposite effect on him. So if I had to take extreme measures to protect him, that's what I was going to do.

James was persistent, but so was I.

"I'm not telling him." I put on my most intimidating face. "*No one is telling him.* Like I have been saying, I will do what I have to do to prove his innocence. This is what I have to do."

He held up his hands. "Fine." He walked to the living room and grabbed his coat. "Get some sleep. I'll pick you up in the morning."

"Okay."

A few hours later when Dee came home, I pretended to be sound asleep. I didn't want to talk to him because I didn't want to have to lie.

Chapter 47

When I woke up the next morning, Dee's side of the bed was cold and empty. He wasn't in the apartment and he hadn't left a note. I thought about calling him but decided against it. Instead I'd give him his space and focus on what I had to do. I had a busy day ahead of me. As I showered and dressed I reminded myself that if everything went according to plan, my life and Dee's would be back to normal when it was all said and done.

Forty minutes later James was waiting outside for me. Pop was with him. But the wrinkle in his brow, the tightness in his face, and the fact that he stared straight ahead without saying a word when I slid into the back seat, told me that he wasn't happy about it.

"Good morning," James said.

"Yeah, I hope so," I said.

Pop turned around and looked at me then. He took the opportunity to remind me, "You can still change your mind about this."

"No. Let's just do this," I told him.

"There has to be another way," Pop mumbled.

We drove the fifteen minutes to the projects in absolute silence except for the news playing on the car radio. I thought about all the people listening to this news broadcast in their cars on their way to work; it was something to make conversation about during the day.

Did you hear about that horrible fire? Oh, did you hear that the police caught that guy that was involved in the robbery.

But none of it would really hit home for them. Oh, they might retain a couple of the details for an hour or two, but that's about it. I couldn't really blame them, it was not their fault, none of it stuck with you until you were somehow personally involved.

I thought about how, if all of the things that had been happening to me were happening to someone else—if I were simply hearing about it on the news—I wouldn't think twice about it either. But it wasn't a news story, I couldn't just change the station and forget about it. No, this was my life and this would be a year that I'd never forget.

We pulled up to the building entirely too fast. This place had been my home for years and now it looked foreign and dangerous. I wasn't ready. I was scared. So many things could go wrong. I said a quick prayer asking that we all make it home safely.

Walking around with a gun should have given me a little bit a confidence in this situation, but it didn't. All it did was weigh me down. It nudged me every time I took a step, reminding me that I was in way over my head.

Pop stayed in the car. James wasn't wearing a wire this time because he knew that it would be found if he were searched, so the two-way radio was out of the question. Instead he had a panic button attached to his watch. The FBI has some of the coolest gadgets, 007-type gadgets. That's what I had thought when James first showed it to me.

If he pressed that button it would alert Pop that we were in trouble and that he should call the police. On that day walking into that building, his gadgets didn't give me peace of mind. All I could think was I wasn't comfortable relying on the police and their slow response time if we got in trouble.

In the elevator my mind was racing. Right before we got off on the seventh floor, James grabbed my hand and squeezed. "I won't let anything happen to you." I nodded. I knew that he would try his hardest to keep his word on that.

All of this was happening so fast. Not that long ago, I was hanging out with Gran and Marie at the mall. But I wasn't complaining, I needed things to happen fast because the longer this situation lasted, the more depressed and worried Dee was getting. I needed the truth to come out for his sake.

Dee had gone from rambling on and on to not talking about it at all. It wasn't just that he wouldn't talk to me about the case. He wouldn't talk to me about anything. I knew the reason though; Dee wasn't just nervous, he was pissed at me.

I couldn't blame him. I thought about it a million times a day, what would have happened if I had just listened to him, if we had just packed up our bags and left town. But I couldn't go back and change my decision; all I could do was clean up this mess. Then the two of us would leave the Bronx and never look back.

When we got off the elevator and started down the hall, my stomach was in knots, twisting and turning. I swallowed hard. My feet followed James, but my mind was someplace else.

I was thinking about how my father had warned me not to go into anyone's apartment without telling him first. That was one of his major rules, that and the no dating rule. What would he think if he saw me now, I wondered, going into the apartment of a known drug dealer to work out a deal to protect my boyfriend?

A dog growled from behind one of the doors and I nearly jumped out of my skin. I took a deep breath and tried to calm down. I needed to play it cool. The dog growled again. I wondered if even through the door it could smell my fear. I assumed it was a pit bull. They were as much a stable for men in the hood as those stupid pink tights were for the women.

James cupped his hand on my shoulder and nodded reassuringly. He knocked on 7C. I couldn't tell the sound of his knocking from the sound of my heart pounding in my chest.

James had shown me a mug shot of Atlantic the day before, so I knew the guy who answered the door wasn't him. We were showed into the living room by a light-skinned guy with some kind of tribal tattoo on his arm.

No one could have predicted what happened next. There was no way to plan for something like that. When I walked into that living room, I got the shock of my life. And that's saying a lot because I never thought anything would outdo that moment sitting at Aunt Jackie's kitchen table and getting the news that my father was a drug dealer.

Her words had been as sharp and precise as a surgeon's scalpel. She cut me open and took out my vital organs, leaving me gasping for air and bleeding out on the kitchen floor. That's how I felt, but walking into the living room of Atlantic's apartment and seeing Dee, the feeling that came over me was unexplainable. It was so much worse than anything that I had ever felt before. That day with my aunt at her kitchen table was like a walk in the park by comparison.

Chapter 48

Atlantic introduced himself. My eyes darted back and forth from Dee to Atlantic, Atlantic to Dee. Atlantic followed my gaze and shrugged his shoulders like he was completely innocent, like he had nothing to do with Dee sitting there, tied to a chair, blood pouring out of a wound on his head, his face swollen to the point that he was almost unrecognizable.

Finally I found my voice and repeatedly shouted Dee's name. There was no response.

"No! No! What did you do to him?"

Casually, Atlantic said, "Don't worry, he's fine." He walked to the kitchen, picked up a cup off the counter, walked over to Dee and poured it over his head. Dee moaned. "See, I told you he was fine."

"What is he doing here?"

Atlantic rubbed his goatee like he was thinking about it and then laughed. "Your guess is as good as mine," he said. He looked at Dee and shook his head in disgust. "He contacted me, said he wanted to talk. To tell you the truth, I thought the two of you were coming together, but here he is. The best thing that you can do for him now is to ignore him and we'll get down to business."

After a brief pause Atlantic turned his attention to James. "Who's this, your bodyguard?" Until this point James had been quietly observing everything.

"Her uncle," James said.

"You were afraid to come alone?" Atlantic said. "That's smart. That's probably a lesson my brother over here should have also heeded."

He was pointing at Dee. Brother? I figured he meant it as slang, just a figure of speech. But I guess he saw the question on my face and said "What? He didn't tell you?"

I searched his face, not looking for an indication as to whether or not he was lying. After all, he *was* a criminal. I was looking for a resemblance, an indication that the two of them could possibly be related.

I'd just decided that he was lying, trying to play mind games with me, when he noticed what I was doing and he smiled. And there it was... that smile. Dee's smile. That same cocky smirk that Dee had given me a million times. The one that had made my insides flutter a little the first time I had seen him on that bus.

At that moment, that same smile made me lose my balance. I reached out groped for something to hold on to, something to keep me from falling. I grabbed the fabric of James' shirt.

How can I explain this? The pain that I felt when I realized the two of them were brothers? The pain was so sharp it had me doubling over and gasping for air. I'm not a guy, but I'd have to say it was probably something like taking a swift kick to the groin.

Atlantic ignored the fact that I was in agony, still coughing and trying to catch my breath. "I'm not surprised he didn't tell you," Atlantic said. "Dee and my whole family pretty much stopped claiming me years ago. It still hurts though. I have feelings too." He held his hand over his chest and made a sad face and then laughed. He was crazier than I had ever imagined. "Like right now," Atlantic said. "I'm feeling a little impatient."

I glanced over at Dee again. If he wasn't sitting there looking so battered and pathetic, I might have taken a few swings at him myself. I could have put some of those fighting skills Daddy had taught me to use and partnered with Dee's brother Atlantic, tag-team style. I couldn't believe that he had been lying to me for months. All of his talk about how dangerous these people were and come to find out he knew that first hand. He knew it for a fact because he was related to Atlantic.

Don't get me wrong, I wasn't upset because he was related to Atlantic. Who was I to judge? I was my father's daughter after all. I was upset because he'd lied. I had trusted him and he'd lied. It was starting to feel all too familiar. I pushed that thought out of my head because I had to focus on the situation at hand.

One thing was true though. Dee had been right about how dangerous and well connected Atlantic was. His reputation had preceded him. I knew that he was more than a drug dealer, he was also violent. He was known for his so called lay-away plan.

He would give potential customers samples of his product free of charge. Then over time he'd get them hooked. The ones who couldn't afford their new habit, he'd put them to work, figure out something for them to do to pay down their debt. And if he had no use for them, they'd simply go missing.

What was another missing drug addict, right? How many man hours would the NYPD expend on that? It was James who had linked these seemingly random disappearances together and made Atlantic his prime suspect.

And there I was standing in front of him as he laughed, his jumpy eyes making me wonder if he had been dipping into his own supply. "I was always the outcast of the family," Atlantic was saying. "The black sheep. Dee was the good one and Jeff was somewhere in the middle, but there was no question that I was the bad seed out of the bunch."

He walked over to Dee and with his full force punched him in the stomach.

"Stop! Please, stop!" I yelled.

Dee was alert now and growling in pain. His head bobbed up and down like a bobble head doll as he tried to catch his breath. He made eye contact with me and said, "Run, Brie. Go... get out of here." I knew he was trying to yell but it came out as little more than a raspy whisper.

"I'm not leaving you here," I told him.

"Someone cue the violins," Atlantic said. He walked back over to me and got a little too close for comfort. "Let's put the soap opera on hold." I could feel his breath on my face. "What you both seem to be forgetting is that I'm in charge here and no one leaves until I say they leave. Now let's get down to business. You want me to tell the girl to drop the charges and in turn you are going to turn the money over to me. Not Jackie, me. That's how we are going to handle this."

"No," I said

"No? Well then why are you here? Why don't you take a minute to think about that while I occupy myself over here." He walked back over to Dee. "Dee and I have some more catching up to do."

"No!"

Atlantic stopped just short of punching Dee in the jaw. "Well, that didn't take long. Did you change your mind?"

"I have a new deal for you."

"This isn't let's make a deal. Our old agreement works perfectly fine for me. You don't have anything else that I want."

James finally spoke. Poised and calm as usual, he said, "You already know she has the money. If anything happens to her, the money will all go to Jackie and you know you will never see one cent of it. So it's in your best interest to listen to her. If you want the money you will agree to her terms."

"He talks like a cop," Atlantic said more to himself than anyone else. "So uncle, are you a cop?"

"No," James answered truthfully.

"It doesn't matter if you are. I get along very well with cops. I actually employ a few. I don't know if you've heard, but the NYPD really doesn't pay enough, so if you ever want a new gig…" He made the universal *call me* sign. "Anyway what makes you think I'm going to hurt her? I don't *want to* hurt her." He folded his arms over his chest. "So what's this new arrangement you want me to agree to?"

I stopped looking at Dee, cleared my throat, and tried to make my demands without letting my voice crack. "First I want you to let Dee go. Then I want you to let Toni go and once they are both outside, I will give you the bank account numbers and you can transfer the money into your account."

He gave me the once over before he said, "I understand why you want me to let Dee go, and that's not a problem. Like I said, Dee contacting me was just a pleasant surprise. But Toni? She is just a teenage crack head. What could you possibly want with her?"

"Why does it matter? You are getting what you want."

"You know, I have this pet peeve." He was walking back toward Dee. "I hate when people try to answer a question with a question." He stopped half way and turned back toward me. "It angers me. So why don't we try this again. What do you want with Toni?"

I had to figure out something to say and it had to be a quick. But I was drawing a blank. I was thankful when James stepped in.

"Brie and I have seen Toni around the neighborhood and we saw what happened to her mother too," he lied. "We don't think it's too late to get her some help. She's just a kid. Brie's father got a lot of young girls hooked on drugs and we couldn't think of a better way to help than to use his money to get this girl out of here and get her some help."

What was James doing? Appealing to the moral sensibilities of a violent drug dealer? That wasn't going to get us far. I chimed in, "I mean, what's one girl? You know you don't have any shortage of customers."

He laughed. "You and my brother are a perfect match. You obviously think that you are some type of Mother Teresa and he has a panic attack every time he is in any type of confrontation. The two of you should live in a little bubble so the reality of life never touches you. From everything that went down with your father, I would think you would have outgrown this fairytale phase."

He walked over to the couch, sat down and patted the cushion next to him. "Come over here and have a seat with me. I want to tell you something."

Reluctantly I sat down next to him. James remained standing at attention. Atlantic said he wanted to tell me a story.

"When I was sixteen," he said, "I drove from Florida, where my family lives, up to New Jersey. The crew I was working for was making a delivery to your father. I got there on time as scheduled, but your father never showed. I waited and waited. I waited until my hotel room got raided. And when I went to jail, I waited some more, all the way until my twentieth birthday. Four years of my life… gone." He waived his hand. "And you know what? The reason your father didn't show up was because he got tipped off about the raid. But instead of giving me a heads up he let me go down alone."

Why was he telling me this?

"That was my first encounter with your father. To this day he has no idea that's why I came after him and took over his hood. That's why I'm coming after his money too. You get what I'm saying."

I nodded. Still having no clue what he was getting at.

"See, its revenge. Revenge is real life. All this crap about wanting to help a girl you don't even know, that's not real life. And you know what else? I don't believe that's why you really want her."

A twinge of panic went through me. Had he seen me shudder?

"I don't trust you any more than I trust your father."

I got up started to move closer to the exit, closer to James.

Atlantic pushed me and I fell backwards into James. James stepped forward, putting his body between me and Atlantic. "You can't judge what she wants to do to help Toni based on what you would do. Everyone is not like you."

"The world would be a much more interesting place if it were filled with people like me, don't you think?"

James ignored him. "Not everyone does things based on revenge and hatred. But you're right, there is something else that we hope to gain out of this situation." While Atlantic was busy reminiscing about his days as drug trafficker, James had taken that time to brainstorm about other justifications for us wanting Toni. He knew that Atlantic would revisit his original question.

"Brie's father betrayed her and her aunt has followed in his footsteps. Putting the money in your hands is the best way for her to send him a message that she is done with him and that not even the money can fix it."

"Really? Why not just spend it?"

"I wouldn't give him the satisfaction," I said playing along, trying again to distract him from his question about Toni, which was obviously James's plan. But we were both unsuccessful.

"Okay, but I still want to know the real reason you want Toni. Why her?"

"What?" I said, and tried to give him a casual shrug. "You got some other strung-out teenagers living here? You can hand them over too. It's almost a million dollars we are talking about. I should get something out of the bargain."

"You are getting Dee's charges dropped."

"Yeah, fictional charges that would have never existed in the first place if not for you and my aunt. I could just turn over the money to her and you can wait and see if she gives you a cut. Either way works for me."

I didn't know I had it in me, that confident, strong, and in-control voice. My words shocked me. I think it was the blood dripping from Dee's head and pooling into a maroon stain on the front of his shirt. I'm pretty sure that's what brought out that side of me. Thankfully, Atlantic bought my act. He didn't want to have to fight over the money with Aunt Jackie. I'm certain that threat was what turned the tables in my favor.

I was glad that worked because I was getting a little desperate. It was not like we could tell him the true reason we wanted to take Toni. That wasn't even an option.

I couldn't tell him that the only way I could get Sandra to testify against him was if we got her sister, Toni, safely out of here. If he knew we'd already spoken to Sandra and didn't need him to authorize her to drop the charges, well, our whole plan would fall apart like a house of cards. The foundation was already shaky.

"So let's do this," Atlantic said.

"Let Dee and the girl go first," I demanded.

Atlantic reached for his gun. I was about to duck and cover when James stepped forward again and stood in between Atlantic and I. James had a calm expression on his face and didn't even go for his weapon; unlike me he was confident that everything was completely under control. Plus I knew that James didn't want to break his cover unless it was absolutely necessary.

Atlantic held his gun, slightly fondling it. "This is Ethel," he said. "Isn't she beautiful? We've been through a lot together." His eyes glazed over and he went silent. I didn't want to think about what memory he was reliving. Abruptly he said, "She has never let me down. I named her after my mother. No nonsense, strong, loyal. Maybe Dee will introduce you to her one day."

He walked over to Dee. I held my breath when he placed the gun under Dee's chin. "Wake up," he said. Dee moaned.

"I've enjoyed catching up with you, but your girl says it's time for you to go now."

Atlantic took out a knife and cut Dee out of his restraints. Dee wasn't able to stand up on his own. When he tried he collapsed right back into the chair.

"He seems to need a little help," Atlantic said, laughing

I told James that he should take Dee and Toni outside and that I would finish up with Atlantic. Of course James protested. Atlantic was the one that stopped our argument.

"Who's in charge here? You or me?" He gestured with his gun. "She had it right the first time. You go." He told James. "And she stays. I'm tired of reminding you that I'm running this."

James pretended to hug me and slid me the panic button. Atlantic went into another room and came back pulling Toni by her hair.

"What did I do?" she cried. "What did I do?"

"It's time for you to go. I don't want you anymore."

She dropped to her knees and begged for Atlantic to let her stay. She grabbed his pants leg. Atlantic pulled her up off the floor. "Hey, you belong to me, right?"

Toni nodded.

"And that means I can do what I want with you, right?"

When she said yes, I thought about that old commercial. You know, the one with the egg, this is your brain...this is your brain on drugs. Her brain must have been totally fried, that's what I was thinking.

"Well, then I am giving you to this man," Atlantic said. "He will take care of you from now on. Now go!"

She scurried toward James. The one good thing about the beating that Dee had taken was that he was in no position to protest when James half carried and half dragged him out of the apartment.

A few moments later, it was just the two of us, Atlantic and I, staring at each other from opposite sides of the room.

Chapter 49

"Alone at last," Atlantic said. "You know, you have some spunk in you. I like that." He closed the gap between us. "Don't be nervous. I told you I wasn't going to hurt you." He handed me his cell phone and a piece of paper with his account number on it and told me to make the call.

I followed his instructions, closed my trust fund, and transferred all of the money into his account. When he called his bank to confirm, they of course told him that the money was there. I knew that's what they would say, and my hand was already resting on the doorknob.

"You really hate your father that much?" he asked, eyeing me suspiciously.

"I don't hate him. I just don't want any connection to him in my life." That was the truth. When I first found out about everything, I thought I hated him, but I realized it was slowly driving me crazy. I was thinking about him all the time. So, for my own sanity, I had to let it go.

"I'm glad his family disowned him, It's only fair," Atlantic said. "That's what happened to me after I went to jail because of him. My parents, my brothers, none of them would even talk to me. About a year after I got out, I got shot. I was in the hospital for a month. I could have died. And you know what? None of my family even came to see me. I blame your father for that."

"Was my father the one that shot you?"

"No. He would be in the ground if he had instead of rotting away in prison. But don't you get it? It's his fault that I lost my family. It's only fair that he loses his too."

His flawed reasoning made me think of those sessions I'd had with Dr. Beekman. She'd helped me understand that just because I'd had some bad experiences with my family I couldn't use that as an excuse for my actions now. I had to act, not react because reacting meant giving up control. She had drilled that into my head week after week, and I guess it stuck because that was the first thing I thought about when Atlantic said he blamed my father for losing his family. He needed to take responsibility, but as he stood there holding Ethel, I thought better than to explain that to him. Instead I asked, "So are we done here?"

"Yeah, everything seems to be in order. And if not I know where to find you." I felt my eyes widen at that possibility. "Don't believe me? Trust me, I'm very well connected." Had my aunt somehow found out and told him? Had Dee told my aunt when he'd gone to see her?

"You can't imagine the things that I know about you already. If I put my mind to it I could probably know what you're thinking before the thought even forms fully in your head. So don't ever think that you can get something over on me. Because you can't. I went to jail once when I was young and stupid and I'm not going back. To avoid that in my line of work, I have to be smart. And I am, very, very smart." He didn't raise his voice, but his threat was not lost on me.

I swallowed hard. Coughed. "Okay." My sweaty hand slipped a little as it moved to turn the doorknob. He stepped forward and placed his hand against the door, blocking my exit.

"One more thing before you go." My back was against the door now and he stood directly in front of me, leaning over me with his hand against the door. I put my hand in my pocket, held my finger a few inches from the panic button. "Just something for you to think about. Do you think that a smart person...an observant person, believes in coincidences?"

I shook my head, remembering the revelation I'd had during my last meeting with Dr. Beekman. All of the things that had happened with my aunt were not coincidences at all.

"Exactly," Atlantic said. "A true coincidence is very rare. You should always view it as happening for a reason, as part of a plan." He walked away from me and into the kitchen I heard the faucet. *Run, Brie! Run now!* That's what I was telling myself, but my feet didn't get the message.

He walked back into the room. His voice was so calm, almost friendly, that I hadn't seen it coming, hadn't been able to brace myself at all before I had the wind knocked out of me.

"So ask yourself this," he said. Out of all the guys that you could have hooked up with, why my brother? A chance meeting, a random exchange on a bus? Do you really believe that? Is that what your gut is telling you? That the two of you just happened to meet that day? Or does he have his own motives? Is he more involved with me than you know?"

His words hit me harder than his fists had hit Dee.

"Your father tried to take down my organization by planting a man in my crew. Maybe I have done the same thing. Maybe Dee has reported your every move to me. Now these are all maybes." He shrugged. "It's possible it doesn't mean anything, but I think they are worth thinking about, don't you?" His eyes narrowed. He walked back over to me, placed his hand back against the door. Why hadn't I run when I had the chance?

"So when you think about whether you can get away with whatever little game you are playing—and I know that you are—you better think long and hard. Like I said these are all maybes. But there is one thing that I can tell you for sure. If I have to come after you, things will not end well for you."

I felt my eyes getting moist. I don't know whether it was anger or fear that was causing that. It took all of my willpower to prevent those tears from materializing and rolling down my face. *Not here, not in front of him*, I told myself.

He moved his hand from the door and I couldn't get out of there fast enough. I ran down the hallway, bypassed the elevators, and took the stairs two at a time. In the lobby I nearly knocked James over as I ran for the door.

Chapter 49

I practically ran James over, like a speed bump, as I made a mad dash for the exit. He grabbed me by the shoulders, shook me. "Brie!" he shouted, trying to snap me out of my panic-ridden trance.

Was that me screaming? Tears were streaming freely down my face now.

"Brie!" James shook me again. "Why...why didn't you press the panic button?"

"I have to get out of here."

James refused to let go of my shoulders. "Tell me what happened. Did he...What did he do to you?" He was looking me in the eyes with such intensity that I had to look away. I wasn't ready to talk about it yet. Wasn't ready to admit what a fool I'd been.

I wiped my cheeks, forced myself to look him in the eye and lied. "I'm fine. I'm not hurt." I couldn't tell if he was buying it. "I just need to get out of here. Can we please just go?"

"Are you sure?"

I nodded.

"Okay, let's go. The car is right out front."

As soon as we walked outside, I spotted Dee slumped over in the back seat of the car. "I don't want to see him." I said it as clear as day, but for some reason there was a comprehension problem on James's end.

"What?" he said.

I pointed to the car. "Dee. I can't see Dee right now."

He stared at me, confused, but I couldn't elaborate, not yet. "I can't see him right now," I mumbled.

"Okay, seriously, Brie, what happened up there? Why are you acting like this?"

I just stared at him, not answering. I couldn't tell him that I was having this all too familiar feeling. Déjà vu. That's what it was, déjà vu. I found myself sitting back at Aunt Jackie's kitchen table yet again. I was having the same feeling I did when I asked her if my father was a drug dealer, and she nodded. All of those questions came back to me. Had I missed something? Were there warning signs that I was too naive or oblivious to recognize? I asked myself those questions, but again I came up empty.

"Okay, fine," James finally said. "But we can't just leave him here. He's hurt. We'll drop him at the closest emergency room."

I tried to keep my cool sitting in the backseat of the car with Toni sandwiched in between Dee and I. Even with her in between us, it was still a little too close for comfort. So when she offered to trade spots with me, I might have answered her a little more forcefully than I should have. I couldn't help it. No longer in Atlantic's apartment, the fear had subsided, what remained was anger.

Dee was moaning in pain. He actually tried to reach for me. I pushed myself so close against the car door that the handle was digging into my side. I did what I had to do to get as far away from him as the confines of the car would allow.

Atlantic had planted a seed in my head, and like Jack and his magic beans, it only took a moment for it to start to sprout. Was it really possible that day on the bus wasn't a chance meeting? I hadn't even mustered up enough strength to get on that bus until that very day. How could he have known I would be there? Had he been following me? What were the odds that we would be attending the same school?

Was that somehow part of Atlantic's plan? Had Atlantic known I would be getting my father's money even before I did?

"Brie, are you okay?" I found myself grinding my teeth at the sound of Dee's voice. His voice was barely audible, but I was even less audible because I didn't respond at all. *Are we there yet?* That's what I was thinking and we hadn't even reached the corner yet. I couldn't get away from him fast enough.

"Babe?" His hand was still reaching out for me.

I could tell that Toni was feeling awkward being stuck in the middle, literally. Fortunately, Mount Vernon Hospital was only about ten minutes away. If it had been up to me, I would have voted for slowing down and pushing him out instead of coming to a complete stop in front of the emergency room. But James was the driver, so we pulled in front of the emergency room and he helped Dee inside. When he got back in the car, James told us that even though he was no doctor, in his opinion Dee looked pretty banged up. He thought Dee might have a few broken ribs.

Were we comparing wounds? I had a broken heart. What was James' point? As if his unwanted opinion on Dee's medical condition wasn't bad enough, James turned around and faced me, "I think he thought you were going to stay with him." He stared at me and waited. That technique might have gotten him some spontaneous confessions on the job, but it wasn't going to work on me. What did he think, that I was going to jump out of the car and run to Dee?

I folded my arms and waited him out. My temper was at its boiling point and I'm sure that James saw that too. He turned around, buckled his seatbelt and put the car in drive. Ten minutes later we hit the highway and were moving at a decent clip, putting some much needed distance between Dee and I.

The problem was the distance hadn't done anything to calm my temper. And that was when it happened. That was when I realized whose fault all of this was: Dr. Beekman.

Every last bit of it was her fault. What a quack. I was even thinking about Dr. Beekman when Atlantic was talking to me earlier, thinking about how he could learn a thing or two from her. But that was before he … before he… let me know that Dee had been part of this whole thing.

All of that advice about giving Dee a chance and not letting my bad experiences in the past influence my relationship with him. Because of her I was sitting here reliving the past stuck in an episode of *The Twilight Zone*. What a load of crap!

Sure it sounded good at the time: *start fresh, give Dee a chance, let yourself love him*. Well, look how that turned out.

You could argue that I was just looking for someone to blame. Yeah, that was true, I can admit that now, and granted, it was not my most shining moment, but at the time it felt right. I had to get the anger out somehow. I felt like it was eating me alive. I could barely breathe.

It could've been temporary insanity or something; it was like I knew what I was doing, but I had no control to stop myself. I fished my phone out of my pocket, punched her number in on the keypad. *Ring, Ring, Ring*, voicemail. That didn't dissuade me. I let her voicemail have it.

I didn't care that everyone in the car was looking at me. Pop turned around and stared at me questioningly. Even James was giving me a look through the rearview mirror. Every ounce of anger that I had for Dee, for Atlantic, for my father, my aunt, every ounce of it, I unleashed it on that voicemail message. The click let me know that I had exceeded my time limit. As soon as I hung up the phone it started to ring. I saw Dee's name on the screen. I pressed ignore. He had exceeded his time limit too. Expired.

Chapter 50

As a guest at my pity party, one of the things I did for entertainment was think about what the look on Dr. Beekman's face would be when she listened to that message. I got a little satisfaction from that. I also mulled over the possibility of letting Dee go to jail. That thought brought a momentary smile to my face, but I was annoyed with myself because I knew I couldn't actually do it. I'd been raised by two criminals, where did this sense of moral obligation come from?

Whatever. I wouldn't let him go to jail, but things were definitely over between the two of us. I'd finish what I set out to do: get Dee's charges dropped, make sure that Sandra and Toni were safe, and then pack up and move down south with my family.

I was sitting in the back of the car, eyes closed, running all of this through my head when Toni started shaking next to me. I opened my eyes. I could tell that she'd been pretty about fifteen pounds ago, before her cheeks had sunken in, before her hair had started to fall out in patches, and certainly before her skin had gotten blotchy and discolored.

She kept shaking and she scratched at her arms, leaving white marks on her ashy skin. I asked her what was wrong, but I already knew the answer.

"I'm sick," she said. "Why did you take me from Atlantic? Where are we going?"

She was sweating, too; a sheen coated the space above her top lip. "We are going to see your sister," I told her. I was surprised when she asked why. "Because she wants you to come home." I was really in no mood to be comforting. I needed comforting myself. But sitting next to her, seeing the fear and sadness in her eyes, my anger slowly melted away. She looked so young, too young to have endured as much as she had.

I took her hand and explained that her sister missed her very much and that she was worried about her and just wanted her to be safe. I couldn't read the look she gave me. I kept talking to her, tried my best to comfort her, but I didn't know whether or not I was succeeding.

Maybe holding her hand was helping me more than it was helping her. Talking to her, seemed to get rid of my anger more than my telephone rant to Dr. Beekman. We rode the rest of the way with her clammy hand in mine.

When we got to the hotel, I was thinking, this could go one of two ways. It could be a knock down, drag out fight, Jerry Springer-style, or it could be all apologies and hugs like the last five minutes of a T.V. sitcom. I honestly didn't know what to expect as we walked through the door of Sandra's hotel room and she came face to face with her sister for the first time in months.

Sandra was sitting Indian style on one of the two beds in her double occupancy room, remote in hand. As soon as she saw Toni, she ran to her, grabbed her, and hugged her tightly. Toni was stiff as a board until she started shaking again. I couldn't tell if it was her withdrawal or emotion that was causing that.

Still holding her sister, Sandra mumbled in her hair, "I was so worried. He wouldn't let me see you."

"I didn't want you to see me like this," she said, crying. "I don't want to be like this anymore."

"I know. I know. We're going to get you some help." Sandra hadn't been given guardianship of her sister until her eighteenth birthday, but

I imagined she'd been playing the mother role for years before that. "You're going to be fine… everything's going to be fine," Sandra said.

Then, in a Dr. Jekyll and Mr. Hyde moment, Toni pulled away from her sister and pushed her down on the floor. She was on top of her throwing wild punches. For someone who looked so fragile and shuffled her feet when she walked, Toni seemed to get some strength from somewhere.

Some of those punches hit their target. Sandra was lying beneath her in a fetal position trying to protect her face. "This is all your fault… you left me… you let them take me!" Toni yelled in between punches.

It was James who broke it up. He grabbed Toni off her sister, lifting her cleanly off the floor and setting her down on the bed. That wasn't hard to do considering Toni only weighed about ninety pounds.

The punching had stopped but not the screaming. "You let them take me! This would have never happened if you hadn't let them take me away!"

Sandra sobbed loudly. I could tell that Toni's words had hurt Sandra more than her punches. "I had no choice!" she shouted. "I had to wait until I was old enough to become your guardian."

Sandra had confided in James that day in the diner that she had never been able to get Toni to open up about what happened to her in the foster home. But something must have happened, Sandra told him, because Toni wasn't the same girl when she came home; she was like a completely different person and it wasn't just the drugs. Even though Sandra had never been able to get Toni to break her silence, James was a professional and he had Toni telling us her deepest darkest secrets within minutes.

I imagined James using those same techniques in an interrogation room. But I could tell that this was more than just a job to him. He really wanted to help her. I wondered if this was still somehow connected to his need to redeem himself for not being able to give Gran and Pop some closure about what happened to my mother. I glanced at Pop, he sat quietly in a chair in the corner. I wondered if he was thinking about my mother, I wondered if he was reliving the worst experience of his life.

James sat down on the bed next to Toni and rubbed her back. He didn't say a word. He just let her continue to yell at Sandra. James nodded at Sandra as if to say, *Hang in there it's almost over*. When Toni was finally quiet, James asked her if she was telling the truth about wanting to get better.

She nodded.

"I'm going to help you then. I need you to trust me, though. Can you do that?"

She nodded, still breathing heavily.

"Good."

James told her that she would be able to put all of this behind her: the drugs, Atlantic, her mother being in prison. I had almost forgotten that what had started this downward spiral in their lives was their mother going to prison. I wondered if my father had supplied their mother's habit. Well, we had one thing in common: a parent in prison, a parent that had screwed up our lives.

"Before you can put this all behind you," James told Toni, "you need to talk about what happened in the foster home. Do you think you can do that?"

He was gentle with her. And after what seemed like a long time, she turned to him and started to talk. It was as if Pop, her sister, and I were invisible and only the two of them were in the room.

Chapter 51

When Toni's mother went to prison, Toni stopped going to school. She pretty much felt like it was nothing but a big waste of time. Then one day when she was minding her own business, not even doing anything, she was stopped by truancy officers. "The education police," she called them. They wrote her up, which was fine. She didn't care, but then later that week they made a follow-up visit at her apartment.

"That's how they found out there was no adult living with us," she said. "And they called child protective services."

She'd begged the social worker, Mrs. Andrea, not to separate her and Sandra. But she was an older woman, the type who was very stuck in her ways. She wasn't even willing to try to find a placement where she and Sandra could be together.

"I can barely get foster parents to take one teenager. How am I supposed to get someone to agree to two?" Ms. Andrea told Toni. She dismissed Toni's concerns. "The system is overcrowded. There's no way I can start taking request like that." She said she'd put Toni and Sandra with whoever agreed to take them.

"She dropped me off at a house in Brooklyn. She didn't even come inside with me. Just rolled down the window and yelled that she'd be back in two weeks to check on me."

Toni remembered that the house had a stale and musty smell. It wasn't even really like a foster home, it was more like an orphanage; kids were everywhere. She counted eight before she even made it past the living room. She felt overwhelmed and scared. She didn't know what she was supposed to do, or where she was supposed to go, and there were no adults in sight. She just sat there in the living room with her hands folded in her lap and forced a smile at anyone that walked past.

Over an hour later, Toni finally spotted an adult. Ms. Taylor introduced herself and told Toni that she could call her Joyce.

"Mrs. Joyce was crippled," Toni said. "She only had one leg and she'd take her prosthetic leg off during dinner and sit it against the side of the table. For the first couple of days, I couldn't even eat. All I could do was stare at it."

On that first day, Toni followed Joyce as she limped down the hallway, gave her a tour of the house, and showed her to the room that she would be sharing with four other girls.

Over the next few weeks children came and went. Ms. Joyce's house was only a temporary placement until children's services could find more permanent homes for the kids. Caleb arrived four days after Toni. He was older than Toni was. But she hadn't made any friends yet, so she was happy when he started talking to her. "He said he was from the Bronx too," Toni said.

He seemed really nice. They'd watch T.V. together or go hang out at the park. They had a good time together until one night she woke up with him on top of her.

Until that point, everyone in the hotel room had been absolutely silent except for the occasional encouraging word from James.

But Toni's last statement made Sandra gasp. And probably for the first time, Toni realized that we were all still sitting there listening to her. It was awkward being there; it was much worse than sitting in the back of Gran's car and listing to her conversation with Marie. In that hotel room, I felt out of place, like I had no business hearing the secrets of a girl I had only met for the first time a few hours ago.

I could see her start to clam up. James gave her his kindergarten teacher smile and told her that she was doing fine and that she would feel better once she let it out.

Toni turned her back to her audience and went back to focusing solely on James. No one could hear her screaming because Caleb had put a pillow over her face, she said. She felt like she was suffocating. Was he trying to kill her? She wondered, feeling herself start to black out. Maybe that would be best. Some days she wanted to die, to disappear, and let it all be over with. Toni turned and looked at her sister. "But then I thought about you," she said. "I didn't want you to have to be alone."

Toni said she started kicking and punching with all her strength, but she was getting light-headed, her arms felt rubbery, and she didn't know how much more she could take. She inhaled pillow foam, coughed, choked, and tried to scream, but there was no sound. The bed springs squeaked loudly, screaming out on her behalf.

And just when she thought things couldn't get any worse, "He stabbed me!" She thought she passed out after that. The last thing she remembered was being stabbed with some kind of needle.

The next day she was sick, she said. She couldn't tell if it had actually happened or if the whole thing was just a horrible nightmare. But the next night, the nightmare came back, and then the night after that, and then every night.

She was afraid to go to sleep; she was afraid to say anything. What if she got sent somewhere that was even worse?

It went on for months. He'd come into her room at night, stick her with a needle, and everything would fade away. She said she had no clue what he would do to her after the drugs started to kick in. Sometimes she woke up the next day in pain or with a funny taste in her mouth. One morning she woke up with a dark bruise on her leg.

She wanted to tell someone. She tried to talk to one of her

roommates, a girl named Latoya who was about her age. She asked her if Caleb had ever touched her, and the girl just stared at her expressionlessly. That's when she realized that there was a Don't Ask Don't Tell policy, just like in the projects. In that foster home everyone was blind, deaf, and mute. There were four other girls sharing the room with her and no one said a thing about it. They knew, she told James, they had to know what he was doing to her. Maybe he'd done the same thing to them, maybe they were just as scared as her.

After a while she started to convince herself that it wasn't so bad. The drugs didn't only make Caleb disappear, they made everything disappear, and that's what she wanted. When she was finally allowed to come home and live with her sister, she was already hooked. She couldn't function without the drugs. That's how she got mixed up with Atlantic.

Toni was finally silent, having come to what she considered as the end of her story. James told her it was not just an end, it was a whole new beginning for her. We'd been sitting there, listening to her for hours. One minute she'd be talking so fast that it sounded like a foreign language, and I was only able to catch about every third word. At other times her voice was slow and barely above a whisper and it was like she was reliving what happened.

"What happened to Caleb?" James wanted to know.

She shrugged. "He aged out."

He'd turned 18 and was no longer the state's problem. Off to go terrorize someone else, I suspected.

Sandra kept telling her how sorry she was. How things were going to be better now. James told Toni that he was going to keep his end of their agreement and get her the help she needed. Which was a good thing, because the tremors that shook her body were becoming more and more difficult to watch.

"Let's go," James told Toni.

"Where?"

"I told you we are going to get you some help."

Sandra gave her a quick hug and told her that she loved her and was proud of her. After James and Toni left, Pop, Sandra, and I just sat there, still shocked by everything we had just heard.

No doubt Caleb played a big part in Toni's suffering, but once she'd escaped that, another nightmare had started at Atlantic's hand. I couldn't help but wonder how many families besides my own had been ruined by Atlantic's and my father's actions.

Chapter 52

By the end of the day James had Toni set up in a residential treatment program in Staten Island, Sandra was safely tucked into her hotel room right next door to James' and Pop's, and I was in a cab on my way home.

On the ride, all I could think about was that the thing that had kept Toni fighting and had given her the strength to survive was the thought of her sister. For months Dee had been that person for me, my family, my strength.

I was still pissed that Dee had made me feel so stupid, but listening to Toni, it made me want to at least give him a chance to try to explain. I couldn't think of one, but maybe there was a reasonable explanation. Now that I was calmer, now that some of the initial shock had worn off I could give him a chance to tell me his side of the story, right?

If there was any possibility of us having a future together, and I still had serious doubts about that, it would depend on how he explained himself. So even though it had been a long day, as I slid my key into the door, I braced myself for a long night.

"Dee?"

No answer. I checked the bedroom, bathroom, nope. "Dee?" I called out to the empty apartment. I sat on the couch frustrated. The least he could do was be here when I got home.

I called Dee's cell phone. Maybe he was out with his brother planning to... my heart started pounding. I didn't let myself finish that thought. There was no answer. I started to get that all too familiar sinking feeling deep in the pit of my stomach. Something was very wrong.

I thought about Dee tied to that chair, bloody. That's when it hit me. "Oh no! No! No!" I jumped off the couch. My mind was racing. We had dropped him at the hospital... *I think he has broken ribs*, I remembered James saying.

I called a cab and went downstairs to wait in front of the building. I ran out of the apartment so fast that I forgot my coat. The cold crisp air tore through me.

I kept seeing Dee in the back of the car, reaching for me, trying to talk to me. I heard James say, I think he thought you were staying with him.

When the cab arrived, I slid into the backseat and rubbed my hands together in an attempt to create some warmth and gain some of the feeling back in my fingers.

"Mount Vernon Hospital," I told the driver.

Dee had lost consciousness sitting there tied to that chair. Of course he wasn't okay. How could I have just left him there like that? I was so close to fixing everything, getting rid of Atlantic and Aunt Jackie once and for all. I couldn't take it if Dee wasn't all right.

"Please. Please just let him be okay."

"Excuse me?"

I didn't exactly know who I was directing my pleas to, but I knew it wasn't the cab driver. "Nothing," I said.

He's fine, Brie, he's here and he's fine, I told myself as we pulled up to the hospital. They made you wait forever in the emergency room, that's what it was. *He had to wait a long time to be seen by the doctor, that's why he's not home yet, but he's fine.*

I ran into the hospital at full speed, dodging a baby stroller and a wheelchair along the way. The emergency room was packed: mothers rocking sick children, a man with an ice pack over his eye, another with a bandage around his head. Someone was talking loudly about the mishap they'd had while hanging Christmas lights. I scanned their faces. Dee was nowhere to be found.

It doesn't mean anything, he's here. He's probably just now being seen by the doctor, I reasoned. But as I approached the front desk, I couldn't prevent the panic that rose in me. I spotted a women sitting behind a Plexiglas window. Above her booth was a sign that listed symptoms and said "Please tell me immediately if you are suffering from any of these symptoms." I had three out of the five listed. My heart wouldn't stop pounding.

Her name tag introduced her as Rachel. She was playing a game of solitaire on her computer. I could see the reflection of the computer screen in her glasses. She didn't even acknowledge me standing there.

"Demetrius Sheppard," I said.

She looked up, noticing me for the first time. At first she just gave me a blank stare and then she had the nerve to cop and attitude. "What about him?" she said.

Daughter of infamous drug kingpin goes on shooting spree at local hospital, that would be the headline. I wondered if the stupid Plexiglas window was bulletproof. It was a good thing that James had retrieved his gun from me earlier, because if I were still walking around with it tucked into my waistband, the temptation might have been too much for me to ignore.

I took a deep breath. "Was Demetrius Sheppard admitted here today?"

She minimized her game of solitaire and typed in his name.

"What's your relation to the patient?"

Okay, now we were getting somewhere. At least I knew he was a patient. "I'm his girlfriend."

"Well, I can't give you any information if you are not family."

Family? If I wasn't so panicked I would have laughed at that. His so-called brother was the reason he was here in the first place! Not to mention he had tried to extort me out of nearly a million bucks. Or how about my family? My aunt had tried to set him up for a felony. Why not give her a visitor's pass?

Breathe, Brie, Breathe.

Rachel tapped one of her Lee Press-On Nails against window to get my attention. "What's your name?"

"Brianna Roberts?"

"Okay. Mr. Sheppard put you down as his emergency contact."

"Was there and emergency? I wasn't contacted."

She ignored my question. "That allows me to let you up to see him. He is in room 306, second set of elevators on your left."

I ran toward the elevator. I turned back for a minute and thought about asking Rachel about Dee's condition, but I decided against wasting time on that when I saw that she had already resumed her game of solitaire. By the time I had made it up to the third floor, all types of thoughts were running through my head.

"306, 306, 306," I turned around in a circle trying to figure out which way to go.

"Can I help you?" a petite blond nurse said. Her smile offended me considering the situation.

"I'm looking for Demetrius Sheppard, room 306."

"That's all the way at the end of the corridor on your right."

"Thank you. Thank you." I broke out into a run.

"Miss!" the nurse called to me. "It's not safe to run in the hospital. Someone could get hurt."

Someone's already hurt, I thought.

"Anyway, he is still under anesthesia," she said referring to a clipboard she was holding. "He'll be out for at least a few more hours, so no need to rush."

I walked back toward her. She seemed to have the information I needed. "What happened to him? Why is he under anesthesia?"

"He came in pretty severely beaten." She referred to her clipboard again. "He had three broken ribs, one of which punctured his lung. He also suffered a perforated spleen, which had to be removed. He had several hours of surgery. That's why he is still under anesthesia." She tapped her pen against the clipboard. "His injuries are both serious and painful, so he will be sedated to help with pain management."

Blondie was thorough in her explanation, but it was all very clinical. There was no indication that he was anything more than another set of medications to keep in order or another set of vital signs for her to keep track of. I thanked her for the information. The sour smell of medication and sickness wafted up my nose as I rushed down the hallway to Dee's room.

From the moment I first suspected that he was still in the hospital, all I wanted to do was see him, but when I finally laid eyes on him, it wasn't relief that I felt. I gasped, covered my mouth with my hand.

The white florescent light at the head of his hospital bed somehow made him look small and fragile. My eyes moved from his swollen face to the clear plastic tubes peeking out from under the blanket and the half-empty IV bags beside his bed.

I sat in the chair next to his bed and held his hand. I watched his eyes move rapidly behind his eyelids. Even through all of the swelling, I thought I saw a scowl on his face. Was he dreaming?

For the umpteenth time since this whole thing started—since the jury said guilty, since my aunt said Daddy was a drug dealer, since the people at the bank said "trust fund"—I cried.

I held Dee's hand and I cried. I let my tears flow freely in the darkness of that hospital room. At some point I fell asleep. I remember dreaming about Dee on a bus. Not the bus that I had met him on; it was another bus. He was there with another family. I sat there invisible and watched him with his arm around an attractive woman. He kissed her on the check and they both laughed at something cute that the baby sitting on her lap had done. My heart was breaking.

Wake up! Wake up! I told myself but the nightmare wouldn't release me. I felt Dee's hand moving, the one that I had fallen asleep holding. I heard him moan. That's what finally got rid of Mr. Sandman.

Chapter 53

Dee was moaning and making a kind of gurgling noise. I squeezed his hand and called his name but got no response. The morning sun had come up and the light that filtered through the window allowed me to see him more clearly.

His face was still swollen and covered with bruises of all shades of purple and blue, and there was dried blood under his chin. His eyes were swollen shut so it was hard to tell if he was awake. But he started to squeeze my hand a little.

"Dee?"

He squeezed.

"Oh, babe. You had me so worried." I clasped his hand in both of mine, rubbed his arm. "I went to the apartment last night and… I had no idea you were this hurt. I'm so sorry, babe. I'm so sorry."

Most of the time my dreams faded away quickly, like a shadow when the sun rises, but not that one. That nightmare, seeing Dee with another woman and a kid, the thought was almost unbearable and it lingered for days. I knew I had to do my best to make it work, no matter what.

"I love you," I told him. It was only the day before that I'd been sitting in the back of the car with Toni sandwiched in between us. I could not have imagined then that I would ever say those words to him again. "I love you."

He squeezed my hand a little harder this time. He opened his mouth but nothing audible came out. He tried again but there was still no sound. He struggled again and let out a little croak.

My nerves were completely shot. When I realized he couldn't talk, I started to panic. I dropped his hand, ran out into the hallway and yelled for a nurse.

It wasn't Blondie who rushed into the room, it was another nurse. This one was tall and slim and wearing way too much makeup. If she ever stopped wearing it, Maybelline's stock would plummet.

"His vitals look good, stable," she said.

"How can he be good? He can't talk!"

"Calm down please," she said. "You are going to upset the patient. This happens a lot when patients go under anesthesia and have been unconscious for a while. It's only temporary." She should have led with the "it's only temporary" part.

"Try feeding him ice chips. That should help," she said. "He'll be able to pick up on your agitation, so I want you to stay calm. Try to talk to him and keep him calm. Okay? Do you think you can do that?"

I nodded.

When she left the room, Dee immediately started struggling to speak again. I ran my fingers across his chapped lips. "Shh. Just relax. It's okay," I said.

Talk to him and keep him calm, I thought. Well, that was easier said than done. Everything that I wanted to talk to him about had the potential of causing agitation. We'd had very few calm conversations recently. Very few real conversations at all.

I laid down beside him in his bed. I fantasized about us lying out on the beach on some tropical island. I was feeding him grapes. I was no longer in that hospital room lying next to him in that uncomfortable bed, feeding him ice chips.

When I was seven years old, my father took me to the Bronx Zoo for the first time. I remember being so excited about it that I could barely sleep the night before. I was standing in front of the bear cage mesmerized; I remember thinking that they looked nothing like Yogi Bear, my favorite cartoon at the time. And when I turned around Daddy was nowhere in sight.

When I first started going to school I use to have serious separation anxiety. I would cry for hours. At the end of the school day I couldn't get into my father's arms fast enough. The school nurse told my father it was completely normal. "Children from single-parent homes often have a more difficult time with the separation than other children," she'd told him.

Over time it got better, but the fear never completely went away. Then, that day in the zoo, my worst nightmare came true: I was lost, alone. I could remember the feeling of terror like it was yesterday. I searched the crowd frantically. I was so little, and people were moving around in all directions. I didn't know where to look, I didn't know what to do.

I guess I did what any kid would do: I burst into tears and started screaming at the top of my lungs. A man and his two daughters approached me. "It's okay sweetie. Are you lost? What's your name?" the stranger said.

"Brianna."

"Who did you come here with?"

"My daddy."

"Okay, let's see if we can find him."

I held on to his hand for dear life. He took me to the security booth. We rode around in one of those golf cart things looking for my father. I sat next to the man and cried into his chest the entire time. We still couldn't find him. I was completely panicked. I was crying so hard that I couldn't catch my breath.

When we returned to the security office, there Daddy was. He looked just as scared as I did. I'd never been more relieved in my life.

Talk to him, try to keep him calm, the nurse had advised. So I decided to tell him something that I had never told him before. Nothing about my aunt or Atlantic or the money.

Lying in the hospital bed next to Dee, I don't know why it was this story that came to mind. Well I guess I do, I told him that he was like that man that helped me in the park. He squeezed my hand when my voice started to crack a little.

"You rescued me," I told Dee. It sounded a lot more sappy when I said it out loud than it did in my head. But whatever, there was no point in holding back now. "You took care of me. I felt scared, lost and alone and you took care of me. I will always love you for that."

Chapter 54

For the next two days, I kept a vigil at Dee's bedside. Pop and James dropped by a few times. They were both getting a little antsy about the Atlantic situation. "We're running on borrowed time," James reminded me. We had to finish what we started.

I saw Atlantic lean close to me and heard him tell me to think long and hard before I tried to get away with whatever game I was playing. It was only a matter of time before Atlantic figured out the truth, and James was right, we had to be prepared. But I could only focus on one major catastrophe at a time. So I told James that Atlantic would just have to wait.

Dee and I had been having communication problems for months, but as the days passed all I really wanted was for his voice to come back. Forget Atlantic, forget my aunt, I just wanted to hear Dee say back to me what I had been telling him, "I love you."

For the first few days, the medicine kept him pretty knocked out most of the time. In between his naps, I had one-sided conversations with him. I told him little stories and things I'd never told him before. I filled him in on everything I'd learned about my family on my trip down south. I'd never gotten the chance to do that because I had rushed back to bail him out, and since then all of our focus had been on keeping him out of jail.

When the swelling in his face started to go down and he was able to open his eyes a little, we channel surfed on the TV that was suspended from the ceiling. I sat in the chair next to his bed, elbow on the armrest, chin in the palm of one hand, remote in the palm of the other, quickly clicking my way through the four channels (one of which was in Spanish).

Unfortunately, there was no breaking news story about a major drug bust at Atlantic's apartment. I often found myself daydreaming about things like that, different scenarios that would solve everything, tie it up in a nice neat little package that could be easily discarded.

Every now and then, in a raspy voice, Dee would mumble something that I couldn't understand. It wasn't until the third day that his voice returned. I knew this because in a surprisingly strong voice, he said, "We need to talk."

From my chair next to his bed, I leaned over, held my hand to his mouth, and told him, "Me first."

Over the last three days, I'd had more than enough time to think about how stupid and selfish I'd acted. Sure, Atlantic had scared me with the idea that he and Dee had been working together, but I knew Dee. I should have given him the benefit of the doubt. It was clear what I had to do.

"When I was a little girl," I told Dee, "I used to watch all of these Disney movies, and the prince and the princess would live happily ever after." Behind his puffy eyelids, Dee rolled his eyes. "I knew even then that it wasn't real. Even though I didn't have both of my parents around so that I could see what a grown up relationship was suppose to be like, I still somehow knew that the fairytales weren't real. Relationships aren't perfect. They're hard work and as you work at it, if you're lucky, you grow more in love with the person you're with."

He pulled his hand away when I tried to touch it, but I still continued, "That's what I want more than anything. I want us to keep working at it. I don't want you to judge me by things that my family has done. And Dee... I promise... I promise from now on I will do the same for you. I don't care who your brothers are as long as you are honest with me. No more secrets. I know that we can make this work."

Okay, I'd finally gotten it out. Said what I'd really wanted to say for the last three days while I was telling him stories and heeding the nurse's advice not to agitate him. Little did I know, he wasn't ready to kiss and make up.

While I had been planning what to say to him, he had been laying there in his hospital bed doing the same thing. But the conversation he had constructed went very differently and he was about to let me know it.

There should have been flashing danger signs or something to let me know that there were hidden landmines. Something to warn me that he was bringing out the heavy artillery. One false move and I could end up splattered all over the walls.

When I finished talking, the first thing he did was laugh. I guess I was seeing what I wanted to see because at first I thought he was happy. I thought he was relieved that we had agreed to let bygones be bygones. I couldn't have been more wrong.

He pushed aside the sliding table that was across his hospital bed, pressed the button on the side of the bed, and adjusted it so that he was sitting up and looking directly at me. That's when I saw it: his clenched jaw, the darkness in his eyes.

"I didn't even expect you to be here." He spat out the words, like they left a bad taste in his mouth. "Isn't that your M.O.?"

So making up wasn't going to be as easy as I thought. I'd had a chance to show him how angry I was, ignoring him in the car, leaving him alone at the emergency room. Now it was his turn.

He glared at me. "You stick around long enough for people to disappoint you and then you make a run for it," he said.

The look he was giving me... if looks could kill, I would have been in worse shape than him.

"When the going gets tough," he said. "Brie gets going. Isn't that what you did with your father?"

Back then, Dee couldn't have uttered more hurtful words, and the look on his face said he knew that. He definitely wasn't fighting fair. He was purposely trying to hurt me. It was his way of ignoring my outstretched hand like I'd done his. That much I'd figured out.

"Your father disappointed you," he continued. "You wrote him off, scribbled him out of your life with permanent marker." He was screaming, gesturing wildly with his hands. "You... you create these ideals that you want people to live up to... but it's impossible."

I tried to let his words wash over me, roll off my back. But I couldn't. I balled my hands into fists; let my nails dug deep into my palms. I tried to concentrate on that pain, instead of the daggers he was throwing at me, but it was no use.

My throat tightened, my eyes burned with tears that ached to be released, and I felt my lip start to quiver. Why did he have to bring my father into this?

I tried, but I hadn't quite mastered my poker face yet. I know he saw the look on my face, but he had no sympathy. "People aren't perfect," he said. "No one can live up to your unrealistic expectations. And this might be news to you, but you're not perfect either. How do you think I felt when I tried to talk to you in the car and you shut me down... like I meant absolutely nothing to you?"

He'd finally asked me an actual question. One that I could answer, or so I thought. When I opened my mouth the only thing that escaped was a squeaky cry.

I felt like I was suffocating, like the walls of the small hospital room were collapsing on top of me. I needed a time out. Just a few minutes, maybe a walk down the hall and back and then I'd be okay. Then I'd be able to answer him.

"There she goes," he said as I moved toward the door. "Make a run for it, Brie."

I never actually left the room, just stood there facing the door, with my back to him and my eyes closed. I was thinking about the best way to handle this. I'd think of things to say, but then I wouldn't say them. I remember wishing that Gran was there. I could have used some of her advice. *You get more with honey than vinegar. Men have a lot of ego.*

This is not how the conversation was supposed to go. In the days that I'd waited for him to regain his voice, I imagined he'd say that he was wrong for not telling me about Atlantic. He'd say he was sorry and that he would never lie to me again. But there was no apology.

After a few cleansing breaths I turned and faced him. I was ready to get this conversation back on track. "This is about you and me," I said. "Not my father. Don't try to take the focus off the real issue. You lied to me. That's what this is about."

He had the nerve to let out a sigh, like I was annoying him, like for some reason I just didn't get it. "You say that I should be honest with you, but I have never lied to you." I watched as he balled his hands into fists, and then winced feeling the pain it caused at his IV injection sight. "Atlantic is not my brother!" he yelled.

I gave him my *you cannot be serious* look. I wasn't a skeptic; I was a downright nonbeliever.

Obviously the pain medication the doctors were giving him was a little too strong or maybe he had been dipping into his brother's drug supply, because he had to be on something if he thought I was going to fall for that.

He's not my brother? Was that all that he could come up with? I mean, Atlantic had practically recited to me their whole family tree, and Dee had the nerve to say they weren't brothers.

I crossed my arms in front of me. I read somewhere that it was a defensive gesture. I felt defensive.

How stupid did he think I was? Maybe there was an explanation. Maybe Dee had some type of undetected brain injury. Or maybe I'd just heard him wrong. "What?" I said, looking for clarification.

"Yes, Atlantic and I have the same parents. But it's been a very long time since we've been brothers." He put the word brothers in air quotes, like that made some big difference to me. "My whole family has disowned him."

"Yeah, Atlantic mentioned something about that. We had a very interesting chat."

He ignored me. "My family disowned him because a guy pulled a gun on my mother over something that Atlantic had done. She wasn't hurt, but it was a close call. That was the last straw for my father. Before the other day, I hadn't spoken to him since the day my father put him out. So he's not a brother to me. I would walk past him on the street like any other stranger. Don't you get it? I didn't lie to you."

"Didn't you basically just tell me that I had turned away from my father because he disappointed me? So how can you justify lying to me by claiming that Atlantic is not your brother because he disappointed you?" It seemed like a valid question to me, but he ignored it completely.

"My brother, Jeff, he has always been a follower. I told you that. He came to New York to be with Atlantic and I'd been trying to convince him to cut his ties with Atlantic once and for all. I told you all of that, too. And I told you how dangerous Atlantic is. I never lied to you. What would telling you that Atlantic and I have the same parents have accomplished? Tell me that. I don't consider him my brother, so I never lied to you."

I was about to answer his question, but he held up his hand.

"And the difference between my relationship with him and your relationship with your father is that Atlantic has been given more than enough opportunities to change. My family did everything they possibly could. Bailed him out of jail, got him counseling, put him into job training programs. We even moved trying to keep him away from the bad crowd he was running with. None of it worked.

"You know, that's the first thing you asked me that day on the bus when I told you my brother was in jail. You asked me if he was guilty, why I still visited him. To you, once you found out that your father wasn't this perfect person… it was too much for you to handle and you walked away." He paused to take a breath. "You say you don't believe in fairytales, but that's exactly what you are looking for. That's why you ignored me in the car. You felt like your fairytale had fallen apart."

He should've given up on the EKG technician career a long time ago, and gone into politics. That was obviously his true calling. He had an answer for everything. The more I listened to him, the more my anger started to match his. By the time he'd finished I was furious.

"You can argue it whichever way you want," I said. "Whatever makes you sleep better at night—"

"I sleep just fine, thank you. How are you sleeping these days, Brie?"

"You can say what you want to say, but you did lie to me!" It's a good thing Dee had a private hospital room. "You lied by omission!" I screamed. "The bottom line is if you were upfront with me about it I wouldn't have been blindsided when Atlantic sprung that little fact on me. It would have allowed me to avoid questioning our relationship."

"Questioning our relationship?" He shifted in the bed.

He was kidding right? "Of course I questioned our relationship! What else would I do when he asked me if I really thought us meeting on the bus was a coincidence? He insinuated that you had been working with him the whole time. Like you two had this master plan and I was your mark. I pictured you and him sitting around laughing about how I had fallen for you so easily. I felt stupid."

"If you really think I'm capable of that, then you don't know me at all."

"I know I messed up too. But I'm not going to let you turn this around on me. Like you aren't even a little at fault, like you didn't consciously decide not to tell me Atlantic was your brother."

I paused, gave him another opportunity to apologize, but he stayed silent. "I know now that I should have given you a chance to explain before I jumped to conclusions, but at that point I didn't know what to think," I said. "And that could've been avoided if you would have just told me the truth like you're doing now."

Just say sorry, just say sorry, I was chanting that in my head. I don't know if I wanted to get that message across more to him or me. I just wanted this argument to be over. We both just sat and stared at each other for a while.

"I'm getting a headache," was what he finally said. I was the one that should have had a headache, considering talking to him was like banging my head against a brick wall. "I don't want to talk about this anymore. You know everything now and you know I love you. I'm not going to make any more excuses. If I could do it over, I would tell you. To me, it wasn't important, but I can see why you would have wanted to know." He paused for a moment. "I'm so tired, Brie. I'm just tired of all the drama. I want us to focus on us. I just want us to get away from all of this mess, so that we can focus on ourselves and our relationship."

Was there an "us"? I wondered. Reading the question on my face, he threw it back at me.

"That's if we have a relationship left to salvage," he said, looking for confirmation. I wondered if he realized that he was nervously twirling his hospital I.D. bracelet. He was waiting for me to tell him that our relationship wasn't beyond repair.

There was a long pause on my end. It was like a moment of silence, mourning the relationship that we might not be able to fix. I managed to tell him the same thing I'd been telling him for weeks. "We'll be okay. Everything will be over soon and we'll be able to leave the Bronx for good."

I had no doubt that we would be leaving the Bronx soon, but my confidence when it came to whether we would be okay, well, both of us knew that the jury was still out on that one.

For a while the silence just seemed to hang in the room, invisible yet obvious. In that silence, I let myself think about my father. Dee's mention of him had made those thoughts surface again.

I hadn't thought about him in a long time. I hadn't thought about *him*, I'd thought about what he'd done, I'd thought about the mess that I was trying to clean up. But it had been a very long time since I'd let myself think about *him*. I thought about how despite everything, I still missed him, how much I still loved him, how much I still needed him.

Emotionally and physically exhausted, sitting in the chair beside Dee's hospital bed, I drifted off to sleep feeling... I don't know what I was feeling, really. Guilty? Annoyed? How could I still have those feelings for my father after everything that he'd done?

Chapter 55

After a four-day hospital stay, Dee had healed enough to be released. He still wasn't a hundred percent; he had trouble getting around on his own and there was still some swelling, but to the naked eye he definitely appeared to be on the mend. What the doctors couldn't see were the emotional scars that he had, that we both had, the open wounds that were infected and festering just below the surface. I couldn't help but wonder how long it would really take for the two of us to heal from everything that had happened this past year.

As the nurse prepared his discharge papers, I stood in the bathroom of Dee's hospital room. I didn't recognize the sleep deprived person that stared back at me when I looked in the mirror.

As we stared at each other, I thought about how much I'd changed in the last year. With the exception of the bags under my eyes, and the much shorter hairstyle, physically I pretty much looked the same, but beyond that I was a completely different person.

It was easy to focus on the people around me, what they had done. It was much more complicated to look at myself. Who was I really? The motherless daughter? The daughter of a convict? The trust fund baby?

I'd thought finding out the answers would make me feel complete, but I felt even more lost. For every answer that I'd found there was another question. As usual I forced myself not to think about that.

The cab dropped us off curbside in front of our apartment building. James had offered to give us a ride, but it was also the first day that Toni could receive visitors at the treatment center, so I insisted that he and Sandra go see her.

Dee leaned his weight against me as we walked gingerly over the slush covered ground and up the stairs to our apartment.

The day before I had taken a brief leave of absence from his bedside. In preparation for Dee's release, I'd cleaned the apartment from top to bottom. I'd stocked the fridge with all of his favorite foods, and I'd picked up some magazines and the first week's worth of his prescriptions.

But when we made our way into the apartment, the first thing we both noticed was the smell. *Oh crap,* I thought. Literally. Crap.

It was actually kind of funny. That wasn't how I wanted to introduce him to my surprise, my peace offering.

I grabbed Dee's hand and walked him over to the crate that I had hidden behind the couch. There he was, our new puppy, a three month old boxer. Dee smiled and thankfully when he did I saw him and not Atlantic.

I smiled back. "What do you think?"

"He's cute," Dee said.

"He's a boxer."

"Yeah, I know. I always wanted a dog growing up, but my mother claimed she was allergic." He tried to bend down to pet the puppy but his body rejected that idea. I took the puppy out of the crate. He immediately stood on his hind legs and placed his paws against the front of Dee's legs. He wagged his tail.

"I never really believed her though…about the allergy," he said while petting the top of the puppy's head. "Every good report card and every special occasion, a dog was all I ever asked for. I would always end up with a video game or something." The puppy was still happily wagging his tail. "Once she even got me one of those robotic dogs.

That's probably when I gave up asking."

I laughed. "Well, I'm glad you like him. Now you don't have to be bitter anymore."

"What's his name?"

"I think we should call him Orlando."

He raised his eyebrow. "Why?" The dog looked at us both, cocked his head to the side a little.

I looked away from Dee. I occupied myself with the puppy and said, "I've been so selfish. I see that now. You were trying to protect me and I didn't listen… we… we should have moved a long time ago, when you first mentioned it. I guess… I guess it's just my way of telling you that I'm sorry about what's happened and as soon as its cleared up…" I looked at him then. "I'm ready" I watched him smile. "So since we're moving to Florida, I thought Orlando would be a fitting name."

"I don't like it," he said. He stepped closer to me. "He looks more like a Raleigh. Don't you think?"

"Really?" A wide smile broke out on my face.

"We've both been selfish," he said and kissed me on the forehead. "Not just you. I think you need to have the opportunity to really get to know your family and I want to be a part of that. Raleigh sounds like a good place for us to settle."

It was always hard for Dee to say he was sorry, but then he did something like that and made me fall in love with him all over again. We still had some kinks to work out in our relationship, but the love wasn't a problem.

I'd wanted to move to Raleigh all along. All I needed to do was finalize the arrangements with Gran. But I would have put that aside to make Dee happy, and obviously he was willing to do the same for me. That was a pretty solid foundation… everything else, we could work out.

It was turning out to be a pretty good day: Dee was home, he liked the puppy, we were moving to Raleigh, everything was falling into place. I remember that's what I was thinking when the phone rang. I had just set Dee up in bed and handed him a magazine.

When I answered the phone, I reluctantly told the operator I would accept the charges. After some brief, not so pleasant pleasantries, my father began to talk to me as if he was in a confessional: *forgive me, Brie, for I have sinned.*

My ears perked up when he said he was going to tell me what he should have told me a long time ago. He said I deserved to know the truth.

Yeah, I thought, *tell me something I don't know.* That's exactly what he did.

He told me that when his mother was pregnant with Aunt Jackie, he caught his father cheating—walked right in on them in his mother's bed. His mother was in the hospital. She was having a difficult pregnancy, high blood pressure or something.

"I was just a kid," he said. "Not even ten years old."

His father told him that it had to be their little secret. His mother was already sick. "You don't want to make her sicker, do you, buddy?" He put on that little voice people use when they're talking to children.

"That's what he said to me," my father said. "Of course I didn't want to make my mother sicker... but I was just a kid. I couldn't keep such a big secret."

He'd tried, though. For days he couldn't eat or sleep. When his mother got home from the hospital, she knew something was wrong. She kept asking him to talk to her and he'd held out as long as he could. He finally gave in and told her what he'd seen.

"When she confronted my father about it... the look he gave me, I was so scared. He wouldn't hit my mother but he didn't hesitate to hit me. That was the worst beating I'd ever gotten."

His mother tried to break it up, but she was pregnant and there was nothing she could do. "When my father had exhausted himself, I ran to my mother. I sat quivering in her arms."

Even though his mother wasn't working because she was sick at the time, she didn't think twice before kicking his father out. She had the locks changed the next day while he was at work. He and his mother packed up his father's stuff in garbage bags and put them outside the front door.

Months went by and they didn't see or hear from him. Then one Saturday morning, my father said, he woke up and his father was sitting at the kitchen table, holding Jackie in his lap.

"He had never seen her before. He looked so comfortable sitting there rocking her. I wondered if I had imagined the whole thing, because the way he was sitting there it seemed like he'd never left. But then he gave me that look, that same look of disappointment and disgust that he'd given me the day he'd left.

"For a while, that's what he did, came and went as he pleased. Then, he stopped coming around all together. And we were on their own."

As I listened to him, I thought he was trying to give me some excuse for why he'd lied to me. But I could tell it was more than that. He seemed to really want me to understand; not necessarily forgive, just understand.

After he finished his story he told me that for a long time he blamed himself. If he had only kept his father's secret, his family wouldn't have had to struggle so much.

"I couldn't take back what I'd done, but I had to take his place, I had to be the man of the house."

The phone was silent for a moment or two. Then the operator let us know that our time was up. Before either of us could figure out what so say, the line went dead.

Chapter 56

O n the first day of the trial, people were packed into the courtroom like sardines. By 9:00 am the court officers were turning people away. Most of the faces I didn't recognize. But what did I
expect? The news had been running the story for weeks. Enquiring
minds wanted to know.

I watched as the defense attorney nodded and whispered something to his client. The defense attorney was a public defender named
Mr. Jacobs. He was a scrawny guy, with a hippy ponytail that hung
midway down his back. It looked as though he'd never owned an iron
in his life. In the interviews I'd had with him, he seemed nice enough,
but he liked to play dumb, give you this false sense of security, make
you think the two of you were on the same side, make you think he
wasn't a threat when he was.

On the other side of the room was the prosecutor, Randy Knox.
I'd had many meetings with Mr. Knox over the last few weeks as well.
He was the polar opposite of Mr. Jacobs. We would meet in his spacious office that was wallpapered with his degrees and awards. He
knew he was smart, and if for some reason you didn't know, he was
not going to hesitate to tell you. I assumed he'd invested a hefty penny
in his wardrobe. There was nothing understated about him.

Between gulps of coffee, Judge Katz explained to the attorneys and
the jury the rules of his courtroom and how the trial would proceed.

When he spoke I was distracted by his turkey neck that flapped loosely and hung down the front of his robe.

Judge Katz was an older guy, mid-sixties if I had to take a guess. He had an enviable tan considering spring weather hadn't even hit yet. He said that he'd been playing a charity golf tournament in Palm Springs but was called back for the trial because another judge had been in a car accident. I saw Mr. Jacobs whisper something to his client again.

During opening statements both Jacobs and Knox sounded like politicians. They made promises to the jury about what they would prove. Then it was time for the first witness. Sandra glanced quickly at the defense table before she took the stand.

Sandra looked mature and trustworthy in the navy skirt suit that Gran had helped her pick out for the occasion. Of course Pop teased that Gran was just using that as an excuse to hit the mall, her favorite pastime.

Sandra in a very calm and clear voice, just as she had practiced, told the court about how she had been forced to make a false criminal accusation to the police. She remained calm even when asked about her sister's drug problem and subsequent admission to a treatment program. She was questioned for over two hours and never once lost her cool, much to the disdain of the defense.

When the judge called the next witness I didn't realize that I was holding my breath until I started to feel light-headed. When Daddy entered the courtroom, his eyes searched the crowd looking for me, like he had done so many times in the prison visitation room. Like then, I waved to get his attention. When he saw me he smiled and mouthed I love you.

Chapter 57

By the second day after Dee's release from the hospital, he was already complaining that I was hovering.

Yes, he had taken his medicine.

No, he didn't need anything.

Yes, he was sure.

So when James called and reminded me that if Atlantic hadn't already figured out the truth, he would soon, I agreed to leave Dee home alone and go meet with the prosecutor on Dee's case.

By that point, Ms. Fleming from the bank also had me on speed dial. She was getting nervous. Atlantic was calling her two or three times a day wondering what the holdup was. Why hadn't the money cleared in his account yet? She said that she was running out of excuses. She said that she could really get in trouble for doing this. A fake money transfer had to be against a number of laws. I told her not to worry, that it was all legitimate FBI business.

But that wasn't entirely true. For our little investigation to be legit, we had to get the prosecutor on board. I didn't think that would be too hard though. Why would the prosecutor go after Dee with such a weak case when we could deliver a much bigger fish? And I planned to deliver Atlantic on a silver platter. I knew that Atlantic had escaped going to prison quite a few times before, so the prosecutor should jump at the opportunity to put him away.

When we arrived at his office, Mr. Knox gave James, Sandra, and myself firm handshakes and instructed us to have a seat. He sat across from us behind his big mahogany desk and eyed us somewhat suspiciously. He wore a fancy suit with a pocket square that matched his tie. He was trying hard to dress the part. Maybe he was trying to overcompensate for the fact that he was so young, *Doogie Howser* young.

His pale blue eyes must have noticed me giving him the once over, because he put a little bass in his voice, and started to talk with more authority. I noticed that he smelled as though he'd been sucking on garlic mints. I'd find out later that it was chronic halitosis.

He threw around some legal words that he knew we wouldn't understand. That's when James adjusted himself in his seat and made sure his badge was visible. It was like an old west showdown. I might have laughed if I wasn't so tense. The bottom line was that all of the work that we had done now rested in the hands of a guy that probably still put on Clearasil at night.

James started the conversation and Sandra and I followed. We each told what we knew. Mr. Knox listened, nodded at times and asked follow up questions.

Atlantic had been the primary focus of the conversation, but I didn't want Aunt Jackie to feel left out.

"Atlantic is a menace to the community," I said. "No doubt about it, but when it comes to framing Dee, my aunt, Jacqueline Roberts—" I spelled her name, he wrote it down. "—she initiated the plan. So by no means is she innocent in all of this."

His eyes widened when I told him about our fight at the bank, about the guns under her couch that Dee had told me about, about my suspicions that she was somehow involved in dealing drugs.

I'd thought about all of it a million times before, but there was something about saying it out loud that made something click in my head. It was like those stubborn and elusive puzzle pieces that I'd been trying to fit into place for months were finally coming together, the picture was finally coming into focus.

I closed my eyes for a minute, right in the middle of talking to Mr. Knox. Segments of conversations and things that I'd seen flickered across the insides of my eyelids.

"I'll kill you."

"She is a very dangerous woman, be careful."

"Your father's flaw was trusting the wrong people."

"It wasn't her husband."

I was finally starting to make out the picture and I didn't like what I saw.

It was Sandra who elbowed me and brought me back to the present, brought me back to Mr. Knox's office.

"Oh, sorry," I said. "Where were we?"

Mr. Knox picked some invisible lint off of his fancy suit. "I was saying that we obviously have no case against Demetrius without Sandra's testimony and since she was coerced into making the false report we are not going to charge her for that offense." As he was talking I noticed how obnoxiously well manicured his fingernails were, perfect and square. I glanced down at my own fidgeting hand with its nails bitten down to nubs, a nervous habit I'd picked up in the last few months.

"We'll go after your aunt and Atlantic," Mr. Knox was saying. "We might be able to get one to flip on the other and build and even stronger case. But I've got to be honest with you. Our priority here is going to be Atlantic."

That wasn't exactly what I wanted to hear. In my mind Aunt Jackie was just as guilty as Atlantic—she deserved to go to prison—but I wasn't the one sitting behind the desk.

The meeting wasn't all bad. I didn't leave empty handed. I walked out of there with signed paperwork that formally dropped the charges against Dee. When I got back to the apartment and casually handed those papers to Dee, the mixture of shock and joy on his face was priceless.

As excited as I was for him, for both of us, I couldn't help but feel unsettled. If the feeling that I'd had earlier turned out to be true, this nightmare that I'd been living for the last year was far from over.

Chapter 58

Later that same evening, as if the day hadn't been eventful enough already, my father called again. He was starting to make that a habit, one that I wasn't sure I wanted to encourage. Talking to him always left me feeling exhausted and confused. Despite all of that, for some reason I still said yes when the operator asked if I would accept the charges.

"I know I was being a selfish jerk," he started.

Acknowledging you have a problem is the first step, I thought.

"I miss you so much, Brie. I've been writing you letters."

I never got any letters. Might have started a bon fire if I had.

"Telling you not to visit... that wasn't to protect you... it's just that... that every time I looked at you staring at me across that table all loving and optimistic... I couldn't stop thinking about how much I'd messed up. How much I'd let you down, you and your mother. You look so much like her... sometimes it hurts to look at you."

The unexpected mention of my mother sent a piercing pain through me. It started in the pit of my stomach and radiated to every inch of my body. My instincts told me to make it stop.

Shut up, shut up, stop talking, I wanted to say but didn't. Instead I took the opportunity to confirm what I'd already figured out.

"She did it... Aunt Jackie. She killed my mother."

"Oh, Brie." He groaned, and that pretty much said it all.

"Your mother was such a wonderful woman," he said. "Being around her made me want to be a better man. When I asked her to marry me I had every intention of turning my life around. I told Jackie that I was out, that I was done with dealing." He inhaled audibly. "She went crazy when I told her that. I mean I knew she was a little... a little...."

I could sure think of a couple of words to describe her.

"...But I never expected her to... to..." His voice trailed off as he started to cry.

Through his sobs he answered the question that I'd asked him all those years ago as a confused kindergartener: Why don't I have a mommy?

"Alecia didn't know anything about my dealing and I wanted to keep it that way. I wanted to quit before she ever found out. I wanted to put that life behind me and start a new life with her.

"But Jackie got so pissed. She said no one was going to mess with her money, not even me. Then Alecia found out. And I thought she was going to leave me, I really did. I couldn't blame her. She'd stuck beside me when her family had doubts about me and here I was proving them all right.

"But she didn't leave me. She said that she still loved me, and we had you on the way. She wanted us to be a family. But I had to promise her that I would stop and I did stop. That's what sent Jackie off the deep end. I knew Jackie would be upset, but I never thought she would hurt Alecia."

I knew it was a stupid question before I even finished asking it. "Why didn't you go to the police?"

"Brie, I couldn't turn her in. It would be like turning myself in. At first when Alecia disappeared, I didn't know what to think. I mean there was no body or anything. I knew something was wrong though. She wanted more than anything to be a mother, so I knew that even if she had gotten fed up and left me, she would never ever leave you.

"I paced around for three days. I called everyone I knew, everyone she knew. I didn't know what to do. And Jackie, she just sat back and watched as I slowly went insane looking for Alecia. She didn't say a word.

"It got to the point where all I could do was stay in the house all day and hope she'd call. It wasn't until Jackie realized that I wasn't staying on top of things, that I wasn't making money, that's when she finally told me... She told me to suck it up because Alecia wasn't coming back. The way she said it, with such confidence... I knew.

"When Jackie finally told me what she had done, of course I wanted to go to the police... of course I did. But Jackie said if she was going down so was I."

I would have still turned her in. I didn't care if I went to jail. I didn't care what happened to me. I already felt dead inside. Then I thought about you. In all of my panic, I seemed to have forgotten about this perfect beautiful baby that I had. If I went to jail, who would take care of you? I owed it to Alecia to be around for you, Brie. That's what she wanted, for us to be a family.

"I loved her so much. I never wanted any of this to happen." His voice trailed off a little. "Brie you know I love you too, right? I know you have doubts about me now because of what's happened, but don't ever doubt that. I'm sorry I didn't come out to see you the last time you visited. I just couldn't handle telling you all of this face to face and seeing the disappointment in your eyes."

He paused for a moment, "I know you used to think I was over-protective with all of my rules but I need you to listen to me about one thing, more than anything I have ever told you. Jackie is a soulless person. She's capable of anything."

I would have thought that was a little harsh if he had been talking about anyone else, anyone other than my mother's murderer. Soulless seemed to be pretty accurate in this case.

"She's desperate to get that money," he said. "I think it was a mistake turning the money over to you... I never thought it would be like this. I just want you to be safe. If that means giving her the money, just do it. Please, Brie... If something happened to you, if you were hurt in any way, I don't know what I would do."

I was already hurt, I told him, right before the operator disconnected the call.

This time when I got off the phone with him, I felt neither exhausted nor confused. I was fired up. I checked on Dee, who was sound asleep, slipped on my coat, and quietly closed the door behind me as I left the apartment. I was on a mission.

In the cab, I conjured up images of my mother, a collage of Polaroids I'd seen over the years. I wasn't sad though; all it did was add fuel to the fire.

Was it premeditated? That was arguable. Did she deserve it? Absolutely. That's what I was thinking as the cab pulled up in front of her building. Jackie and Brie, round two, and this time I was ready.

I banged on her apartment door. "Jackie!" I yelled. "Jackie!" My voice echoed down the hallway.

I was operating on anger and adrenaline, a lethal combination. I didn't know what I was going to do when she opened the door, but I figured it wasn't going to end well.

That's when Trevor, Jackie's oldest, cracked open the door. His brother peaked from behind him.

"Brie!" they yelled in unison.

They were so excited to see me. I knelt down and took them both into my arms and hugged them tightly, I hoped that a little of their innocence would rub off on me. I had all but forgotten about them in the chaos of the last few months. My nerve melted away. They told me mommy wasn't home. Maybe that was a blessing. If she had answered the door, there was a good chance the two of us would end up cellmates.

I held onto the boys a little longer than necessary. I tried to comfort them in advance because I knew that before this was over, they would lose a mother too.

Chapter 59

O n the second day of the trial, as my father walked toward the witness stand, I couldn't help but think that he was a far cry from the man that used to chase away anyone that so much as looked at me cross-eyed. He was no longer the strong and intimidating man whom I once knew.

That didn't stop him from giving Dee one of his infamous intimidating looks. Dee nodded and smiled nervously when he saw my father, and my father responded by giving him one of those looks that fathers give their daughters' boyfriends.

It seemed like a lifetime ago that he and I had bargained over when I would be allowed to start dating. He had spoken to Dee briefly on the phone and tried to give him the third degree. Even with everything that had happened, it was kind of nice to think that he was still trying to look out for me.

But I couldn't get past the fact that he looked so old and frail. It was like he'd aged ten years since the last time I'd seen him. His hairline wasn't receding; it had pretty much retreated all together and the little that was left had turned white. He was sort of hunched over when he walked. And he'd gotten so thin. He seemed to be swimming inside the suit he was wearing.

And the suit he was wearing? That was an issue in itself. The prosecutor had argued for my father to be able to wear a suit to the trial instead of his prison issued jumpsuit.

"It would be prejudicial. The jury wouldn't see him as a credible witness if he came to court with an inmate number written across his back," Mr. Knox had argued.

I didn't see the big deal. "The jury's going to know he's in prison anyway, right?" I asked.

"There is a big difference between hearing something and seeing it. What we need to do is prevent the visual image."

With that argument, Mr. Knox won over both me and the judge. But I was pretty sure my father in that ill-fitting suit wasn't exactly the visual image Mr. Knox was going for.

The charcoal gray suit had seemed perfect when I spotted it on the hanger in the Macy's men's department. But he'd lost so much weight that he looked like he was wearing someone else's clothes.

As he took the witness stand, my father didn't even glance at the defense table. If he had, he would have seen his sister scowling at him. Aunt Jackie's scowl was fleeting. If I had blinked I would have missed it myself.

She sat, legs crossed, hands folded in her lap, completely calm and collected, like she was oblivious to the myriad of felony charges she was facing, like the hippie with the ponytail was just some old buddy and not the guy that was fighting for her freedom.

Optimistic—that's what she was. Even after sitting in jail for months waiting for trial, she was optimistic. Her optimism was likely fueled by her thinking she would get off the same way Atlantic had.

When I got the news that Atlantic's high-priced lawyers had gotten him off on a technicality, I was livid and petrified. I knew for sure that he would be coming after me and Dee. I pictured us entering the witness protection program and living out our days on a farm in Montana.

Thankfully, James had other plans. Within an hour of his release, Atlantic was taken into custody by the FBI.

"And we're not going to make the same mistakes that the local police made," James assured me.

My father held up a shaky hand to take the oath to tell the truth, the whole truth, and nothing but the truth. Better late than never, I thought.

Dee leaned forward in his seat directly behind me and squeezed my shoulder. "Everything's going to be okay."

I guess that feeling of optimism was going around. I wasn't entirely optimistic. But I was hopeful that the time that Jackie had spent in jail so far was just the tip of the iceberg.

No matter how calm and collected Aunt Jackie looked sitting there, I knew she was at least a little scared. I had seen it in her eyes, although not that day in court; that day her eyes were glazed and emotionless.

But when the cops had dragged her out of her apartment amidst flashing cameras and reporters, I'd seen the fear. I had watched the news streaming live her 7:00 am perp walk. Morning puffiness, no makeup.

NY1 ran her mug shot at the top of the hour for days, informing the public of whatever new development had transpired in the case. The guns and drugs uncovered in her apartment, her own brother scheduled to testify against her, the surveillance tape of our fight in the bank—that one was hard to watch.

It seemed like every day there was some new angle to the story. So I knew she was scared, but I had to admit, seeing her sitting there next to her attorney with that confident expression, it unnerved me a little.

My father dabbed his eyes with a handkerchief as he talked about my mother. When he started talking about how Aunt Jackie had stolen from the medicine she was supposed to dispense to the elderly people she cared for, when he told how she smashed up those pills and mixed the powder into a meal that she had prepared for my mother, when he told how she had been disappointed that her first attempt at killing my mother had succeeded only in making her violently ill, when he told how she had resorted to hiring someone to get the job done, no one was looking at him.

The judge, the jury, and everyone else in the courtroom had turned their attention to Gran. Gran sat flanked on either side by Pop and I, but neither of us was able to quiet her sobs.

She sobbed loudly, screaming incoherently in between each sob. She rocked herself back and forth, perhaps in an effort to quiet her own cries. A court officer came over and politely offered to escort her outside, but she refused to budge.

The whole family had flown in for the trial and the closure they had been waiting so many years for. It was Marie who finally convinced Gran to step outside for a few minutes to compose herself.

Aunt Jackie's lawyer was objecting to something. I didn't understand any of that part. I was probably one of only a handful of people who didn't watch *Law and Order*. I hated the way they recycle their characters. One episode an actor is playing a criminal and in the next the same guy is the lawyer; that's just annoying.

Anyway, the judge ruled on the objection and when my father continued, he was talking about Jackie's dealing. He had kept meticulous records over the years.

My father would have been a shrewd and successful businessman if he had only decided to use his powers for good. He had kept stacks of marble notebooks dating back twenty years with dated entries of all of Jackie's out of state trips, all of her drug buys, and even the names of some of her suppliers.

I was exhausted by the end of the day, when the judge finally told my father to step down from the witness stand, so I knew he must be too. That's why I didn't think too much about it at first when he hesitated. He sat there for another moment, took a deep breath, but still didn't move.

"Sir?" The stenographer typed, recording the judge's impatience for posterity.

My father clutched his chest. He had a look of panic and fear on his face. The microphone in front of him amplified the sound of his labored breathing.

The jury was quickly rushed out of the room. As they exited single file, the last few saw him collapse. He doubled over right there on the witness stand. Someone had already called for an ambulance.

I pushed my way out of the aisle and ran toward him. The courtroom was in a frenzy. Reporters and photographers were immediately on their feet. The court officers had their hands full with crowd management, so I was able to get closer to him than I had since the day the cops came to our apartment and took him away. I touched his limp clammy hands, no plate-glass window or chain link between us.

With his hand in mine, I closed my eyes. That would be the picture that the photographers would chose for the cover of *Newsday* and *The Daily News.*

When I closed my eyes, we were at the beach. I smelled the salt water, felt the sand between my toes. I smiled at him with my missing front tooth. We were so happy. That was so long ago, but in that moment none of the things that had happened since seemed to matter.

When I opened my eyes I knew he was gone. I knew that all we would ever have were those memories, no chance to make new ones. That didn't stop me from begging him to hold on. "The ambulance is on its way," I told him. I told him that I still needed him. Then I told him something that I hadn't been able to say during all of those collect phone calls we'd had recently. He'd said it, and all I'd ever given him in return was dead air.

"I love you, Daddy, I love you."

Chapter 60

It was as if everything was moving in slow motion. I wanted to turn back time, but all it did was creep forward at a torturously slow pace. I'd heard people talk about having outer body experiences, but I'd never actually experienced it myself before that day. I knew what was happening, it just didn't seem completely real. It felt like it was happening to someone else, like it wasn't my father's body they'd just put on the gurney and wheeled out of the courthouse.

Dee tried his best to shield me from the reporters, pushing away microphones that were shoved in my face. Once we made our way through the reporters and were able to get out of the courthouse, Gran said she and Pop would meet us back at our apartment.

"I just want to be alone right now," I told them.

She frowned.

"Please, I'm tired. I just want to go home and go to sleep. I will talk to you tomorrow."

"Okay," she said reluctantly. "If that's what you want."

But I didn't sleep. I sat on the couch for hours staring at nothing in particular. I was waiting for the tears. I hadn't cried yet. I was waiting for it to hit me. I sat there and I waited.

I thought about how, when Dee was in the hospital, he'd told me that I had abandoned my father. At the time, I thought that he was trying to hurt me. I wasn't ready to admit it then, but Dee was right. I had abandoned my father just as much as he had abandoned me. That's all I could think about. I kept running that thought through my head over and over. Now he was dead and I had wasted so much time being angry with him.

Chapter 61

The next few weeks are kind of a blur. My memory is a collage of pictures and sound bites, with huge gaps of time that I simply couldn't account for.

"There was nothing anyone could have done," I remember the coroner saying.

His skin was nearly as white as his lab coat, but there was something disturbingly dark about him, the result of spending the majority of his time in a room with cabinets full of dead people.

I don't remember how many arteries he said were blocked. Massive heart attack. That's what the coroner identified as my father's cause of death. But I knew that wasn't true.

I had no doubt that my father had in fact died of a broken heart. But it wasn't the way the doctor's thought. It wasn't the type of heart condition that would be revealed by their medical tests.

Finally saying out loud, in front of witnesses, what his own sister had done to his wife, the love of his life, it was all just too much for him to bear. My father died of a broken heart.

When I told Mr. Knox that there was no way I could set foot back in that courtroom, I remember him saying that he understood and that he'd keep me posted on the progress of the trial.

I remember sitting on the side of the bed and Gran dressing me in a navy-colored dress.

"Raise your arms... good," she said in a gentle voice.

It rained the day of the funeral. Dee held my hand and balanced an umbrella over both of our heads. The wind caused the rain to blow diagonally and hit us in the face. I'm sure everyone assumed that the rain droplets on my face were tears, but they weren't.

I remember looking down into the fancy wooden box with the pearl white satin fabric inside. Up close Daddy looked even older. His arms were folded over his chest. I would have given anything to feel his arms around me.

Gran cried and I wondered why she would cry over the death of the man she had spent so much time hating, a man she had wrongfully accused of her daughter's death.

"At a funeral people cry for the person that has died, but they also cry for the people that have been left behind," Dee told me. "She's crying because you lost your father. She's crying for you."

As for me, some of the numbness had faded away, but I was so angry with myself that I couldn't cry. I was angry that I had wasted so much time being mad at him, time I would never be able to get back. I had so many regrets. I guess that's something that my father and I had in common.

Chapter 62

After my father's funeral, I thought Gran and Pop would head back to Raleigh like the rest of the family had, but they didn't. They came by the apartment every day. Dee, Gran, and Pop took shifts sitting with me, talking to me, trying to get me to eat. I didn't talk, and despite Gran's persistence and superior culinary skills, I could barely eat.

I just wanted to be alone with my misery. But they wouldn't leave me alone; any moment that I had to myself was only because they'd gone off to some corner of the apartment to talk about me. I overheard them a couple of times as they huddled together in the kitchen.

"She still hasn't cried yet," Dee whispered.

"She can't keep it bottled up inside like this," Gran said.

Pop agreed. "She needs to let it out if she's going to be able to move past it."

It was Dee who called Dr. Beekman. I could only imagine what that conversation had been like. "My girlfriend is on the verge of some type of breakdown. Do you make house calls?"

Whatever he said to her, it worked and she agreed to come over. When Dee told me that Dr. Beekman was on her way, I was both nervous and embarrassed. What would I say to her after that horrible message I'd left on her answering machine?

When she arrived Dee let her in. I stayed sitting on the couch where I'd been for at least two weeks. I was losing track of time so I couldn't be sure, but the cushions had a permanent imprint of my body.

I couldn't even look at her. "I'm ... I'm..." I started to stutter.

She sat next to me on the couch and hugged me. It was weird, all of the things I'd confided in her during our sessions and she'd never done more than shake my hand. But there she was sitting in my living room with her arms around me.

That's when it finally happened. That's when the tears came. I didn't just cry, I wailed, like a wounded animal. I cried so hard my whole body hurt. Poor Raleigh whined along with me, not knowing what else to do. I cried until I was dehydrated. Once I started I thought I would never be able to stop. Maybe that's what I'd feared all along.

Chapter 63

After several more house calls by Dr. Beekman, I started to feel a little better. I would get up in the morning, shower, get dressed, and walk the dog. I was slowly starting to get into a routine.

But everything took so much more effort than it used to. From the moment I opened my eyes in the morning, before I even swung my legs over the side of the bed, I was had to start telling myself that I was okay, everything was okay. I did that at least a hundred times a day, and those were the good days.

There were bad days too. I could be in the middle of doing something and my father's death would just hit me like a ton of bricks. Knock the wind out of me. There was no warning. Out of nowhere it would be like I was falling off the edge of a cliff.

There was no point in fighting it. It was these moments when I would just have to stop what I was doing, whatever I was in the middle of, and sit down. Just sit, try to catch my breath and wait for it to pass.

Doctor Beekman said they were panic attacks and completely normal for someone who had witnessed the death of another person. We started working on ways for me to cope with them. Gradually, the good days started to outnumber the bad.

One of the really good days was when Mr. Knox called to tell me that the verdict was in. Jackie had been found guilty on all charges. She was sentenced to life in prison. To me that meant that the judge had realized what I already knew: there was no fixing her, no chance of rehabilitation. All he could do was protect the rest of us.

Social services had contacted the father of Jackie's boys. He seemed to have turned his life around once he'd got away from Jackie. He was married and living with his wife and daughter in a house in New Jersey. He took custody of the boys.

It seemed like everyone was moving on, and my move from the Bronx was long overdue.

Dee and I packed our things and headed down south. When we hit I-95 and put New York in the rearview mirror, I hoped that our move would give us the fresh start we were looking for.

That day when I was sitting on the couch with Dr. Beekman's arms around me, my tears came in an unexpected flood. For a while after that I thought I'd never be happy, thought that there'd never be anything funny enough to make me laugh again. But I was wrong. My laughter, just like those tears came in a sudden, unstoppable waive.

Gran and Pop were more than happy to open up their home to Dee and I. Pop even built Raleigh a dog house in their backyard. They set up two twin beds on opposite sides of the guestroom for us. I couldn't help but laugh when I saw it. The sound of my own laughter seemed unfamiliar to me.

Gran realized that it was the first time I'd laughed since my father died. She looked at me with sad eyes but gave me an encouraging smile.

"I like what you've done with the place," I told Gran.

She snorted. This was all Pop's idea, she told me. Imitating him she said, "I know she's sweet on that boy of hers, but I ain't never let none of my children shack up under my roof and I ain't about to start now. So this is the compromise I came up with." She laughed. "I told him that Demetrius is not a boy, he's a man, and you are a young woman, not a little girl. I told him that you have been on your own for a while already."

That's for sure, I thought.

"But he just kept going on and on about you not being married. And that when he was coming up, kids didn't live together like this. I told him that there was no record of civilization that long ago. He laughed at that but he's as stubborn as a mule. He just wouldn't let it go, he kept rambling on about cows and milk… oh, yeah, why buy the cow when you can get the milk for free? That's what he said. So it was either this or setting up a tent for Dee in the backyard. I hope you're not too uncomfortable in here."

"We'll be fine," I told her, still laughing.

Chapter 64

When Dee and I lived in the Bronx, we never really went out on dates much. When we first got together we went to the movies a couple of times and out to dinner, but we quickly got wrapped up in school and didn't have much time for that sort of thing. Then of course we couldn't go out for fear that someone would see us together.

In Raleigh we made a point of having date night at least once a week. We went to restaurants and shows and we even took a long weekend and visited his parents down in Florida.

Things were going really well between us. I told Dr. Beekman as much when she'd call to check up on me. She had become more than a doctor to me, she was a friend. Dr. Beekman said she was happy for me. I waited for the but.

"But," she said. "I want you to work on something."

"What's that?" I asked

"A little assignment. I want you to think back over everything that has happened and figure out what you've learned from the experience."

"You mean besides the fact that for someone who's not a teacher you sure give out a lot of homework assignments?"

I tried to make light of it because I hadn't thought about any of that stuff for a long time and the idea of dredging it all up again wasn't appealing. I still thought about my father a lot, but the rest of it I just put behind me, left it in the Bronx when I rode away in the U-Haul.

As usual Dr. Beekman was persistent. Week after week she'd ask me the same question? *Have you figured it out yet? Have you figured out what you've learned?*

Chapter 65

Time has passed so quickly. It's hard to believe that it has already been four years since Dee and I moved from the Bronx.

A lot has changed in that time, but some things are still the same. I still have my trust fund, and the interest alone is ridiculous. I sometimes wonder how I would have been able to negotiate with Atlantic if I hadn't been able to convince Ms. Fleming to make that fake wire transfer into his account.

I haven't spent one cent of the money. I couldn't just go buy a house or a car or something, I needed the money to mean something. I don't know, maybe one day I will start a charity or maybe a drug rehab center. I haven't figured it out yet, but I want it to go to a good cause.

I'm feeling a little nostalgic, because today was such a big day for me. It was my college graduation. I decided to leave the nursing program behind and instead I got my degree in psychology with a minor in English. My whole day was pretty much perfect, but it was surprising too.

Not the fact that I graduated; I knew that I would. Not even the fact that I'd graduated *magna cum laude*; I'd worked really hard for that. The surprise came later, back at Gran and Pop's house, after my celebratory dinner.

I was alone in the bedroom with Dee, a rare occurrence in that house. Pop is always watching us like a hawk, but he was nowhere to be found. I guess that should have tipped me off.

On that day in the hospital when Dee regained his voice, that first conversation was hard, and we both let our anger out. But after that, the liquid that dripped through Dee's IV was like truth serum. He opened up to me more than he ever had before.

He told me about his family, the whole story. By the end of that conversation, once the demons had been forced out of their hiding places, we were both in tears. He told me that he would never lie to me again. That if I gave him another chance he would do everything in his power not to disappoint me. And he hadn't.

We'd vowed never to speak of it again. And the only reason that I even mention it now is because that's what I thought about when he told me that he wanted to make another vow to me. When he got down on his knee and asked me to marry him.

It has taken a while, but I finally finished Dr. Beekman's assignment. I have narrowed it down to three things. This is what I've learned:

Forgive freely

Love unconditionally

Truth

This was the most difficult lesson of all. Truth, is always a mixture of different perspectives, that's what I've learned. You can never know the complete truth by talking to one person. It's a patchwork, one piece of fabric gets sewn into another and then another. I've heard the story from more than one person—Daddy, Aunt Jackie, Gran, Pop, Dee, Ms. Fleming, Sandra, Toni, and even Atlantic, each clarifying something or adding to the whole.

And just like the truth is connected by individual parts, each thing that I have learned is also connected.

Truth leads to understanding. Once you understand, you can forgive freely and the ability to forgive freely gives you strength. So when Dee asked me to marry him, I knew it was right and there was no voice in the back of my head that disagreed. Because now, now that I'm stronger, I can love unconditionally.